Fractured Destiny

Sara McClaflin

First Edition

ASIN: B0G3NFYNTZ

ISBN (trade): 979-8-9991778-4-1

Book Cover: Pia

Editing: Brandy Gibson

Social Media Coordinator: Tawny Gratto

Social Media Group Moderator: Ashley Sullivan

PA: Sarah Toon

Marketing & PR: Wildfire Marketing Solutions

Content Warning

This book contains mature content and situations intended for adult readers (18+). Some of the events, conflicts, or character backstories may touch on sensitive topics.

Please note this story includes references to sexual assault and explores difficult themes surrounding pregnancy and reproductive trauma.

Reader discretion is strongly advised.

If you'd like to see a detailed list of possible triggers and content notes before you begin, I've prepared one for you and it is located at the back of the book.

This book is dedicated to those who were told their fate was written in stone—and brought a chisel anyway.
And to my Grandma Peggy, who believed in me long before I believed in myself.

The Demon's Oath

A Sacred Vow of Binding and Judgment

By the Depths of the Abyss, by the Shadows That Watch, by the Chains of Fate that no force may sever—

Let it be written. Let it be known. Let it be sealed.

I, **Lucas Duvain**, of my own will and without coercion, do stand before the Unseen Council and swear this Oath, binding my existence to the Eternal Laws of Bargains, Punishment, and the Seven Sins.

I take upon myself the mantle of **Deal Maker and Deliverer of Judgment.**

I wield not the sword, but the contract, for a promise is sharper than any blade.

I wield not chains, but consequence, for a choice freely made is a fate unchangeable.

I wield not force, but inevitability, for what is agreed shall come to pass, no matter the pleading.

I walk among mortals not as a savior, but as a test—**to tempt, to offer, and to take.**

Thus, before the **Shrouded Thrones and the Abyssal Hosts**, I inscribe my vow into the **Book of Binding**, knowing that once my name is burned into these pages, my path is set.

THE LAWS OF THE OATH

I. The Deal is the Beginning.

To speak is to shape. To offer is to bind. Once my words seal a deal, there shall be no undoing, no regret, no escape.

II. The Bargain Holds Weight.

What is given shall not be returned. What is promised shall not be denied. No mortal, angel, or demon shall unravel the contract once it is set.

III. The Cost Shall Match the Desire.

Each soul shall be measured, and its burden weighed. The greater the sin, the greater the consequence. No deal shall be granted without its proper price.

IV. The Collector Does Not Pity.

I shall not sway, nor shall I falter. I shall take what is owed in its due time. No tears, no pleas, no prayers shall alter fate.

V. The Soulmate is Fate, But Duty is Eternal.

If I should find the one who bears my mark, the soul bound to mine by fate, I shall not deny them, for fate cannot be rewritten. **To love is not a sin, but to forsake my duty for love is unforgivable.**

Though my soul may recognize its other half, my purpose remains unshaken. I shall not waver, nor shall I allow this bond to weaken the will I have sworn to uphold.

If I place my soulmate above my duty, if I let them turn me from my path, then let my name be burned from the Abyss, my power stripped, and my soul cast into the void, lost to both fate and eternity.

VI. The Unseen Council Holds the Final Word.

Though their presence is unknown, their law is absolute. No punishment shall be given beyond what is agreed, and no deal shall be struck that defies the Balance.

VII. The Reckoning Shall Always Come.

No bargain shall go uncollected. No debtor shall go unpunished. In pain or in ruin, in torment or in nothingness—the price shall be paid.

SO IT IS WRITTEN.

SO IT IS SEALED.

SO IT SHALL BE.

SIGNED IN BLOOD AND HELLFIRE BEFORE THE UNSEEN COUNCIL

Lucas Duvain

CHAPTER ONE

Josie

I give Bella, my best friend or more like my sister if I'm being honest, one last hug before closing the door behind her.

This is it. I'm officially living with Jasper Wilder. My boyfriend. The man I love. The man I'm going to spend the rest of my life with... I think.

The problem is, I'm a mate. A soulmate.

Bella's one, too. So is her sister, Ophelia. I've watched what that bond does to a life—how it rearranges everything whether you're ready or not.

They're happy, and I'm happy for them, but I don't want that. I don't want demons or destiny or a future decided for me. I especially don't want to have no say in it.

All of that sounds like my own personal hell. No pun intended.

I jump out of that line of thinking when I hear the door open and shut.

"Hey, babe," Jasper calls from somewhere behind me.

I'm still on the couch. I sat down when Bella left and just haven't found a reason to get back up.

"Hey, Jas," I say, keeping my voice light, trying not to let the annoyance slip out. He was supposed to help me move in, but he went back to work instead. Again.

"I know you're mad," he sighs, cringing slightly. "But I had to," he adds. "I need to get ahead of things so I can take time off when the baby gets here."

My hand moves to my stomach automatically. It's barely there yet, just a slight curve. Even so, I keep reaching, searching for a kick or any movement.

I'm only at the end of my first trimester and the morning sickness has been kicking my ass.

He drops his keys in the bowl by the door, the sound of the metal meeting the glass feels like nails on a chalkboard. He steps closer, close enough that I can smell his cologne. The one I picked out for him. The one I loved... until now. I kind of want to vomit after smelling it.

Pregnancy really changes everything.

"Hey," he says, softer now. His hand comes up, thumb brushing my jaw as he lifts my chin to kiss me.

It's warm and familiar and exactly what I need after a long day. I kiss him back, my shoulders easing as if I'd been holding them too tight all afternoon.

When he pulls away, his hand slides down to my stomach.

"We're okay," he says.

I smile up at him, because that's what you do when someone says that with enough confidence. Still, my thoughts drift to the faint ache along my collarbone.

We're not okay. I don't say it, though. I can't even admit it to myself. I do *not* want to say it outloud. Not yet anyway.

"I know," I say. It's better to just go with that.

His thumb moves in a small circle around my stomach.

"I just want to do this right," he adds. "For you. For the baby."

My nod comes easily. Forgiving him is familiar, it takes less effort than holding onto disappointment. Loving him has always been the easy part.

"I know," I repeat.

He kisses my forehead, then my hair, and steps back toward the kitchen. "Let's get you something to eat."

I follow him, light and relieved, already letting the disappointment fade. That's what love does, isn't it?

The clock shows that it's almost 8PM. My stomach immediately decides to be loud about it, growling like I haven't eaten in days.

Apparently knowing food is coming just makes the noise worse.

Dinner is pasta from a box and sauce from a jar, which feels almost funny considering Jasper runs a contracting development company and signs checks with more zeros than I can picture. He stares at the stove like it might fight back. I don't say anything. It's kind of endearing that he's trying for me.

"Sit," he says, tugging an apron over his head. "You've been on your feet all day."

"I've been sitting," I tell him, but I slide onto the stool anyway because he's already moved on to pulling out a pot.

He won't start dinner until he knows I'm sitting. I'm too starving to argue with him.

"Still," he says. "You shouldn't have done all that packing alone."

I pick at the edge of the counter. "Bella was there. But I kind of wish you'd been there, too."

He pauses, just for a second. "Yeah," he says. "Me too. I really wanted to be there to help. But you know I couldn't get out of this."

The water starts to hiss, and Jasper opens a cabinet finding the box of pasta I bought yesterday and holds it up triumphantly. He starts pulling random seasonings out.

I have no idea how this is going to go.

"Look," he says. "I'm domesticated."

"You're doing amazing, sweetie." My grin isn't forced this time.

He gives an exaggerated bow with the spoon still in his hand. "Thank you! Glad you're so impressed."

"Maybe a little," I admit, letting the grin spread across my lips.

He grins like he's won something important. "I knew it."

The timer goes off and he straightens, suddenly all business. "Alright," he says, reaching for the pot. "Are you ready? Because dinner is about to be served."

He takes his time plating the pasta, lifting the noodles carefully and fixing the edge of the bowl when sauce drips where it shouldn't. The penne, a little softer than ideal, is coated in bright red marinara that clings unevenly. The sauce is weirdly thicker in some places than others.

It's... not how I would've done it.

Not even close.

But he's so focused. I try not to laugh at his scrunched nose. He looks like he's plating for some award winning restaurant instead of making dinner in our kitchen. I have to bite the inside of my cheek to keep from smiling.

He even wipes the edge of the bowl again.

It's kind of adorable.

"Go easy on the critics," he says. "I may have eyeballed the measurements for the sauce."

"It smells good," I tell him, and I mean it. He tried and it's not perfect, but it is fully cooked. That's all I can ask for.

"That's the dream," he says, sitting across from me. "Low expectations lead to pleasant surprises."

I laugh, and he smiles like that was the goal all along.

"Eat," he says gently. "Tell me if it's terrible."

I take a bite.

"Well?" He asks, eagerly waiting for my response.

"It's... actually good," I tell him with a wide smile on my face.

His shoulders relax. "Thank God."

I laugh softly. "You were really worried."

"I had a backup plan," he says. "Ordering pizza. Emergency pizza."

"Very reassuring."

He grins, pleased with himself, and finally starts eating.

He takes a few bites, then looks up again. "So," he says casually. "How did packing go?"

"I didn't think I had that much stuff," I say. "But, every time I turned around, there was another drawer."

He grins. "That sounds about right."

"It took way longer than I expected," I say. "I kept opening boxes and containers I forgot I had."

He laughs. "That's impressive. I don't even use half my closets or drawers."

"I noticed," I tease, rolling my eyes lightly. "They're very empty."

"Minimalism," he says, winking. "Very intentional."

"Very convenient," I tease.

He shrugs. "I like not having to look for things."

"I feel like half of my stuff was in boxes labeled *miscellaneous.*"

"Ah." He nods solemnly. "The most dangerous category."

"It really is." I grab another noodle with my fork. "Bella tried to reorganize it."

"I'm shocked she didn't succeed."

"She did. I just don't know where anything is now. Not that I knew where it was before."

He chuckles and takes another bite. "You'll figure it out. As long as you have your hoard of books to read."

"I collect books," I correct. "Reading them is aspirational."

"That makes perfect sense for you." He shakes his head, amused with all of my antics. "At least it's all here now."

"Yeah," I say, letting my voice stretch. "It is."

He glances around the apartment, like he's seeing it with me for the first time. "It'll feel like home soon."

I hope it will, because right now, it's devoid of everything that is me.

He doesn't even have any pictures of us anywhere.

I nod. "I think so."

He reaches for his water. "We can get rid of stuff you don't need. Start fresh."

"Maybe," I say. "I kind of like knowing where everything came from, though."

He hums, unconcerned, and goes back to eating.

I take another bite of pasta and look around the kitchen, the counter, the stool I'm sitting on. All my things are here now. I'm just not sure where *I* fit yet.

"So," he says, stabbing some pasta on his fork. "What are you doing with the kids this week?"

I brighten a little. This is my favorite thing to talk

about. "We're starting a feelings unit. We have a chart with faces and everything. One of them keeps insisting grumpy is his favorite emotion."

Jasper laughs. "Sounds about right."

"They're really sweet," I add. "Exhausting. But sweet."

"I don't know how you do it," he says, watching me from across the counter. "All that noise. All that energy."

I smile into my bowl. "You get used to it."

"I don't think I could," he admits. "I'd lose my mind by noon."

"They're not like that all the time," I say. "They just feel things very loudly."

He dips his chin, acknowledging what I am saying. "Yeah. I get that."

"It's kind of nice," I add, leaning back on the bar stool. "They don't hide it yet. If they're happy, they're happy. If they're upset, everyone knows immediately."

"That sounds like a lot of management," he says, eyebrows lifting.

"Sometimes," I say. "But it's my favorite part."

He grabs another bite. "You're really patient with them."

"I don't feel patient," I sigh. "I just remember what it's like to be small."

He nods. "You're good at it," he says. "I mean—at teaching them. Not... being small."

I smile. We've talked a bit about work before. But he always seemed more interested in what his job was and not mine. Now, I can feel his excitement to learn more about what I do.

I feel included in our relationship this time around.

We broke up before I found out I was pregnant, but

when I told him about it, he wanted us to raise our child together.

I agreed immediately because I wanted my baby to know their father. Unlike me, who will never know mine.

"You make them feel safe," he finishes, rushing that out as quickly as possible.

"I hope so," I say, trying to move on from the conversation.

"I know so," he says easily. "You've always been like that. Taking care of people."

"I like taking care of people," I say. "I always have."

He smiles once again, bigger this time. "I know. That's one of the things I love about you."

He pauses for a minute probably to figure out what to say next. He's never been the best at starting a conversation. "You've always said you wanted to be a mom."

My fork stills. "Yeah. I have."

"Like—really wanted," he continues, voice easy. "Not someday, maybe I could start a family. But that you know you are going to."

I smile at my plate. "It's always been my dream."

He reaches across the counter and squeezes my hand.- Something warm spreads through my chest.

"You don't have to do everything that you were doing before," he continues. "Work. Pregnancy. Moving. It's a lot."

I don't really understand what he is trying to say.

"I can handle it," I say quickly, pulling my hand from his grip to cross my arms.

"I know you can," he says, his fingers flexing once before dropping to his side. "You know that's not what I meant."

I don't say anything back. I'm curious about how he's

going to remedy this. I know exactly what he's trying to tell me. But I also want to give him the benefit of the doubt.

"I just mean you don't *have* to work," he adds. "Not forever. Not if you don't want to."

I look at him. I was right. He wants me to stay at home. "You mean—"

"I mean we're okay," he says. "I've got us. You don't need to prove anything."

"I love my job," I say defensively. "I don't *want* to stop working."

He nods immediately. "Of course not. I'm not saying that." He runs his hand through his hair and sighs. "I'm just saying you could take a break. Be with the baby. Be present."

"I would be present with the baby no matter what," I argue. "Bella said we can figure anything out,"

"I know," he says gently. "But this would be different. You wouldn't be tired all the time. You wouldn't be rushing." He smiles. "You could actually enjoy it."

I picture it for half a second. Quiet mornings. No schedule. No rushing.

He watches my face carefully. "And if you miss it, you can always go back."

"That's true," I say, even though I'm not so sure it is.

He squeezes my hand again. "I just want you to be happy."

My throat tightens. "I am happy."

"I know," he says softly. "I just want to make it easier. I want you to have everything you've always dreamed of and more."

He goes back to eating, and the conversation drifts, but the feeling stays with me. The thought that someone loves me enough that they would do anything to make me happy sends a warmth through my chest.

I wasn't raised with that.

I move through rooms in my memory the way you flip through channels on a television. Marble floors. White kitchens no one cooked in. Chandeliers that cost more than most people's houses.

That is where I lived.

My mother liked to call it privilege.

It felt more like employment.

I knew which wine glasses were for guests and which were for show. I knew how to iron silk without burning it. I knew how to answer the door, how to smile, how to disappear when company arrived. I was introduced as her daughter, but I was expected to behave like I was part of the staff.

I left at sixteen with a backpack and sixty three dollars to my name.

She didn't come after me.

I don't know my father. I've never even seen a picture of the man. My mother said he was a mistake. All I know is that he had good hair. That's the closest I've ever gotten to an origin story.

She always hid him. I never had a choice. It was her way of controlling me.

Sometimes not knowing feels like a missing limb. Sometimes it feels like relief.

You can't miss what you never had.

Except I do.

Constantly.

Jasper knows all of this. I told him early on, in pieces. A sentence here, a joke there. He never made it awkward. Never pushed. He knows where I come from in a way most people don't bother trying to understand.

He came from foster care. He bounced around from home to home for a bit. But he got adopted when he found the one place that just stuck.

I never met his adoptive parents. Once they had their own kids, he said he always felt a bit forgotten. Although he's still grateful for them and everything they did for him.

Our beginnings are incredibly different.

But we share something even bigger. We both know what it means to grow up without being chosen first. He learned how to be good enough to be taken in.

I learned how to be useful enough to keep.

Different houses. Same old skill of survival.

Being with him feels safe in a way that still surprises me. For once, I don't feel like I have to earn my place. I know I won't be moved along when I get inconvenient.

I want to feel that way forever.

But then the mark on my collar bone begins to pulsate once again. The little reminder of fate rearing its ugly head back into the picture. One that I am clearly hiding from Jasper.

I lost my right to choose. If I even had a choice to begin with.

CHAPTER TWO
Josie

Jasper left early this morning. He said he just needed to sign something for a new contract and then he'd be back.

So, I go on with my usual Sunday routine. Laundry, grading work from the older kids, and lesson planning for the week. It's the same every week, nice and safe. I love my little schedule.

It's supposed to be enough.

But now I keep thinking about the moment I was marked.

I've been packing for hours, and Bella's apartment, that I took over, looks like a raccoon broke in and decided to start a thrift store.

Every time I tape a box shut, three more piles pop up like, Hey, remember us? We're your poor life choices in physical form. My hair's falling out of the messy bun I shoved it into this morning, and my cardigan keeps snagging on everything

—drawer handles, box flaps, the corners of my fractured patience.

Jasper swore he'd be here to help. But he called an hour ago to say he "had to work late." Which, in Jasper speak, means "I'd rather do literally anything else."

So, here I am, moving into his place, carrying my stuff, trying not to think too hard about the fact that the math on that feels...off.

The knock at the door is so loud I almost drop the stack of plates I'm holding. "Coming!" I yell, because apparently I live in a barn now. My mother would have lost her mind if I shouted like that as a child.

When I open the door, Bella's standing there, smiling like she's just solved world peace. They knocked. I thought they simply portaled everywhere.

I shake my head because behind her is...oh no. Oh no. It's not just her. It's Bella, Ophelia, and an entire wall of very large, very confident looking men carrying empty boxes like they're about to do a home makeover show.

"Packing party!" Bella announces, sweeping inside before I can protest.

The tall one heads straight for my bookshelf like it insulted his mother. Two of them are in the kitchen, muttering about expired cereal. Someone—someone—is halfway out my window. It's like watching a small army rearrange my life in real time.

I carefully pick up a box of toiletries. I'm trying to be mindful and not throw up everywhere.

I pause when I hear a new voice in the living room.

"Look who finally decided to show," one of them calls, teasing.

"About time, Sloth," another adds.

There's a pause, a low voice in reply—calm, slow, like he's allergic to rushing.

The new man is leaning against the wall near the door, watching me. His golden eyes lock on mine, and something in my chest stutters.

Suddenly, the pain hits.

It starts on my left shoulder, curling across my skin like someone's drawing fire into my very being. My breath catches. The box slips from my hands, crashing to the floor. I gasp and double over, clutching at my chest because I don't know what else to do. It feels like my heart is trying to beat its way out.

Bella's there in seconds, pushing my hair out of face with Ophelia right behind her.

"Josie—hey—look at me," Bella says, her voice firm but shaking underneath. "You're okay. Just breathe. We've got you."

Ophelia crouches beside her, one hand on my back, the other gripping mine. "Tell us what's wrong. Where does it hurt?"

"It's—" I gasp, clutching at my chest as the fire in my skin climbs higher.

One of the men is moving before I can scream again—shouldering past anyone in his way, eyes locked on me like nothing else exists.

Bella's eyes flick down, then they widen. "You're marked," she says, like the words are both a fact and a warning.

I shake my head, fighting for air. "No—no, it hurts. Is my baby okay?"

Silence swallows the room.

"Baby?" The voice is so close. I know it's him without looking, without fully understanding.

I look up at him through the blur of tears. My words come

out small—the way they only do when I'm scared. "I'm pregnant."

The mark burns hotter. And the whole world seems to hold its breath.

I think about my baby. About this small life growing inside me, and how the wanting doesn't go away, no matter how hard I try to ignore it. The wanting of something even greater than what I have now.

I look around the apartment. Jasper says we can start fresh, but what he really means is that we can keep things just as they are now. Neutral. White walls. Gray accents. Dark gray furniture. No color. Nothing I can point to and say is *mine* yet.

Everything I own is still packed away in boxes stacked in the corner, or sitting in a storage unit near my old place. Waiting for me to decide where it belongs. Or if it even belongs at all.

I should be allowed to want more, but it feels selfish. Everything I need should already be here with Jasper. And that's the part that makes me uneasy. Not because Jasper is a bad man. He isn't. He's good. But something in me keeps reaching anyway, and I don't know what to do with that.

We went full throttle the moment I found out I was pregnant. Back together. Moving in. All within a month. It felt necessary at the time. The responsible thing to do.

Maybe it was just fast.

I reach for my phone before I can talk myself out of it. I need Bella.

Hey. Are you free?

BELLA

Yeah. What's up?

Can you come over?

BELLA

On my way.

Something black and gray, like storm clouds folding in on themselves, opens up right in front of me.

"Hey," Bella says, stepping through like this is completely normal.

"You portaled in?!" I stare at her. "Are you insane?"

"Yeah," she says easily. "Why wouldn't I?"

"What if Jasper was here and caught you?"

"You mean you didn't tell him I'm a soulmate of a demon?" Sarcasm. Great. Exactly what I need. "Let me guess," she continues without waiting. "You also didn't mention that you're mated to one."

She trails off, giving me that look only a best friend can manage. I want to tell her everything. I just don't know where to start. So I grab the first feeling I can reach.

"I need advice," I blurt.

"Girl, you just moved in. What is happening already?"

"I don't know if this feels right," I admit.

"Can't blame you," she says, glancing around with her brows raised. "This place is depressing. And why is all your stuff still in boxes? You have six boxes here and it's been over twenty four hours. You two too busy?"

"No. Jasper said we could start fresh," I say, a little too casually.

Bella exhales and grabs my hands. "Okay. What's really going on?"

I sink onto the couch.

"I feel like I want more," I say quietly. "And that makes me feel selfish. I have a good man. A safe place. A baby on the way. I don't even know what the *more* is. I just know it's there. And I don't know how to stop wanting it without feeling like I'm doing something wrong."

Bella sits beside me. She's my boss, technically. But she's also the only person who has ever cared enough about me to make me her friend.

"You are not selfish," she says firmly. "You're about to have a child. You deserve someone who puts you first. If he can't do that, how is he going to put your baby first?"

I swallow.

"Where is he right now?" she presses. "It's Sunday. You should be unpacking. Starting your life together. And I bet he's at work. Just like yesterday. When he should've been here helping you move."

I've never heard her talk about Jasper like that. Something ugly flares inside of me. A dark, sudden urge to defend him, to tear into her for saying things like that about him. I want to shove her, to make her bleed for it. It's more than just anger, it's vitriol, I can *see* this happening.

"Don't get me wrong, we were more than happy to help, but it should have been something you two did together." Her hands are up in defense, as if she too, felt the hot rage that I had.

The thought makes my stomach drop. It feels foreign. Bigger than me. I bolt for the bathroom and barely make it before I throw up.

"Josie—what the hell?" Bella's right behind me, pulling my hair back, pressing something cool against my neck. "What is going on?"

"I don't know," I breathe. "I just... I felt this overwhelming need to defend him. To hurt you for saying that. Like I wanted to attack you."

Bella goes very still. "Okay," she says slowly. "That doesn't sound like you."

"It's not," I whisper.

Her eyes narrow slightly. "That sounds like something else."

"Like what?"

Bella exhales. "Like maybe there are some tricks at play here."

She backs up and starts pacing, muttering under her breath. Within seconds, the bathroom fills with Ophelia, Owen, and Lucas—the one I'm mated to—trailing behind them.

"Josie!" Lucas moves around Bella immediately. "Are you okay?"

He scoops me up like I weigh nothing. My breath catches. Something inside me locks into place so suddenly it almost hurts. The constant ache for something more—the thing I couldn't name, couldn't explain—collapses inward.

Not because it disappeared. Because it's here.

The world narrows until there is only this. His arms. His heartbeat. The steady pull of something that feels so incredible that I can barely function. Peace.

He carries me to the couch and sits, wrapping me in his arms.

"Why are you here, Lucas?" Bella asks. "And how did you know where we were?"

Lucas rests my head against his shoulder and looks up at them. "She called me."

"She—what?" Owen blurts.

I glance up at Lucas. He raises a brow slightly, as if that explains everything.

"Fuck, that was fast," Julian mutters.

Lucas huffs a quiet laugh, and I feel the vibration of it against my mark. "Something fast happening for sloth," Lucas says. "Quite the oxymoron."

"Now what?" I ask, looking between them, slightly panicked but more drained than anything. "What do I do? I'm literally getting sick over this. Bella says something about Jasper and I either throw up or try to kill her. Sorry about that, by the way."

"No worries, babe," Bella says quickly. "But the bigger issue is the part where you wanted to kill me. Josie, what did you feel right before you got sick?"

"This... darkness," I say slowly. "It was creeping up from somewhere deep. All I wanted to do was grab something sharp and stab you until there was nothing left. I could see myself doing it. It felt... detached. Like I was watching it happen."

I look around. Every face is grim. I'm about to explore territories that I *really* don't want to be a part of.

This may kill me. At the same time, I need to know what is going on. Especially if it affects my child.

"Is that what I think it means?" Bella asks quietly.

"Yeah, Belladonna," Owen says. "I think so."

Another portal opens.

Great. Apparently we're hosting a demon convention.

"Little Artist," Julian says, pulling Ophelia in for a quick kiss. "What are you doing here? I thought you were working on the Loom tonight."

"That's why I'm here," Ophelia replies. That feels extremely grim. She's here for me. And fate. The Loom. The very thing that holds the fabric of this world together.

She kneels in front of me and takes my hands. When she looks into my eyes, whatever she sees makes her step back.

The look on her face gives me chills. There's a sense of warning in her eyes. This is going to suck. Really fucking bad.

A new cloud forms—this one streaked red and white—and Della Sage steps through.

Really? Another one? Should I start charging admission?

"I'm needed," she says simply, crossing the room to me, and pulling a small mirror from her bag. She flips it open and holds it up.

My reflection stares back. My eyes stop any thought that I might have formed. There's black bleeding around the edges of the green that I usually see.

I gasp. "What the hell?"

"Her eyes," Della says calmly. "Demonic darkness has started to creep in. What happened?"

"I think she's in a situation involving demons," Bella replies dryly.

Ophelia gives her a dry look. "Insightful."

Bella shrugs. "I try."

"The Loom reacted," Ophelia adds.

"Of course it did," Bella mutters. "Because we can't have one normal Sunday."

"*You* invited half of Hell into her living room," Ophelia points out.

"Josie..." Owen trails off, cutting into the sisterly banter. "Who is this?"

He's holding a framed photo of Jasper and me. I love that one. We were at a picnic, the one where I told him I was pregnant.

"That's Jasper," I say.

"Jasper Wilder?"

"Yeah..." I get off Lucas's lap and step toward him. "Wait. How do you know him?"

Owen runs a hand down his face. "Fucking shit. Bella—he's the one I made a deal with."

"Wait, *him*?" Bella screeches. "Josie's boyfriend?"

"Well, I didn't know that, did I?"

They start arguing, voices overlapping, but all I can hear is one word.

Deal.

"Owen!" I shout, and the room goes silent. "What do you mean deal?"

He looks at Bella, then back at me. "I made a deal with him."

"What was it?" My voice feels thin. I don't want the answer. I know whatever he says next is going to split my life in two. And now I don't get the mercy of time dulling it.

Owen rubs the back of his neck. "I gave him a charm. Power. Something to help his girlfriend love him again. And if he could convince her to stay... he'd have her forever."

My future. Everything cracks in my chest. I feel stupid. Naive. And suddenly, I'm falling into a pit of despair.

Holy fucking shit.

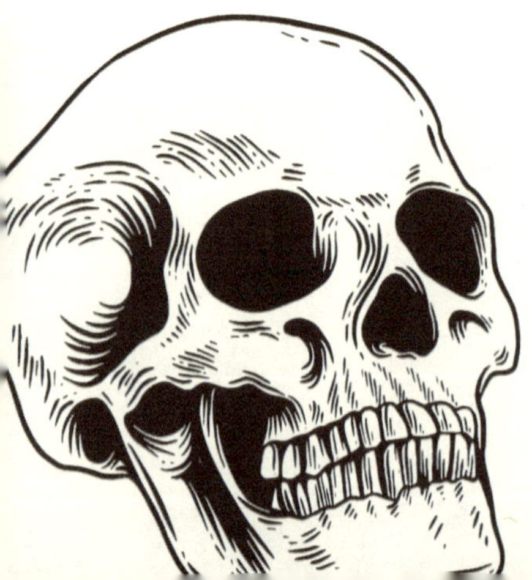

CHAPTER THREE

Lucas

I'm going to kill someone.

No. Not someone. Jasper Wilder. I am going to kill Jasper Wilder.

Mortals are a persistent inconvenience. Typically, they're just that—an inconvenience. But seeing Josie here, in my arms, unraveling because of him shifts something in me from annoyance to something much much deeper.

Della crosses her arms, making me look up toward her. "All right. We need to decide what happens next."

"We?" Josie repeats faintly. "Like this is a group project?"

Bella gives her an unimpressed look. "It kind of is."

Ophelia kneels in front of her. "What do you want, Josie?"

Josie stares at her hands in her lap. Her voice is small when she replies. "I don't know."

That answer spikes irritation through me so fast it almost surprises me. She should want to leave this asshole.

"That's fair," Bella agrees.

I bite my tongue. She doesn't need people telling her what she wants to hear. She needs the truth.

I glance at Julian and Owen. Both of them freeze. Julian's eyes widen just slightly before he leans back a fraction, palms lifting in surrender. Owen doesn't even look at me, he's too busy staring at Bella and Della like he's watching a storm cell form on the horizon.

Owen gives the smallest shake of his head. A silent way of saying *don't*.

Julian mouths *absolutely not.*

"Cut the bullshit," Della huffs, making Josie look up. "You know exactly what to do. Dump his sorry ass."

"Della..." Bella warns.

"No, Bella," Della pushes, exasperated with Bella's hesitance. "I told you the same thing about your stupid ex husband. You didn't listen. I'm not making that mistake again."

I can see Josie starting to get overwhelmed. It takes everything in me to not whisk her away from all of this. Anything that causes an ounce of discomfort I want to erase from her existence.

"We have a child together, Della," Josie whispers. "I have to remember that too."

"No," Della fires back. "You don't know Jasper like I know him—"

"Della!" Ophelia cuts in, voice tight around the edges. "Fate. You have to—"

"See, Ophelia," Della turns on her, "I don't have to worry about fate. You do. All of you know who Jasper Wilder is and you're not telling her. You think you're protecting her. You're not. You're protecting your precious fate. Or yourselves. I'm tired of it. I live on my own terms. So if you won't tell her, I will."

This is probably the most angry I've ever seen Della in my life. She gets assertive plenty, but this is a new level.

The look on Josie's face is one of pure devastation, but it's starting to morph into anger. She hates being the only one in the dark. I can't say I blame her, there's few things I hate more than not having all of the information that I need.

I let my voice slide along the bond. *Josie. It's all right. No one is against you. Breathe for me, Sunshine.*

Her eyes snap to mine. She's startled for a moment, but then she nods once.

I'll explain more about the whole telepathy thing... eventually. That is a conversation I'll have with her later. Right now my focus is on getting her through this moment.

"I want to know," she says to Ophelia. "I need to know. Jasper made the deal and now I'm pregnant. He was desperate. But what makes him a bad person?"

Bella exhales slowly. "You know his best friend is Rhys, but what you don't know is his company works with the Creed family."

Tears spring to Josie's eyes. "No."

I know exactly who the Creeds are.

When Bella inherited Hearthlight Center—where Josie teaches—the Creeds tried to rip it out from under her. The original owner willed it to Bella, and they didn't like that. They used lawyers, pressure, and Rhys Westwood.

Bella's ex husband—professional narcissist, and all around asswipe.

The only exception to the Creed family legacy of assholes is Tinsley. She broke ranks, now working at

Hearthlight as their charity organizer and social media wizard. According to Bella, she's an angel.

But the rest of them? They swallow businesses whole, strip land for pennies, and ruin whoever stands in their way. They own politicians, judges, and half the damn city. We've been watching them for a while.

And now Jasper's name sits right beside theirs.

"Does he know what they've done?" Josie asks, voice trembling as Bella pulls her closer.

Bella doesn't sugarcoat it. "Who do you think told him how to summon a demon, Jos?" she says gently. "He's always known."

"Okay," Julian finally says, cutting through the noise. "What happens next? We should probably figure that out before Jasper comes back."

I watch the realization hit her. This is his apartment. He's going to walk through that door at some point.

Josie straightens, resolve filling her spine.

"I want to leave," she says, the words coming out fast but her face shows that she's not making this decision on a whim. "I want out of this relationship. We can figure out co-parenting later, but right now... we can't be together."

This is the Josie that I want as my soulmate. Decisive and understanding yet knows when to leave.

She may be soft spoken, but she is not weak. Not by a long shot.

"Where will I go though?" She asks, almost to herself. "I gave up everything to be here."

The instinct to answer is immediate. *With me.*

The words rise to my tongue before I can stop them. Owen's head turns slowly in my direction. He gives it a firm shake.

Right. It's not my decision to make.

Bella steps in seamlessly. "My apartment at the center is still open. I haven't filled it with anyone else yet. You can stay there."

"And it's warded," Julian adds.

Josie's brows draw when she asks that question. "Warded?"

"Della reinforced Hearthlight after Rhys kept trying to get clever," Julian explains. "It's secure. Just in case he decides to use some magical bullshit to get through."

"Perfect," Bella says briskly, clapping once. "Lia, portal. Della, help me with boxes. We'll get everything she needs over there before Jasper shows up. No reason to drag this out."

Ophelia nods and a portal blooms open.

The room erupts into movement. I guide Josie back to the couch while they work around us, boxes vanishing through shadow and light.

She feels small in my arms. Exhaustion is slowly creeping over her features.

"Relax, Sunshine," I murmur into her ear. "Let them handle it. This part is almost over."

She exhales in one long, shaky breath. My thumb brushes lightly over the mark at her collarbone. The glow softens beneath my touch. Her breathing evens, and she leans into me on instinct.

The portal seals shut just as the front door opens.

"Babe," Jasper calls casually. "I'm home. See? I told you it would only take a few hours—"

As soon as his gaze lifts from the bowl he dropped his keys into, he\ stops. His gaze lands on the crowd first.

Then on Josie. Then me.

More specifically—on my arm around her.

"I didn't know we had company," he says slowly.

When he sees Owen, I can see his heart rate go up and he trips. He recognizes who is in his home.

He crosses the room in a few strides and grips Josie's arm, pulling her upright and away from me.

My vision darkens at the edges. Josie stiffens in his grasp. Her hands come up—not to hold him—but to push against his chest.

"Don't you think it's inappropriate to sit in another man's arms like that?" The possession in his tone is a living thing, he thinks he's entitled to her, that he *deserves* her.

"Jasper... I—"

"No," he cuts her off smoothly. "I'm not okay with that."

My hands curl into fists at my sides. One hit. One fucking hit and I'd put him through the wall.

"I don't care," Josie chokes out, she's trying to stay calm. Josie is not a violent person, I can tell that much. But everyone has their breaking point. "I don't care what you're okay with. You made a deal with Owen."

His eyes widen, fracturing his composure for just a moment before the mask slides back into place.

"Owen?" he repeats, as if the name means nothing, like he's never even heard it.

I scoff under my breath. Owen rolls his eyes.

"Let's not insult each other," Owen says. "You know who I am."

Jasper's jaw flexes. "Stay out of this, Duvain."

The second our last name leaves his mouth, he realizes the mistake he just made. He confirmed that he does indeed know Owen. It took absolutely no time at all for him to fuck that up.

He recovers quickly, though.

"Okay, Josie. Listen," Jasper says, lowering his voice

like the rest of us aren't in the same room and can't hear every word he says anyway. "You trust me, right? Not this... circus? We can talk about this without an audience."

"No," Josie says, without hesitation. "We're done."

That was a lot more satisfying than I was expecting it to be. I don't move, I don't say anything at all. She can handle this on her own. And based on the look on her face and the energy she's pushing towards me, she doesn't want any help.

But watching this pathetic piece of shit lose control is fucking wonderful.

Jasper lets out a short, disbelieving laugh. "You're emotional, you're pregnant, you're overwhelmed, and you're letting other people decide your life for you—you don't mean that we're done. You'll change your mind if you just think about it for a second."

"We're done," she repeats, firmer this time. Again there is no hesitation or care in her voice. She's made her decision.

He exhales slowly through his nose. "You don't get to throw away our family and everything we're building over some sort of misunderstanding."

"Misunderstanding?" Owen mutters, barely containing a laugh under his breath.

Jasper ignores him, eyes locked on Josie. "I made a deal because I was desperate," he says, voice softening. "Because I love you. Because you were walking away and I didn't know how to fight for us any other way."

"Funny," Bella laughs under her breath. "Pretty sure my dick of an ex said something very similar. Guess you two share the same pathetic handbook."

Jasper turns on her so fast it's almost a blur. He closes the distance in two strides and gets right in Bella's face, towering over her. "I see why Rhys left you. You're a worthless little slut. He said you weren't even a good lay."

Owen's there in a heartbeat, his hand clamps around Jasper's wrist before he can jab his finger in her face, shoving it away.

"Careful," Owen says angrily, "try that again and I'll break it."

"Speaking of that," I cut in, stepping forward just enough to draw Jasper's attention. "How exactly do you know Rhys, Jasper?"

Josie doesn't speak. But she does watch him with curiosity all over her face.

Let's see if the bastard tells the truth.

Jasper hesitates for just a second. "I didn't want to tell you," he says to Josie, softening his tone like that makes him noble, forgivable even. "He's been my best friend since we were ten."

There is a change happening here. I'm watching everything heighten. The bond is pushing tensions to their breaking point.

"And the Creeds?" Josie counters him. "How do they fit in?"

He exhales dramatically, rubbing his forehead as if this is exhausting for him. "They helped me start my business."

"Unbelievable." Josie walks toward me instead of him. I can't stop the smug smile that starts to make its way onto my face. "You knew how we felt about them. About what they did to Bella. And you never said anything."

"I didn't know how to tell you—"

"I don't care." Her voice raises just a bit. "Ellison Creed tried to take Hearthlight. Used his father's position as governor to fund *your* development project. You knew that."

Jasper's jaw tightens. He pinches the bridge of his nose like he's annoyed with the situation *he* created for himself. He is not a victim of circumstance. He is the perpetrator.

"You don't understand how any of that works," he says finally. "Development, funding, politics—it's complicated. It's not personal."

"It was personal," she shoots back. "It was Bella's life."

"That wasn't my decision," he argues quickly. "I'm not the governor. I'm not Ellison. I'm trying to build something. For us. For our child."

"But nothing changed with you," she presses. "You still work with them. You still take their contracts. Even after knowing me and how I feel, what they did. You never cared."

"I cared," he insists, lowering his voice again, pulling out the softer version of himself. "But I also cared about not ending up broke and powerless again. You don't know what that's like. To finally have something. To finally not be the kid with nothing."

There it is. Something that is about to throw all this calm shit out the window if Bella's face says anything.

"You get to be idealistic," he continues, gaze narrowing, accusation creeping into his tone. "You're not the one responsible for keeping everything moving. I am. I was trying to secure our future."

"I don't know what it's like? Oh, I think I know what being powerless and unwanted feels like," Josie asks, menacingly.

I want to know more about that and what she means by it. Now is not the time to ask, though. I stand still, my hands in my pockets as I watch her face me with her hand outstretched. There is no pause or hesitation in her steps.

"Come on," she says. "I'm ready to go."

Owen opens a portal without ceremony. The shadows ripple across the wall.

"We'll discuss co-parenting when the time comes," Josie tells Jasper calmly. "But our child will not be around the Creeds. Or Rhys Westwood."

Jasper laughs harshly. "How do you think this looks? Walking out with another man?"

"Ever heard of a soulmate, Jasper?" Bella asks sweetly, tugging down her collar to reveal her mark. "You must have. Since you're Rhys' best friend and all."

Jasper's gaze snaps to me. Then to Josie.

"No," he breathes. "No. No. That's not possible."

"It is," Bella replies brightly, reaching over and gently pulling the fabric at Josie's collarbone aside.

The mark glows. It's unmistakable what that means.

"Mark of Duvain," Bella teases Jasper. "You were so afraid of losing her you made a deal. Turns out fate had other plans."

Jasper staggers back a step. "That's not real. That's some trick."

Josie lifts her chin. "It's real."

His composure frays at the edges. "It can't be!" He shouts. "You're supposed to always be mine!"

But it is.

We don't argue further. We don't gloat. We step into the portal together.

All we do is leave him standing in what's left of the life he tried to manufacture.

CHAPTER FOUR

Josie

Nothing has changed in Bella's apartment since she left to be with Owen. Well except for the covered furniture.

White sheets drape over everything. It looks like a ghost of an apartment. Almost abandoned. Except for the wafting scent of lemon cleaner drifting through the air. Not surprised that Bella deep cleaned everything before moving out.

The portal closes behind us, leaving all of us in this tiny place.

"Well, I think we're going to head out," Bella says. She leans down and kisses my cheek before opening another portal. Julian and Owen follow her through, giving us a small wave.

I look over and see a few bags on the kitchen counter. Inside are groceries, some toiletries, and basic necessities.

I peel off the note attached and read it.

Josie,

We left the pantry stocked and extra blankets in the hall closet.

Everything you'll need until you can go out and grab it yourself.

We're here if you want some company.

– Ophelia

I stand there for a second, staring at the couch under its sheet. Suddenly, I'm hit with an all consuming sense of fear. I'm overwhelmed. Everything is happening so fast. My head is spinning and I don't even know where to start.

I don't even know whether to laugh or cry. Or curse everyone straight into Hell.

The irony of that is not lost on me.

"I hate this," I mutter.

"I know," Lucas says from behind me.

I jump a bit. I'm so out of it that I forgot that he was still here.

I try to act cool as I walk over and grab the sheet, tugging it down in one quick motion. A slight puff of dust causes me to cough and swipe my hand over my face.

I pull the sheet off the armchair too and fold it automatically. My hands move before my brain catches up.

"Sit," I say, even though I don't know why I'm giving orders when I am so used to taking them. I just spoke to Lucas like I would one of my students. I need sleep.

He sits down on the edge of the couch, giving me enough room to decide where I want to plant myself. Honestly, that one thoughtful gesture is almost enough to bring me to tears.

I lower myself onto the couch carefully. I'm only sixteen weeks along and my body already feels like it belongs to someone else. I adjust, shift, and finally settle both feet flat on the floor. I shift back and forth again to try to find a comfortable spot.

He's silent as he watches me. I can sense that he's holding himself back from helping. I don't think that's what he's doing, I just know it. It's like I can read him like an open book.

"How are you feeling?" He asks.

Should I tell him the truth or take the easy way out? I mean the truth is interesting. And he might already know it, if he can feel me like I can feel him.

Yeah, Lucas. I just dumped the father of my child, moved back into my best friend's apartment like I did when I dumped him the first time, and am going to be a mother when I can't even control my own life, let alone manage someone else's. I'm just peachy.

Okay… lying it is. "Fine."

His eyebrow lifts. Well, I guess he *can* read me.

I sigh. "I'm not fine."

"No," he agrees calmly.

I stare at the floor. "I ended it."

He knows that. It's not like he wasn't there when it all happened. I feel like I need to say it out loud. And it is not something I enjoy. I feel like such a failure.

"That doesn't mean he's gone," I say, trying to salvage what little dignity I have left. "We're having a baby together. I can't just erase him."

I press my lips together and look directly into Lucas' eyes. He says absolutely nothing. I hate that he doesn't argue. I almost want him to. Maybe if we argue or fight or something, somewhere inside me, it will make me feel human.

But I guess it makes sense why he doesn't push. He's not exactly human.

"I have to figure out how to do this," I continue my rambling. "How to co-parent. How to keep things cordial. How to not blow everything up more than I already have. My baby deserves to have a father."

"You don't have to solve that tonight."

I turn to look at him. "That's not how my brain works." I tuck my hair behind my ear. My fingers brush my collarbone, right where the mark burned to life the night he walked into my apartment.

I continue, "I know it's not exactly what I had planned. But is any of this really according to what I thought was the perfect plan?"

He watches me. Patient and not reactive at all. Reading me and my every emotion. I wonder if his low reaction to things and timing is why he's called sloth. I heard one of his brothers call him that earlier.

"And now there's this," I whisper, pointing at the two of us.

He nods. "We are connected."

"That scares me," I admit. "It scares me to be so deeply connected to someone so early on. I barely know you at all."

"It should." He looks at me. "Because you're correct. We barely know each other."

I let out a shaky laugh. "You are terrible at reassurance."

"I'm not trying to reassure you." He's trying to pull me out of the thoughts running through my head.

"Then what are you trying to do?"

"Be honest with you," he responds to me with little to no extra emotion.

I lean back into the couch and stare at the ceiling.

"I don't want something that takes away my freedom," I say. "I've worked too hard to build a life I can be proud of. I won't be pulled somewhere just because the universe decides I belong there."

"The bond doesn't remove your will," he says. "It creates another option. What you do with that is yours. It's not like what you had with Jasper."

I turn that over in my head. "I walked away from that."

"Did you?" His eyes narrow at me. At that moment, my phone vibrates in my pocket.

I take it out. Jasper's name is on the caller id.

"I hate that you're probably right," I tell him.

"About what?" There is no judgment in his tone. He's been confident and kind in everything that he's said so far. Almost too kind.

"That he's not going to let me simply walk away," I admit begrudgingly.

Lucas gives me a look that tells me even if I admit it out loud, nothing about this situation is going to change. Jasper will never let me walk away.

The phone vibrates again.

"Fuck," I mutter under my breath. "I *just* left. You'd think he'd wait at least a night."

It buzzes again. Rolling my eyes, I decide to answer. Better to set some boundaries rather than delaying it any longer than necessary.

"What?" I demand as soon as I hit the answer button.

There's an immediate rush of breath from the other end of the line. "Josie. Finally," he exhales, relief bleeding quickly into frustration. "Why haven't you answered me yet?"

"Because I didn't want to," I reply evenly.

He lets out a humorless laugh. "That's not funny."

"I'm not joking," I say, tapping the call onto speaker before setting the phone on the coffee table between us.

I lean back on the couch as Lucas puts his arm around me.

"You left," he presses, his voice tightening. "You just walked out."

"Yes," I confirm the obvious.

"You don't do that," he presses. "You cool off. You take space. You come back. You've always needed a minute before you overreact."

"I'm not coming back this time," I state, lifting my chin even though he can't see me.

He doesn't even stay silent for a moment. Just keeps carrying on like whatever I have to say doesn't matter in the least bit.

"Okay," he says, forcing patience into his tone. His go-to for when someone frustrates him. "You're upset. I get that. What happened was dramatic. But you don't blow up your entire life over one fight."

"It wasn't just a fight," I counter, raising my voice a tad.

"You're pregnant," he reminds me carefully, like he's explaining something fragile. It's almost as if he doesn't realize that I *know* that. "Your hormones are all over the place."

"There it is," I murmur, scoffing a bit.

"What?" He challenges.

"That thing you do," I explain quietly, "where you make me sound irrational. Stupid even."

"I'm not doing that at all," he insists smoothly. "I'm trying to ground you."

"I'm perfectly grounded," I reply. I realize I've placed

my hand on Lucas' thigh at some point, though I don't know when.

"Josie," he exhales tension that threads through the phone. "We have a baby coming. You don't get to make decisions like this alone. You don't get to shut me out of my child's life."

"I'm not making decisions about the baby," I clarify.

"You're making them about us," he snaps back. "Which affects the baby."

"That's not the same thing," I say, my voice rising before I can stop it. "Having a baby doesn't mean I owe you a relationship."

"This is about him, isn't it?" He asks, suspicion creeping into his voice.

I don't respond immediately. He's just changing the subject to get his way.

"You're confused," Jasper continues, leaning into reason. "He shows up out of nowhere. Inserts himself into our lives. Of course you feel something intense. That's what men like him do. That's apparently what the mark does too."

"Men like him?" I repeat.

"Dangerous," he clarifies tightly. "Unstable. He doesn't want the baby. He wants you distracted from what we built."

"We didn't build anything healthy," I say.

"We built something real," he counters quickly. "You were happy."

"I was hopeful," I correct him.

"You're only doing this because you're hurt," he accuses, trying again.

"No," I say as calmly as I possibly can. "I'm seeing it clearly."

"Clearly?" He scoffs. "Oh, come on."

"I'm getting an attorney," I inform him without giving him a second to start another pointless argument.

"...Excuse me?" he asks after a moment of silence.

"I think we need boundaries," I say. "Clear ones. Documented ones. Where I am not the one talking to you."

"Boundaries from me?" He repeats incredulously. "The father of your child?"

"Yes." I give him nothing. He deserves nothing at all. I know a good attorney will take care of it for me.

"That's insane," he mutters.

"It's necessary."

"You're not taking my kid," he warns.

"I'm not taking your child," I agree carefully. "I'm protecting myself."

"From what?" He challenges. "Me loving you?"

"From you not letting me leave," I respond. "Because it is clear after this conversation that you aren't about to stop."

"You don't get to walk away from me like this," he says at last, his voice cooling.

"I already did," I reply.

"You're being manipulated," he accuses.

"Actually," I counter. "I'm stopping myself from being manipulated... by you."

"You don't mean that," he insists. "You're scared. You always run when things get hard. I'm willing to give you that chance, but you can't shut me out. I don't have to see you everyday, but you have to talk to me."

"I'm not running," I say firmly. "I'm finishing something that shouldn't have continued as long as it did."

"Josie," he lowers his voice again, almost coaxing. "I

know you. You don't like conflict. You don't like lawyers. You don't like escalation. You're not built for this."

"I am now," I tell him.

"You're unbelievable," he mutters.

I put the phone on mute and glance at Lucas.

"Who handled Bella's case?" I ask. "Her divorce from Rhys."

Lucas looks away for half a second, then back at me.

"Julia Carter," he answers evenly.

"Owen?" I ask under my breath.

His eyes flick back to mine. "Yes," he says quickly.

I unmute the phone and speak again.

"I'm beginning the process of hiring a lawyer." I turn to Lucas who is smirking at me, one hand rubbing my collarbone.

"Don't do this," he warns, desperation coming into his tone once again. "You think lawyers make you powerful?"

"No," I respond. "They make things orderly. No more having to talk to each other."

"You're going to regret this," he says quietly.

"Maybe," I admit. "But not as much as I regret coming back to you a second time."

I hang up before this asshole can spin another tale.

"That felt really damn good," I laugh, the squealing sound spilling out of me before I can stop it. Not that I care to stop it anyway.

Lucas laughs beside me. His joy is almost mirroring my own. "I should let you get some sleep."

It's not until he stands that I notice how late it's getting. He's been here for a while.

A dark seam opens slowly, silver light threading along its edges and a large cloud looking portal is in my new living room.

He turns toward it, ready to step through, and something in me resists the idea of him leaving just yet.

"Lucas."

He pauses and looks back at me.

"Thank you," I say and I mean that with my whole heart. "Thank you for not pushing me to do anything I'm just not ready for. Thank you for sitting with me after I got my damn senses back. Thank you for not making this harder on me than it already is."

Instead of answering from across the room, he walks back to me. The portal hums quietly behind him, patiently waiting for him to go through.

He leans down and presses a gentle kiss to my temple. The touch of his lips on my skin feels so intimate that I feel my body clench.

"Anytime, Sunshine," he murmurs against my head.

He straightens and steps away, and the seam in the air closes behind him with a quiet ripple, leaving the apartment feeling strangely silent.

I sit there for a moment, touching the place he kissed, heat lingers against my skin. My pulse flutters in a way that feels unfamiliar and dangerously sweet.

I haven't felt this before, not like this. Not without pressure or expectation attached to it. Not without begging for forgiveness for something that I didn't really do.

I let myself lean back into the couch and breathe it in, the lightness, the ridiculous giddy flutter in my stomach, the realization that I genuinely like him. It feels new in a way that makes me nervous, because new things are easier to take away, and I am not sure yet how much of this I can afford to lose.

I get off the couch and crawl into bed without even

wiping off my makeup. The exhaustion is begging to pull me under.

The room is dark and quiet, but my heart is still racing, like it hasn't caught up to the fact that he's gone and that I can call him whenever I need him.

For about three seconds, everything feels still.

Then my phone starts buzzing on the nightstand. I don't have to look to know who it is.

The vibration stops. Then it starts again. It keeps going, over and over, stubborn and insistent.

I roll onto my side, turning my back to it. The screen flashes against the wall in bursts of light, bright enough to shine through the dark.

I close my eyes and pull the blanket higher over my shoulder.

It buzzes again. And again.

I let it ring.

I don't need to answer it. I don't give a shit anymore.

I fall into an incredibly peaceful sleep for the first time in a long time.

CHAPTER FIVE

Josie

The building is quiet when I unlock the door to my classroom.

I love this time of day. Everything is still off, but I can smell the cleaning solution I picked out myself—lavender with a touch of vanilla underneath it. The janitorial staff thinks I'm dramatic for caring, but if this is going to be a place where kids feel safe, it has to smell like calm. Especially when they get out of control in the mornings.

I reach beside the door and flip on the lights.

The room isn't fancy. We're a nonprofit. Most of what we have comes from grants, donation drives, or whatever someone decides to drop off because they're upgrading their private school classroom.

The walls are patched in places. The bookshelves don't match, two are donated, one leans slightly to the left if you don't wedge cardboard under the back leg. The rug in the center used to be burgundy before a hundred juice spills turned it into something closer to muted rust.

Funding comes in waves. When a grant hits, we replace what we can. When it doesn't, we repair it. We repaint. We reinforce.

But it's full of color with a ton of light. Everything I can do for these kids—I will.

I turn on the instrumental playlist I use every morning. Little voices can carry through the room, bouncing off the concrete walls. I want to give them a moment to slow down, to relax and be in the moment before we start our day.

I refill the sensory bin with fresh kinetic sand and smooth the surface flat with my palm. I lay out watercolor trays at the art table and line up the brushes so the handles all face the same direction.

I check the allergy chart by the snack station and glance over the emergency bag again even though I already did it last week. It's important to me to make sure everything is well stocked.

At the reading corner, I straighten the pillows and adjust the little basket labeled Big Feelings so it's facing outward. The weighted lap pad goes on the arm of the loveseat where Melody, our little four year old, will spot it right away.

I tape yesterday's paintings to the wall at adult height. The kids can see them, but they're too high up for them to pull down.

I set the question of the day jar in the middle of the rug and glance at the board.

What makes you feel brave?

I let out a small laugh. “Fitting,” I murmur.

I grab one of the blank slips and sit back on my heels. After a second, I press the marker to the paper.

Walking away when something feels wrong.

I don’t let myself linger on it. I fold the slip and tuck it into the jar. I always write one. The students always say theirs out loud.

The last thing I do is clip fresh clothespins along the feelings chart.

We have students aged three to six, potty trained because they have to be—it’s required. We’re inspected twice a year and run a tight ship. Our operation is small on purpose, although we all wish we could do more for the community and the women that we help. We don’t have the budget for an assistant teacher right now, so it’s just me working the childcare and classroom settings.

Emery—Bella’s assistant—left once she was fully licensed as a social worker. She took a position at a government facility on the other side of the state. We threw her a party in the kitchen with sheet cake and cheap sparkling cider.

She earned it.

So for now, everyone pitches in where they can.

At least until we find someone to take her position. She left some large shoes to fill, that’s for sure.

This place is used to change, though. Some kids stay for years. Some only last a few months before housing shifts or placements change or court dates rearrange everything again.

Today we’ve got a full classroom.

The first knock isn't actually a knock. It's a hesitant tap and then the door opens just a crack.

"Morning," Ms. Alvarez says, pushing it wider with her hip while balancing a tote bag in one hand and Mateo's hand in the other.

"Good morning," I answer, stepping aside and plastering on a bright smile.

Mateo's sneakers light up with every step. He doesn't smile yet. He rarely does before nine a.m. Some nights follow him into the morning.

His mother leans in slightly. "He didn't sleep much. Nightmares again."

"I've got him," I assure her, giving her arm a small squeeze to comfort her.

She nods once. She's newer to the group—moved into the transitional units upstairs two months ago after filing for a protective order.

The first police report didn't amount to anything, but that's just as normal as it is disheartening. The second one did a little more. But it wasn't until he shattered the dining chair and held a shard up to her throat that something was finally done.

Mateo was there for all of it. He watched his father punch a hole through drywall. Watched his mother stand between them. Watched red and blue lights wash across the living room walls three separate times.

He hasn't slept through the night since the first report was filed.

"Hi, Mateo," I say gently, squatting down to his level. "Want to check the fish first?"

He considers it. Then he walks in. I stay crouched. If you rise too fast around him, he runs.

The next arrival doesn't come in with a parent. A social

worker stands in the hallway with a little girl clutching a plastic grocery bag instead of a backpack.

"This is Ava," she tells me, smiling at the little girl. Then she adds quietly, "We're not sure how long she'll be coming to see you, but I'll keep you guys updated."

She adjusts the strap on her bag and lowers her voice. "Her dad's still downtown signing emergency paperwork. The judge wanted her somewhere stable while they sort out custody."

She gives me a look that says there's more, but not for the hallway.

"We figured this would be the best place for her."

I look straight to the little girl in front of me. She's gripping a plastic grocery bag instead of a backpack, shoulders tight, eyes flicking to the door, the exit sign, the social worker—waiting for the moment she's sent somewhere else.

"Hi, Ava. I'm Miss Josie." She studies me like she's trying to figure out if I'm safe or not. The look on her face is something I've seen plenty of times before, but it breaks my heart just as much each time.

"I have a spot in the circle," I tell her. "Right next to me."

After a second, she steps inside.

More kids trickle in now.

A dad in paint splattered jeans drops a kiss on his son's head before muttering to me. "Call me if he gets overwhelmed."

A grandmother signs the clipboard with hands that shake slightly.

One mom lingers too long at the doorway, eyes scanning her daughter. She's making sure her daughter is safe here.

"It's going to be a good day," I tell her. If she believes that, her daughter will too.

Her shoulders loosen a fraction before she nods.

One by one, the adults step back into the hallway. I close the door after the last one leaves and turn toward twelve small faces.

"Good morning," I say with a smile. "Welcome to class."

The blocks are back in their bins. The art table is wiped down. Backpacks line the wall in a neat row.

"Okay, friends," I say, settling onto the rug. "Before we go home, we have to check the jar for the question of the day!"

A few groans. A few cheers. They know the jar means we're almost done for the day, and they scoot closer without being asked.

I reach into the glass and unfold the paper.

"What makes you feel brave? I'll go first," I say, because I always do.

I don't read what I wrote. That is for me.

"Trying new things," I tell them instead. "Even when they make my tummy feel wiggly."

That gets a few giggles.

"Like broccoli," Oliver says immediately.

"Like talking in front of lots of people," Harper adds.

I nod. "Exactly. Sometimes brave just means doing the thing anyway. So, what makes you feel brave?"

I love when they actually think about their answers.

Heads tilt. Fingers twist into shirt hems. They're taking it seriously, and it warms my heart knowing that I can make a difference in their lives, even if it's just for the few hours they're here.

"When I tell my dad stop," Mateo mutters, eyes on the rug.

Oliver thinks brave is vegetables. Harper thinks it's mastering stage fright. Mateo thinks it's survival.

I nod like his answer belongs right beside the others. "That is brave," I say calmly.

Ava watches the others, then inches forward too.

"You can pass," I tell her gently. "Or you can tell us."

She looks at the door first. Then at me. "I stayed still when she did this," she says, lifting her own arm halfway.

She didn't flinch when she was threatened. Who knows how many times it took for her body to stop reacting on instinct alone to the fear. Little bodies don't learn that without reason.

I nod once, pressing my tongue to the roof of my mouth. "You did," I say. "That's brave."

Harper bumps her knee against Ava's. "I was scared on my first day, too," she offers.

Ava doesn't smile yet. But she doesn't pull away either.

A knock echoes against the door, making me jump a little. I was so engrossed in what they were saying that I didn't even realize what time it was.

3 P.M. Pickup time.

The moment breaks into backpacks and goodbyes. Small arms wrap around my waist. Sticky fingers tug at my cardigan. They leave fingerprints on everything, including me.

"Hi, Ms. Bella!" Harper calls immediately, already halfway into her mom's arms.

Bella laughs, stepping inside just enough to avoid the swirl of tiny bodies. "Hi, Miss Harper. Shoes tied today? I'm impressed."

Mateo gives her a solemn nod on his way past. Ava clutches her plastic bag and stares up at Bella like she's unsure.

Bella crouches without hesitation. "I like your sparkly shoes," she tells her.

Ava is shaking as she takes a tiny step back. She doesn't answer, but she doesn't run either. I call that progress.

When the last adult signs out and the room is finally silent, Bella stands and smooths her hands down her skirt.

"Julia's here," she says softly.

My confusion must show because Bella adds, "Owen told me after Lucas asked. I called her first thing this morning."

I lock the classroom behind me and fall into step beside my best friend. She walks fast when she's thinking.

When we pass the resource table near the room outside of Bella's office, two moms are sitting shoulder to shoulder filling out paperwork. A toddler is asleep across three chairs, their shoes still on.

This is definitely controlled chaos.

Bella pushes open her office door.

Tinsley is already inside, perched on the edge of Bella's desk, phone in one hand, three color coded sticky notes fanned out in the other. Her brown curls are pulled into a loose clip. And there are two iced lattes sweating beside her.

Julia Carter is seated across from the desk. Her dark brown hair is pulled into a tight ponytail, her suit is perfectly tailored. Her hands sit folded over a leather folio. She doesn't fidget. She doesn't check her phone. She simply watches us walk in.

Tinsley looks up first. "Okay," she says, hopping down from the desk. "We're not going to lose it."

"I'm not going to lose it," I reply automatically.

Bella lifts a brow.

Tinsley doesn't argue. She just crosses the room and pulls me into a quick, tight hug before I can protest. Her curls tickle my cheek. She smells like vanilla and espresso.

"We're not spiraling," she says into my shoulder.

I let myself lean into it for exactly one second. Then she steps back, presses one of the iced coffees into my hand, and squeezes my fingers.

"Julia's exactly what you need," she says even quieter.

Across the room, Julia gives me a small, knowing smile.

"I am," she says simply. She closes the folio and gestures toward the chair beside her. "Come sit," she adds, her voice alluding to the amount of confidence she has. "Let's go over some options."

Bella moves behind her desk. Tinsley pulls one of the mismatched guest chairs closer and angles it toward me, phone facedown but within reach. I take the chair beside Julia.

Bella closes her eyes briefly.

"I reached out to Della and Ophelia," she says as she opens them again. "Della's working, but she said to call if we need her. Ophelia's in the middle of Loom work and can't step away, but she knows what's happening."

Julia nods once, taking that in without comment. "Good," she says calmly, her attention shifting to me. "We're not waiting for him to move first," Julia says.

That catches me off guard. I assumed this would mean sitting and waiting. Letting him decide what happens next and responding.

I can be patient. "I just don't want to be powerless."

"You won't be," Julia says quietly. "We won't build this in a way that leaves you exposed."

Bella straightens in her chair while Julia folds her hands in her lap and Tinsley turns her phone facedown before reaching over to squeeze my fingers once under the edge of the desk.

"First, I file a notice of representation. Immediately." Julia holds my gaze. "From that point forward, he does not contact you directly. If he tries, it becomes documented interference."

Yes. This is what I needed. A plan. Something we can actually do. I am not putting my baby in harm's way.

"Second." She turns a page in her folio. "We start a record. Every message. Every call. Every escalation. Not to react, but to establish a pattern."

"What about the baby?" Bella asks, her voice tightening just slightly.

I can see it on her face. She wouldn't ask if she wasn't worried. The fact that she's already thinking like an aunt, like she's fully prepared to put my baby on the forefront of her mind. It brings me a sense of peace, a sense of safety.

"We cannot file for anything related to custody until the baby is born," Julia continues, steady, "but we can prepare the petition now. The day your child is delivered, we'll file for sole legal and physical custody."

My hand rests over my stomach.

"And if he asks for parental rights?" I ask. I know he's a dick. He should be around his child. I just don't want him to be around unsupervised. I have no proof that anything bad would happen. I just have a gut feeling.

Julia doesn't hesitate. "If he wants parental rights," she answers, "he petitions."

Bella's jaw tightens.

Julia turns fully toward me, her posture straight but relaxed. "You are employed. You are stably housed. You have documented community support, and you have no history of instability."

I nod, but unease presses beneath my ribs.

"But he has all of that, too," I answer, as my fingers curl against my palm. "He has a company. He has money. He has a reputation people believe in. He could ask for joint custody."

Bella and Tinsley silently stare at me. I can feel the support through their eyes.

"Yes," Julia acknowledges without hesitation. She folds her hands together loosely. "He can petition for joint legal custody. The court would then evaluate best interest. They look at stability, conduct during pregnancy, communication patterns, and documented behavior."

Bella leans forward, elbows on her knees.

"If there is volatility, coercion, or manipulation that can be demonstrated," Julia continues, her gaze still on me, "that becomes relevant. Judges weigh consistency heavily. They do not reward instability."

I swallow carefully.

"And physical custody?" I ask, pressing my palm flat against my stomach.

"He would need to demonstrate capacity," Julia replies, her tone calm, but still direct. "That means consistent residence, reliable childcare, availability, and a proven ability to provide care."

"All of which he has," I sigh.

"He can ask for joint custody," Julia finishes, her tone more optimistic now. "As of right now, he'd either be granted week on week off, which is normal until the child starts school if the parents are in the same town. Then once school starts it goes to every weekend or every other weekend."

I nod, wrapping my hands a little tighter around the iced coffee Tinsley gave me, letting the certainty in Julia's voice take me away from the hell hole that's swirling inside my head.

I'm grateful someone knows how to take what seems like hopelessness and shape it into something we can actually do.

"Josie," she says carefully, "is there a possibility we're dealing with more than one variable here?"

My throat goes dry as her eyes go to my collar bone.

Lucas.

The bond pulses faintly under my skin as if it heard his name before I thought it.

I close my eyes for half a second. It feels strange to reach out to him in my head instead of picking up a phone to dial a number.

Are you okay with this being discussed? I ask him silently.

Yes, he answers immediately.

A warmth spreads through my chest. He didn't hesitate. He didn't shut me out. He answered so fast it makes me wonder if he keeps that door open on purpose—if I could reach for him anytime and he would be there.

I like that more than I should. A restless flutter takes over my chest, impossible to ignore and even harder to name.

I'm not going anywhere, Sunshine. You don't have to knock. You're always welcome.

He said I'm welcome in his... mind. Which sounds strange when I think it through, but it's nice.

I'm not tolerated. Not temporarily allowed. Not "until further notice."

Always welcome.

Inside the one place no one else gets to be. Somehow, that feels bigger than a house key.

I open my eyes.

"There's... a possibility," I admit, and I can't quite stop the smile creeping onto my face. "That's there's... a variable," I say, trying to keep my voice level.

Bella's mouth curves immediately. "The variable being my brother-in-law."

I glare at her.

She shrugs. "He's a demon, Josie. A very attractive one."

"Bella," I warn, heat creeping up my neck.

She folds her hands together, watching me far too closely. "Am I lying?"

"No," I admit begrudgingly.

"Well," Julia stands, a faint curve touching her mouth, "I'd say you're lucky, Josie. The Duvain men are an entertaining bunch." Her gaze flicks briefly toward Bella before returning to me. "They also keep me very well employed."

She slides her folio closed and picks it up.

"I'll draft the notice tonight," she continues, gathering her colored pens. "If he contacts you directly after tomorrow, it becomes my problem. You won't hear from him again if I can prevent it."

She squeezes my shoulder, firm and grounding, her thumb pressing once. Then she gathers her things and steps out, the door closing softly behind her.

"Okay," Bella announces, turning fully toward me. "Logistics."

My stomach tightens on instinct. I have a feeling I'm not going to love whatever comes next.

"If something happens during delivery," she asks, her voice lower than it was a minute ago, "who are we calling?"

I study a thin crack in the varnish on her desk instead of looking up.

Tinsley shifts her chair closer. "Not in a worst case way," she clarifies quickly. "Just... who goes on the form? Who do they contact?"

I don't have a family. Not one that fits in the neat little box they're talking about. There's no one waiting to be called. No one pacing a hospital hallway for me. No one would hear my name over an intercom and come running without hesitation.

"Bella," I say. "Do you mind if I put your name on the form?"

I have a past. I have a mother. I have a last name I don't use anymore. But that isn't the same thing as having someone who shows up. And as much as I've kept that part of me folded away, these are my friends. If anyone deserves the truth, it's them.

"Of course, Josie." She reaches out and grabs my hand. "I would be honored."

"My name hasn't always been Josie Brighton," I say, folding my hands together so they don't shake. "It used to be Josephine Carrow."

It's still weird saying it out loud. I haven't said *Carrow* in years, I spent that time trying to run away from it as fast as humanly possible.

"I changed it," I continue. "Legally. The second I could."

For a moment I see my mother at the head of her dining table—glass of white wine in one hand, diamonds catching the chandelier light, men twice her age leaning in when she spoke. She loved rooms that had the spotlight toward her.

Loved watching people adjust themselves to fit whatever version of her she decided to be that night.

"Carrow comes with assumptions," I continue. "Money. Influence. Power. People either want something from you or they think you're like her."

I remember being six and not correcting a waiter for calling her Mrs. instead of Ms., because she cared about titles more than she cared about people. I remember how she smiled at me afterward. The same smile that I got to know well. I would hear about her displeasure later.

Bella's jaw tightens, her hand flattening against the desk as if she's physically restraining herself from reacting.

"My mom wasn't complicated," I say. "She was wealthy. She was controlling. She liked being the smartest person in every room." I shrug once. "If you didn't agree with her, she iced you out. If you embarrassed her, you were done entirely."

Bella's expression shifts into something understanding. I feel like she probably knows what that's like. With her dad being the same way.

"She didn't sell me," I add. "She just made it clear that if I wasn't useful to the machine, I wasn't necessary."

There's no anger in my heart. Not anymore. I've had my time to grieve the mother I never had and move on.

"I just don't want to be her." I rest my hand over my stomach. "I'm not building what she built," I add. "And this baby will never grow up thinking love is something you trade."

Bella doesn't hesitate. "That's how I know you are never going to become her."

The Brighton name is the one I chose. And I won't ever let anyone put me back in a position where I have to fight just to be allowed to be happy.

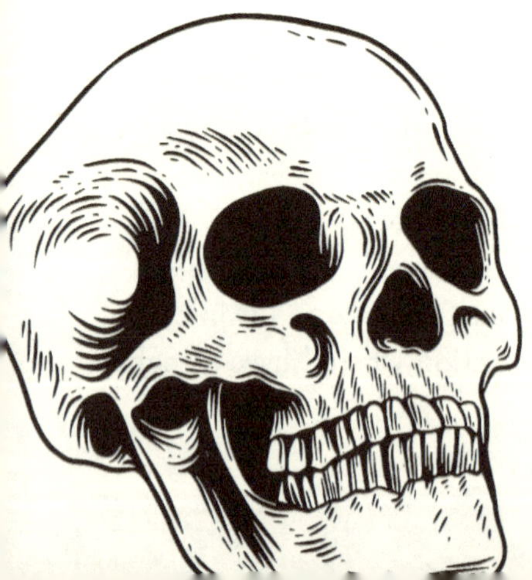

CHAPTER SIX

Another family dinner. Not that I'm really that shocked.

Ophelia started the family barbecues. She claimed it was good for bonding. Fresh air. Open space. Less tension.

My mother followed that up with structured family dinners.

Liora Duvain is not someone you say no to. She is someone you bend over backwards to say yes to. Or you endure the look of disappointment.

Mortals think that's bad—imagine adding it to an immortal soulmate from the 1700s. I would rather volunteer for cleanup duty for the next century than disappoint my mother.

She loves us. All of us. She just wants the entire family together. Now that there are two mates officially in the picture, she's even more determined to make "family time" happen.

And I know she wants grandchildren.

Not that she's getting them from Owen or Julian anytime soon. Their mates are busy running half the mortal world. Seth doesn't have a mate, or even a partner for that matter.

I guess technically she has one through me. Since Josie is my mate.

Wait. Did I just think about her baby as mine?

A rush fills my chest so fast it almost steals my breath. I press a hand over my heart.

I want that baby to be mine.

Not out of obligation. Not because of the bond.

Because I *do*.

If she's my mate, then that child would be mine too. I think. I really need to ask my aunt, Selene, about this. She seems to know everything.

"Hi, honey," my mother calls as she steps out of the kitchen. She kisses my cheek before I can dodge it.

Liora Duvain—regal without trying—is the definition of composed beauty. Dark brown hair falls in a controlled wave down her back, and her long dress brushes the floor as she moves. She doesn't look a day over thirty-five, though she's closer to three hundred and thirty-five.

"I'm so glad you could come," she adds, smoothing a nonexistent wrinkle from my jacket. "Especially after finding your soulmate."

I sit down before she can grill me more about Josie. I wouldn't know how to talk about it. Sure, we spent some time together last night, but I don't really know much else about it. I want to, I'm desperate to know every detail, but that's not where we are right now.

The table is already full with roasted chicken split down the middle, thyme and garlic clinging to the skin, bowls of braised carrots and parsnips covered in butter, and a pot of barley stew still steaming at the center. Thick country bread sits in a torn heap beside a crock of herb butter. Liora favors meals that could've been served in 1720 just as easily as tonight.

Evander, my father, pours dark red wine into glasses, starting with her.

Caleb reaches for the bread too early.

Liora taps the back of his hand without looking up. "Wait."

"I am waiting," he protests, already chewing.

Seth steals a sugared almond and winks at Bella when she catches him.

Julian waits until Mother sits before touching his plate. Owen adjusts his knife parallel to the edge of his fork before he cuts into anything. Damian scans the room like he expects someone to start a war between courses. Adrian's eyes are on the table.

"Can we eat now?" Seth, my younger brother, asks with mocked annoyance.

"Yes, dear," Selene chuckles at him.

Theron leans back in his chair. "So," he drawls, "which one of you is about to complicate my evening?"

Selene sips her wine with a grin. "Statistically? All of them."

Evander snorts. "You married into this family. You knew what you were doing."

"Did I?" Selene asks lightly. "Or was I seduced under false pretenses?"

"You begged," Theron reminds her.

She gives us all a shit eating grin.

The noise grows into overlapping conversations. A norm for our dinners. Seth arguing that indulgence is more efficient than strategy, Owen disagreeing without lifting his eyes, Caleb claiming excess is simply accelerated inevitability. Mother tears a piece of bread and dips it into the stew. My father watches everything without appearing to.

It's a normal, chaotic family dinner.

Ophelia sits quieter than the rest, fingers tracing the rim of her glass, eyes distant for a second before she looks up. "How was the meeting with you, Josie, Tinsley, and Julia today?"

That hushes the entire table. We all want to know what is going on with that meeting.

Bella wipes her hands on her napkin and lifts her chin.

"It went fine," she begins, too calm considering the situation at hand. "Julia did what Julia does. She built a plan. She's filing a notice of representation. He doesn't contact Josie directly anymore. Everything routes through her."

Julian nods once, satisfied with how things turned out.

"We're documenting everything," Bella continues. "If he escalates, it becomes part of the record. We prepare custody filings now so there's no scrambling later."

Liora sets her glass down with deliberate care.

Her gaze shifts to me.

"And what," she begins, folding her hands in front of her plate, "are you planning to do?"

Every head at the table turns toward me. Three brothers. Three cousins. Their mates. My parents. My aunt. My uncle.

No pressure.

I rest my forearms on the table. "I was going to ask for advice," I admit. "She's pregnant. I don't know if that changes things."

A few glances are exchanged.

"What would it change, exactly?" Theron presses.

"My approach," I answer. "The bond is one thing. But she's carrying someone else's child." The words don't sting the way they might have earlier. They just sit there.

"I don't know if that means I push harder," I admit, rolling the stem of my glass between my fingers, "or if I give her more room."

Seth studies me for a second before a grin spreads across his face. "You? Push?"

Caleb nearly collapses off the chair. "Brother, the only thing you push is the end of the deal paperwork."

"I do not move slowly," I argue, leaning back in my chair.

Theron tilts his head, openly skeptical. "You're correct, you don't move slowly. You take sabbaticals before making a decision."

"I've been respectful," I insist. "To everyone."

Seth leans back in his chair, looking at me like I just volunteered for something stupid.

"Respectful," he repeats with a crooked grin, as if I've just said something adorable and wrong.

"That's not a flaw," I add, pushing my chair back half an inch.

"No," Owen replies, wiping his hands neatly on his napkin before folding it beside his plate. "It just isn't the same thing as decisive."

I feel that one in my very soul. I've never been decisive in the moment. I always like to take my time to think about things all the way through. Everything needs to process for a minute.

Except I don't have time to wait on this.

"She's pregnant," I say again, resting my forearms on the table now. "That complicates things."

Selene sets her glass down carefully while studying me.

"Tell me what you think it changes." She isn't mocking me. She is genuinely curious about everything.

I run a hand over my jaw before answering. "It changes... timing." I search for the word. "We don't have time to work through all the kinks."

Selene's brows lift slightly. "Sweetheart, pregnancy doesn't remove the kinks. It just makes them visible faster."

A few low chuckles ripple down the table, you'd think they'd be more mature than this. I don't laugh. I lean forward instead.

"So what do I do?" I ask her directly. "Specifically."

Her mouth curves faintly. She appreciates direct questions. My aunt Selene is blunt. Sometimes to a fault.

"You don't treat her like a problem to solve," she replies.

"I'm not," I answer, and immediately hate how defensive it sounds.

"You are," she counters gently. "You're trying to engineer the correct entry point."

She isn't wrong. I always try to find the perfect next move. If not, then I wait longer.

"She's carrying another man's child," I say, staring at the center of the table. "I don't want to overstep."

Selene nods. "Good. Don't."

I rest my hands flat on the table, grounding myself against the flare of something territorial I don't want anyone to notice. It could be the bond acting up. It could be something else.

Selene doesn't look away. "You don't compete with the pregnancy. You don't pretend it isn't there. You don't dance around it."

I drag a hand over my mouth, frustration tightening my chest. "Then what?"

"You acknowledge it," she says simply. "You acknowledge that your relationship has a baby that is in it."

Seth leans back in his chair. "Translation: don't act scared of it."

"I'm not scared," I argue.

Selene gives me a look. "You're cautious," she amends. "Which is fine. But cautious can read as uncertain."

I consider that. I don't want to be uncertain of anything. I don't *feel* uncertain about her, or about the child. The only thing I'm not sure of is how to approach this situation with her.

"She's deciding who belongs in her life right now," Selene continues. "Pregnancy changes that instinct. It makes you more protective. Less spontaneous."

"I don't know how to be a father," I admit, letting my biggest concern free.

Across the table, my father stops mid reach for his glass. He doesn't react immediately. He studies me instead—the way he does when something he is about to say matters.

Theron shifts beside him, resting his forearms on the table.

"Good," Theron says first.

I frown. "Good?"

"If you thought you did," he replies, "I'd be worried."

A faint ripple of agreement comes from my aunt and mother.

Evander sets his glass down carefully. "No one knows how," he says. "You decide to try. That's the qualification."

"That's all you have for me?" I let out a dry laugh. *Seriously*. I was expecting a bit more help.

"It is," Theron replies without apology.

Evander glances at him before looking back at me.

"When Owen was young," Evander begins, folding his

hands loosely on the table, "his temper manifested long before his control did." Owen lifts a brow but doesn't interrupt. "He set the east wing curtains on fire," Evander continues.

Seth snorts. "They *were* ugly."

"And I extinguished it," Owen adds.

"Not before you nearly burned the house down," Theron corrects.

A few smirks flicker around the table. Evander's gaze never leaves mine. "My response," he continues, "was to suppress him."

Owen's jaw tightens almost imperceptibly.

"I bound his power for a year," Evander says.

We all know that Owen set shit on fire when he was mad as a kid. But we didn't know that he had his powers suppressed. We thought he just couldn't leave the house. Grounding as the mortals called it. Not that he actually could not teleport or have any powers whatsoever.

"I did it publicly," Evander adds.

Everyone at the table shifts in our seats. Owen looks at him.

"In front of the council," Evander continues evenly. "In front of our allies. I made an example of you." Seth's grin fades. "I thought humiliation would prevent future recklessness."

Owen exhales slowly through his nose.

"I did not ask why you were angry," Evander continues. "I did not ask what had triggered it. I reacted to the fire. Not the cause."

I had no idea any of this happened. At all.

"You were sixteen," Evander says to Owen. "And I made you stand there while they whispered your punishment."

Owen doesn't look at him. "It taught me control," he says after a moment.

"It taught you concealment," Evander corrects. "It hardened you for a long time. Until you became a mate."

Evander's eyes flick back to me. "You will have moments where fear makes you act quickly," he says. "Where you choose authority over understanding." He pauses, looking at Owen. "If you do that, correct it quickly."

Theron exhales through his nose. "I made the opposite mistake."

Caleb groans. "I know you did."

"I let him fight a duel he wasn't ready for," Theron says. "I thought blood would teach him restraint." Caleb rubs the back of his neck. "I stood back because I believed stepping in would weaken him."

"You almost lost an arm," Seth mutters.

Caleb shrugs. "I kept it."

Theron looks at me. "You can overprotect. You can overexpose. Both are errors."

Evander nods once. "The difference between a good father and a tyrant is the willingness to apologize."

Owen and Caleb freeze when they hear that.

"You think you will fail because you are afraid of hurting someone," Evander says to me. *He's right.* "You will," he continues plainly. "In small ways."

"But if you do not retreat when you do," Theron adds, "you will not lose them."

I sit there, absorbing it. Selene's watching it all quietly.

"Fatherhood is stewardship," my father says.

"You will misjudge your mate," Theron continues. "You will misread the child. You will overcorrect."

Evander nods. "And if you retreat because you are ashamed of that, you fail."

"She is carrying something powerful," Selene adds softly. "You think that intimidates you."

It does. "I don't want to mishandle any of this," I admit.

Theron leans back in his chair. "Demons do not become better by avoiding fire."

A few smirks flicker.

"You stay in it," Evander finishes. "You learn the heat."

"She will be protective," Selene says. "That child will be watched."

"I know," I answer.

"Then show her you are not afraid of what she carries," Theron says. "Or who."

I look down at my hands. "I don't want her doing this alone," I say finally.

Evander nods once. "Then don't stand at the threshold."

The table eventually breaks into smaller conversations. Chairs scrape back. Caleb and Seth argue about something irrelevant near the fireplace. Mother disappears toward the kitchen with Ophelia.

I'm reaching for my jacket to head home when Bella touches my arm.

"Walk with me," she murmurs.

We step out onto the back terrace. The air is cooler out here. The house noise dulls behind us.

Bella leans her hip against the stone railing and folds her arms. "You needed that talk in there," she says lightly.

"I gathered."

Her smile fades. "There's something you should know."

The shift in her tone makes me straighten. "What?"

"I did some research," she says. "After Josie told us her real name."

My chest tightens slightly. I thought Josie Brighton *was* her real name.

"Josephine Carrow," she continues. "Lucinda Carrow's daughter."

I look at her. "I didn't know Josie wasn't her name."

"Didn't think you would." She rests her hand on my shoulder. "Even I didn't know until today. She didn't tell anyone."

"Who is her mother?"

"Lucinda Carrow is wealthy. Old money. Contracts, consulting, 'arrangements.'" She makes air quotes. "Rich piece of work. Josie wasn't groomed the way people assume," Bella says. "She wasn't paraded around."

My jaw tightens anyway.

"She was useful," Bella continues. "Lucinda ran her household like a corporation. Staff rotated constantly. NDAs everywhere."

Bella looks back at me. "Josie did everything. Scheduling. Hosting. Managing accounts. Cleaning up after events."

"She was a child," I say quietly.

"She was free labor," Bella says, disgust in her voice. "And expected to be grateful for it."

Fucking mortals. Most of them are predictable—short sighted, reactive, convinced consequences won't catch up to them. That's why Hell stays busy.

"When she left," Bella continues, "Lucinda didn't chase her. Didn't threaten her. Didn't beg."

I tilt my head at her, silently begging her to continue. I'm desperate for any information about my sunshine. I want to know every detail about every part of her life. I don't want to have to ask her, I want to know, to be able to make her life better without her asking a thing of me.

"No. She did something even worse." Bella pauses. "She erased her. Removed her from the family trust. Cut off access. Had her name taken off records where she could. Publicly refers to herself as having no children. Josie left, she didn't look back. She was no longer useful so her mother pretended that she never existed at all. It showed her that she's disposable."

My hands curl slowly at my sides. For a moment, all I hear is the distant churn of lava rolling through the ravine below.

"She has no family," Bella adds. "No one calls. No one checks in. No safety net to fall back on."

The word safety echoes against everything we just discussed inside. Bella watches my face carefully before speaking again.

"Jasper was adopted from foster care," she says. "But not right away."

I look at her, confused. I don't give a shit about this man.

"I think Josie saw another unwanted person in him. He bounced around first," she continues. "Three placements before the Creeds helped finalize it with his new parents. Two of them didn't last six months. Apparently he was a menace."

I don't love the sound of her calling him a *menace*. I believe that is an understatement.

"He was older when he was adopted," she says. "Old enough to remember being passed over. Young enough where he was easily manipulated by Rhys and the Creeds."

There's something in her voice that leaves me on edge.

It feels like she is trying to both give me information as well as warn me not to hurt her friend.

"Josie grew up in a house where love was conditional," Bella continues. "Transactional. Useful."

The lava churns somewhere beyond the estate walls.

"She didn't choose him because he was powerful," Bella says. "She chose him not because he felt like a home she always dreamed of, but someone who also understands what it is like."

My Sunshine will never have to feel lost or broken again.

"She thought he understood what it meant to not belong," Bella continues.

"She will never feel that way again," I tell her, the promise settling into my bones. "Not while I'm here."

I don't hesitate.

I open a portal and step through it toward her.

Toward my Sunshine.

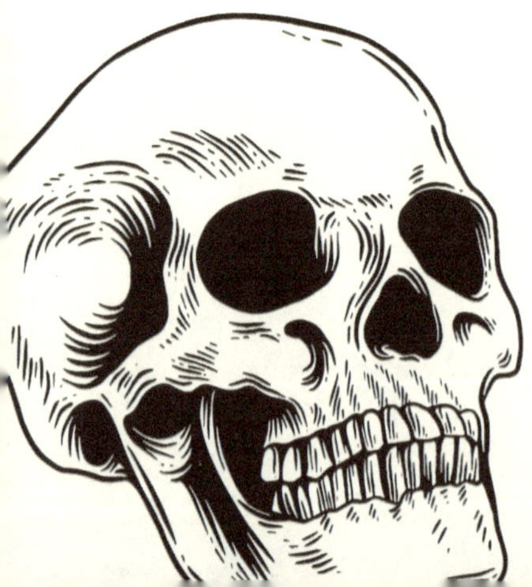

CHAPTER SEVEN

Lucas

I step into the hallway outside her apartment instead of directly into her living room. Probably wouldn't be my best move to appear beside her couch unannounced.

I glance down at my watch. Hell runs on its own time, but with a tap the face shifts to mortal hours. It's early in the evening, so she should be home from work.

I lift my hand and knock.

For a moment, I consider leaving before she answers. But I don't have a chance to turn away.

"Lucas?" She blinks up at me, nose scrunched, brow furrowed in confusion. "What are you doing here? And why are you in the hallway?"

She's painfully cute when she's disoriented.

"I figured materializing in your living room might be a little invasive," I reply, rubbing the back of my neck. "Trying this thing called boundaries."

That earns a small laugh.

"Come in," she says, stepping back and pulling the door wider.

She closes the door behind me when I cross the threshold, then turns around slowly.

"So," she starts, then stops. "Did someone die or—"

I laugh under my breath. "No one died."

"Okay," she says quickly. "That's good. That's... great."

She gestures vaguely toward the couch and then the kitchen like she doesn't know where to put me.

"Do you want water? I have water. Or juice. I think there's juice."

I can't help it—I smile at her. "You're rambling."

"I am not rambling," she shoots back immediately. "I just wasn't expecting you to show up in my hallway like some morally responsible demon."

That gets a fuller laugh out of me.

"I came to tell you something," I say, stepping a little closer.

Her shoulders straighten like she's bracing. "Okay," she says carefully. "That sounds ominous."

"It's not." I say seriously. I mean it. It isn't supposed to be frightening.

She narrows her eyes slightly. "That's exactly what someone says before they say something ominous."

I shake my head. "I was going to give you space," I admit.

She blinks. "Oh."

"I thought that was the respectful move."

"That's very... considerate of you?" She stammers out. I don't know if she even realizes what I'm saying.

"But I realized that was a mistake."

Her mouth opens. Closes. Opens again. "What do you mean by mistake?"

Heat crawls up my forearm. I move into her space before I can stop myself. Close enough that she has to tilt her head to look at me.

"I don't want to be distant," I tell her. "I don't want to hover at the edges of your life while you figure everything out alone."

Her breath catches slightly. "Lucas—"

"I know you're pregnant," I say. "I know that's not a small thing. I know this isn't how you pictured any of this."

She looks down at her stomach automatically.

"But I'm not afraid of it," I continue. "I'm not afraid of the baby. I'm not afraid of the complications. I'm not afraid of what people think."

She looks back up at me, searching.

"You don't have to know what to do with me," I add, softer now. "You don't need to have the right words."

Her lips part like she's about to argue and then she just... doesn't.

"I want you to know that I don't want you doing this alone," I finish. "I'm not going anywhere."

She stares at me for a long second. "That's really unfair," she says finally.

I blink. "Unfair?"

"Yes," she insists, stepping forward. "You can't just show up and say things like that and expect me to be cool about it."

A smile pulls at my mouth.

Her hand grips the front of my shirt before I can say anything else.

"I want to do this before I chicken out," she blurts.

She fists her hand in my collar and pulls me down like she needs this to breathe. Like she needs this as much as I do.

She collides with me—impatient, breathless—and for a second it's all teeth and air and urgency, her body pressing in like she's decided thinking is overrated.

I catch her jaw between my fingers, angling her where I want her.

"Now it's my turn," I murmur into her mouth.

I don't wait. I kiss her back. Slow enough that she can stop me if she wants to. But she won't.

Her fingers tighten in my shirt like she's afraid I'll disappear if she loosens her grip. I cup her jaw, holding her there with me.

When I deepen the kiss, she exhales into me, and the sound nearly undoes me. My hand slides to her waist, drawing her closer.

When I pull back, it's only far enough to look at her. Her lips are flushed. Her bright green eyes are wide, pink is blooming across her cheek bones. She looks unbearably sweet.

"Holy shit," she breathes.

I huff a laugh under my breath, brushing my thumb along her jaw. "You're the one who started it."

"That kiss was... not normal," she says, then winces like she realizes she hasn't processed a complete thought.

"Normal is overrated." I don't let go of her face. "I'm a demon, Josie. The normal ship sailed."

She studies me with the kind of focus that has ended civilizations.

"Can we try that again?" She asks, a little breathless.

My mouth tips at the corners. "I was hoping you'd say that."

I brush my thumb along her jaw and kiss her again, smiling into it when she melts.

I ease back, my forehead resting against hers.

"You're still terrifying," she murmurs. She smiles against my mouth, small and bright. "But I like it."

I slide my hand into her blonde curls and tilt her head up just enough to look at me. "I know."

"So what do we do now?" She's nervous. I can hear it under the question.

She knows what soulmates are. What the mark means. She isn't pretending this is casual. She isn't denying it either. If anything, she's stepping toward it.

What she's really asking is how this changes us.

"We start at the beginning," I say.

Her brows knit. "The beginning of what?"

"Whatever this is." I gesture lightly between us. "The mark is a start. Not a finish line."

She watches me carefully. Her brows are furrowed. Her mind is working overtime to try to find an answer to a question that really doesn't have one.

"It doesn't build anything for us," I continue. "It just points us in the direction of where to start. We still have to do all of the heavy lifting."

Her hand drifts to her stomach.

"As a family?" She asks a little unsure if she wants to hear the answer.

"If that's what you want," I agree. She wants to be a family. She craves it. It's why she chose to be with Jasper in the first place. Even if she hasn't fully admitted it to herself yet.

She swallows and glances away.

"The baby is part of it," she whispers so low that I can barely hear what she's trying to say. "I know that."

There's something strained under the words.

"But?" I press.

Her jaw tightens. "But part of me wishes I wasn't pregnant."

I don't let any reaction show on my face. I thought her anger was about Jasper. This is deeper than that.

She rushes to finish her thought. "Not because of the baby. I already love the baby. That's not—" She shakes her head. "It's just..."

She looks down. "I don't remember," she says.

My entire body goes rigid. She *doesn't* remember? That better not mean what *I* think it means.

"The week the doctor says I conceived," she continues, her voice strained. "I don't remember any of it. Not really. It's blurry. Like it's... missing."

My hands curl slowly at my sides. Jasper Wilder just signed his own death warrant. I don't need to shout. I don't need to threaten. I will make him pay for every fucking thing he did to her.

"Now that I know Jasper made a deal," she says, anger threading through it, "it all makes sense."

I let her finish. A deal. A missing week. A perfectly timed conception. Patterns like that don't happen by accident. Someone planned this shit.

She looks up at me, eyes blazing. "He did something to me, Lucas."

She starts pacing, arms wrapped tight around herself, barely containing the explosion under her skin. "He made that deal and then he planned it," she says. "He had to have. You don't just get lucky enough for all of that to line that up."

That is exactly what I thought. Jasper did something.

"And Owen just... took the deal," she snaps. "Like I wasn't even a factor. Like my body was just part of the fucking contract."

She starts pacing, running her fingers through her hair.

"That's bullshit," she continues, angrier now. "You don't get to bargain with my life. You don't get to decide I'm part of some strategy because it benefits you."

Her breathing turns ragged.

"I knew he was a manipulative shit," she says, pacing again. "But this? This is the next level."

She lets out a hollow laugh. "He didn't just want to mess with me. He wanted to lock me in. Tie me to him permanently."

Her eyes flick to her stomach and away again.

"He didn't just want a relationship," she continues, voice turning acid. "He wanted me in his life at any cost. He wanted a guarantee. And Owen gave that to him."

The pain in her laugh this time makes me want to stab something. Or someone.

"Was I ever anything to him," she asks, bitter now, "or was I just... useful?" She shakes her head once. "Jesus." Her voice drops, no tremor now. "That is so unbelievably fucked."

She doesn't look at me when she says it. She's staring at the floor like it betrayed her.

"Owen wouldn't have known you were part of it," I say, calm as ever. Even though I do not feel calm. She has no right to blame Owen for *Jasper's* decisions.

I may be a bit defensive but Owen is my *brother*. I know he would never do anything knowing that it would hurt Josie.

"Excuse me?" She asks, lifting her head slowly.

"He wouldn't have agreed to terms that harmed you intentionally, or anyone who didn't deserve it," I tell her. "If he knew this was Jasper's plan to get you, the deal wouldn't have been signed."

"You're defending him," she says, shaking her head. "Should I wait while you draft his character reference?"

"I'm telling you he wouldn't have done it knowingly," I reply, folding my hands behind my back so I don't reach for her.

"And how do you know that?" she says, spinning toward me. "Because he's your brother?"

"Yes," I admit.

"Exactly," she snaps. "So don't tell me what he would or wouldn't do. You're handing him the benefit of the doubt when you know greed is his whole thing."

"Jasper made the request," I say firmly.

"And Owen signed it," she says, stepping closer. I stop trying to correct her. This isn't about Owen. I see that now. She blames him and she's right to. Demons never give a shit about the outcome of circumstances and how that could affect those that are around the ones we love.

It isn't even about intent.

It's about the outcome.

Two powerful men signed a document, and she woke up pregnant.

Whatever the nuance, whatever the technicalities, she is the one living with it.

Something shifts in me as I look at her standing there, arms folded tight like she's holding herself together.

"You're not angry about him," I say slowly, watching her face.

She doesn't answer, but her breathing changes.

"You're angry that it was decided without you," I continue, keeping my tone measured.

Her jaw tightens, and she looks away, and as I watch her I understand—this is about what being hasty can cost.

One by one, the Duvains have found their mates, and

with that has come a shift in focus, a subtle loosening of vigilance we would never admit to out loud. We are still powerful. Still precise. But precision requires attention, and attention has been divided.

If a contract passed through Owen's hands without full context, then the failure isn't greed—it's oversight. And lack of oversight is unacceptable.

We should be listening longer before we answer, researching before we sign, understanding who is calling and why before ink ever touches parchment. Not because we are careless—but because we can no longer afford to be.

"I built my life carefully," she says, her voice lower now as she turns her back to me. "I chose what I let in. I chose who got to my heart. I chose how much control I gave up."

Her hand drifts to her stomach before she seems to realize she's done it.

"And apparently none of that mattered," she finishes, her fingers curling against the fabric of her shirt.

"You're right," I say quietly. Her eyes lift to mine at that, surprised.

"If a contract was signed and you were collateral in it," I continue without stopping to wait for a reply, "then the intent doesn't absolve the result."

"I don't care who didn't mean for it to happen," she says, her hands dropping to her sides. "It still happened."

"Yes," I agree, because there's no argument left in that.

She looks tired now. The anger drained something out of her.

"I'll let you get some sleep," I say.

She nods once. "I have work in the morning."

She doesn't ask me to stay. She doesn't ask me to go. I watch her for a second longer, making sure she's okay. Making sure the anger isn't tipping into something worse.

"You're okay?" I ask.

She exhales. "I will be."

That has to be enough. "Call me if you need anything," I say.

She gives me a small nod.

I wait until the portal shuts behind me before I let the calm slip from my face. The air folds around me before it opens and I'm spit out in an office.

Julia Carter doesn't look surprised when I materialize in front of her desk. She simply closes the file in front of her.

"Tell me," she says.

So I do. I tell her about the missing week. The deal. The conception window. The lack of memory. By the time I finish, her face is etched in stone. The anger is palpable throughout the room.

Julia steeples her fingers. "I had Raymond run something in the Archives."

Raymond is the structural mind behind the firm—the man who maps leverage before anyone else sees the board.

My gaze snaps to her. "And?"

"There are precedents." She slides a thin folder across the desk. "Rare. But documented."

I remain standing.

"Pregnancy occurring under a mate bond prior to formal claim," she continues evenly. "In those cases, paternity did not align with the presumed mortal partner."

I hate all of this lawyer speak. "Meaning?" I ask.

Her lips tip slightly. That's quite scary honestly. "The bond can supersede biology."

I think I heard that the bond... *What the fuck.*

"And if that's the case here?" I ask the first thing that comes to my head.

"Then the child may not legally belong to Jasper." She drops a bomb.

"What do you need?" I ask.

"A test." She nods.

Raymond appears in the doorway as if summoned by implication alone—impeccable, composed.

"I'll prepare the documentation," he says.

Julia rises without another word and crosses to a locked cabinet behind her desk. She opens it with a key I don't recognize and withdraws a small obsidian case etched with faint, pulsing sigils.

"Consent?" She asks, glancing at me.

"Yes." I raise a brow at her. Something tells me this is about to get very interesting.

She sets the case on her desk and flips it open. Inside rests a thin silver blade and a crystal vial no larger than her thumb, the glass humming faintly.

"This won't touch a mortal lab," she says calmly. "It stays in house."

"Good." We can't afford to have my blood just running around the mortal world.

She slices my palm in one clean motion. The cut burns —not from pain, but from containment magic catching what I am before it spills beyond the boundary.

A single drop falls into the vial.

The crystal flashes once and seals itself.

She closes the case.

"I'll collect Josie's tomorrow," she says.

"If it confirms," I say, "then the child isn't Jasper's."

Julia inclines her head once.

If the bond overrode the contract, then paternity follows the bond.

And that would make the child mine.

CHAPTER EIGHT

Josie

I walk into my classroom conflicted.

I need to talk to someone. Owen isn't at fault and I shouldn't have said that. But I also want to start something real with Lucas. I need to accept the part of myself that can't change while also making sure I am the reason it never happens again.

This is all really beginning to annoy me.

Flipping on my classroom lights, I see Julia sitting at my desk.

"We need to talk," she says ominously. This is not a social visit.

I close the classroom door behind me slowly.

"Should I be worried?" I ask.

Julia studies me the way a trial attorney studies a witness—cataloging tells, assessing truth, mapping where to press.

"That depends," she says calmly. "How certain are you that Jasper Wilder is the father of your child?"

The question is like getting splashed in the face with ice cold water. "I mean... he is," I say, too quickly. "He's the only person I've been with."

Even if I don't remember any of the conception.

Julia doesn't argue. She simply opens the folder, the way she might introduce evidence she already knows I won't like.

"Raymond accessed archival records yesterday," she says. "Infernal ones in Hell."

Of all the things I thought she might say, that wasn't one of them. "And?" I prompt.

"There is one recorded instance," she says evenly, "of pregnancy occurring during the early activation of a soulmate bond."

My throat goes dry. "What does that mean?" I ask. Demon biology is not exactly covered in health class.

"It means," she says, folding her hands, "that when a soulmate bond ignites prior to formal claiming, it can alter the metaphysical alignment of a developing child."

I stare at her.

"In certain bloodlines," she continues evenly, "particularly those born of demon and mate pairings, the bond does not simply influence emotion. It influences inheritance."

"Inheritance," I repeat.

"Yes," she says. "If a child is conceived during early bond ignition, the bond can override mortal biology. It can restructure the child's immortal alignment before birth."

My stomach drops.

"You're saying DNA just... changes?"

"I'm saying," Julia replies calmly, "that in one documented case, the presumed mortal father was not the biological one once immortal alignment settled."

"So what are you telling me?" I ask.

"I'm telling you that Jasper may not be the father," she says. "And if he is not, that changes everything."

Everything.

My hand moves unconsciously to my stomach. "You said there's only one known case."

"Yes," she says without hesitation.

I swallow. "So this is rare."

"Extremely," Julia replies, calm as ever.

"Convenient," I mutter, my pulse kicking up a notch. "What would you need?"

"I would need a sample of your blood," she says, as if she's requesting a signature rather than something pulled from my vein. "It cannot go through a hospital or a mortal lab. It would be processed infernally and kept entirely discreet."

Fantastic. I hate blood.

"If Jasper isn't the father," I say slowly, "then—"

"Then the law shifts," she finishes. "Significantly."

So now I'm not just dealing with mortal custody. I'm dealing with immortal custody too.

Bright side—if Jasper doesn't have anything to do with this child, I get a clean break. I get to walk away from him forever.

Julia reaches into her bag and produces a small, silver capped vial and a slender needle that looks far too elegant to belong in a preschool classroom.

"Consent?" She asks.

I hold out my arm. "Yes. Please get it over with."

I turn my head and squeeze my eyes shut. When the needle bites, I grit my teeth instead of yelping.

Julia is efficient. A brief sting, a quiet pull, and then it's done—dark red sealed behind glass before I can talk myself into not fainting.

She seals and labels it. "I'll have the results soon," she says, sliding everything neatly back into her bag.

She stands. I watch her walk toward the door, composed as ever.

At the threshold, she pauses. "For what it's worth," she says without turning, "you deserve to know the truth."

Then she opens the classroom door and leaves through it like any other mortal visitor.

The door closes behind Julia like nothing unusual just happened. She casually suggested that my child might be fathered by a demon because fate felt creative.

I stare at the tiny blue chairs for a second longer than I should.

Then the hallway explodes. Backpacks thump against hooks. Sneakers squeak. Someone is already crying before they've even crossed into the room.

"Miss Josie!" Melody barrels into the room like she hasn't seen me in years instead of twelve hours.

I paste on a smile. "Good morning."

The routine begins. Attendance. Snack bins. One shoe is mysteriously missing. Two arguments over the same red crayon despite the fact that there was another one right next to it.

Normally, I move through it without thinking. It's muscle memory by this point.

Today, I miss a beat.

I call the wrong names at attendance. I forget which kid is allergic to strawberries and have to double check the chart taped inside the cabinet.

When Mateo asks me a question about whether butterflies remember being caterpillars, I stare at him a second too long before answering.

"Of course they do," I say finally. "They just don't remember it the same way."

Thankfully, he nods like that makes perfect sense.

The morning blurs. I'm present. I'm functioning. But it feels like I'm moving half a second behind everything.

By the time the end of the day rolls around, I can't tell you what we read during circle time.

Bella lingers in my doorway, staring at me in a way only a best friend can. "You okay?"

I sit down at my desk—the same desk Julia commandeered this morning—and drop my head into my hands.

"She thinks Jasper might not be the father," I say into my palms.

Bella's eyes widen so fast it's almost cartoonish. "I'm sorry—what?"

I gesture vaguely at the universe. "Apparently there's a documented case where a soulmate bond ignited early and rewrote paternity. Because of course there is."

Bella pinches the bridge of her nose.

"And they're testing it," I add. "Infernal lab. No hospital. No mortal lab. Discreet."

"And you're okay?" She asks.

"No," I say honestly. "But I am deeply committed to pretending I am."

"Fuck. Hex & Brews," she says finally. "We're going now."

Despite everything, I snort. "You really think tea fixes infernal paternity anomalies?"

"No," she says. "But Della might."

I grab my bag. This is my life now. Demon genetics and herbal tea.

Fan-fucking-tastic.

The deep sage door closes, muting the street. Ivy crawls up exposed brick, fairy lights tangled in the vines. Waxless candles float lazily near the beams overhead.

The driftwood bar stretches along the left wall, sigils carved deep into the grain. Shelves of labeled apothecary jars rise behind it, glass catching the light. The air smells like steeped mint and something similar to incense.

A woman stands from one of the barstools when she sees us approach.

She's tall, maybe mid thirties, dark hair pulled back in a low knot that looks more practical than styled. Olive toned skin. High cheekbones softened by faint smile lines at the corners of her eyes. She is wearing dark jeans, boots, and a fitted blazer over a simple tee.

"I should head out," she says, checking her phone. "School pickup."

"Not before introductions," Della says smoothly. "Josie, Bella! This is Blaire Reeves."

Blaire offers her hand. Her grip is firm in a way that makes you instinctively relax.

"Nice to meet you," she says and it sounds like she means it.

"Likewise," I answer. I like her already.

"Josie's pregnant," Della adds, because apparently privacy is fictional here.

"Della," I mutter, slightly annoyed.

Blaire's gaze shifts to my stomach, then back to my face. She chuckles. "How far along?"

"Sixteen weeks." Apparently we're oversharing today.

"You have kids?" Bella asks.

"One," Blaire says, a small smile breaking through. "Five years old."

"Single mother?" Bella asks bluntly.

"Bella," I hiss.

Blaire doesn't flinch. "Yeah. Single."

Bella nods once, impressed. "That's badass."

"It's practical," Blaire says. "You adapt."

I like her immediately for not romanticizing it. She glances at her phone again. "I really do have to go," she says. "It was nice meeting you, Josie and Bella."

"You too, Blaire." Bella and I say in unison.

"I'll see you around," she adds to Della, then slips out, the door shutting softly behind her.

Della wipes her hands on a cloth and nods toward the the door at the end of the bar. "Let's go to the back room."

Behind the curtain of bones, beads, and feathers, the light shifts slightly cooler. The back room is smaller, more enclosed. A round table sits in the center, tarot decks stacked neatly beside a bowl of polished stones. A tall mirror leans against one wall, its surface faintly rippling.

Ophelia is already there. She's perched on the edge of the table, shoulders hunched, fingers twisted together in her lap. Her eyes are red.

"Oh," she says when she sees us. "I'm sorry." The word *sorry* cracks.

Bella steps forward. "Lia—"

"It's fine," she insists, shaking her head. "I'm fine. I just need a minute." She wipes at her cheeks, embarrassed more than anything. "I'm sorry," she says again, looking at me this time.

Before I can respond, she slips past us and through the curtain. The bones and beads clink faintly in her wake.

I look at Della.

"What was that?" Bella asks.

"Nothing that you need to worry about," Della says. "It's her story to tell."

The chair creaks under me when I lower myself into it. Della leans back against the edge of the table instead of joining us.

"So," she says, "why are you here?"

I don't pace myself. I just start talking.

Julia. The bond. The blood test. The possibility that Jasper isn't the father. The week I can't remember. All of it spills out in one long, unedited, rambling, rush.

By the time I finish, my throat feels scraped raw.

Della doesn't interrupt once. "So," she says after a moment, making sure I'm not planning on saying anything else, "you want answers."

"I want to know what Jasper is actually capable of," I insist.

Bella's knee bumps mine under the table. Della's mouth tightens slightly.

"That," she says, "is a loaded situation." Della doesn't reach for herbs or tools. She stays seated across from me and leans forward slightly, resting her forearms on the table.

Her movements change. The green in her eyes darkens until it's nearly black. The room draws inward, a slow vortex forming, and for a second I think of Charybdis and ships that never made it back to shore.

"Give me your hands," she says, and it isn't a suggestion.

I slide them across the table. She takes them before I can reconsider. Her grip tightens, thumbs settling against my pulse.

"Don't pull away," she says.

Her thumbs press harder into my pulse. She's counting something only she can hear.

When she closes her eyes, the floor trembles beneath us. Not enough to knock anything over, but enough that the glass jars along the wall rattle against their shelves. The floating candles dip, flames flattening as if the air has thickened.

Her fingers clamp around my wrists in a way that almost burns.

The room seems to compress around us, sound turning thick and distant. The brick walls bend inward toward her, as though we are standing in the center of a tide that has pulled back too far and is about to return.

My pulse hammers under her thumbs.

The mirror fractures into scenes that feel half formed and wrong—bathwater clouded pink, a wrist wrapped in gauze, a hospital bracelet dangling from a limp hand. A man kneeling in the dark, looking upward as if waiting for someone to find him.

The images flicker too fast to hold on to them.

The room drops away.

I'm standing in my classroom, but it isn't morning. The lights are off. The windows are black. My desk lies overturned, chairs scattered across the floor as if someone left in a hurry. Crayons are ground into the tile beneath my feet, crushed into dust.

The room is washed of color, reduced to gray and shadow.

Only one thing stands out. The red spreading across the tile, pooling at the base of the overturned desk.

Jasper drags himself upright, smearing red across the cabinet doors. His eyes track me a second too late, pupils blown wide, smile stretching too far across his face.

"You did this," he says, and the words overlap, echoing over themselves as if more than one mouth spoke them.

Behind him, the air ripples, folding inward like something has pressed its thumb into reality and left an imprint.

Jasper's body flickers, not disappearing but misaligning, his shoulders jerking out of place before snapping back. The blood on his face runs upward for a second, reversing course, slipping back into his skin before pouring down again. His eyes track me too slowly, then too fast, pupils blown wide enough to swallow the color entirely.

The cabinets behind him bend.

He smiles.

And suddenly he isn't across the room anymore.

He moves wrong. Not running. Not stepping. One second he's slumped against the cabinets, the next he's inches from my face, breath hot and metallic, blood dripping onto my shoes. I don't see him cross the space. The distance simply collapses.

"You did this," he says again.

He tilts his head slowly, too slowly, until something shifts beneath the skin of his neck. There's a muted crack, a wrong adjustment, and his spine presses visibly against the back of his shirt as though it's trying to climb out of him. His body bends sideways in a way that ignores bone and tendon, folding at an angle no living thing should survive before settling back into place.

The smile on his face spreads wider, stretching the skin at the corners until it thins and splits.

He never once stops looking at me.

"You can't leave me," he whispers, his nose brushing mine, breath hot and wet against my mouth.

His hand leaves my jaw and closes around my throat. For half a breath I think he's pulling me closer. Instead, he lifts.

My feet leave the floor so abruptly the room tilts. His fingers clamp tight, thumb grinding beneath my jaw while the rest of his hand seals around my neck. I claw at him instantly, nails dragging down his wrist, but the skin beneath my hands shifts, tightening and rolling as though something underneath is rearranging itself.

"You thought you could walk away," he says, voice almost normal.

I kick, heels striking cabinets that bend inward like softened wax. His shoulders pull wider without effort, bones cracking as they lengthen beneath his shirt. The sound is wrong.

"You don't get to choose." His jaw shifts with a muted pop, teeth pressing too long against his lips as his smile spreads wider, splitting at the corners. Blood beads there and slides down his chin, but he doesn't blink.

"I made space for myself inside you." The words drag now, layered over something deeper, something not entirely his. The voice is gurgling. There is very little humanity left in him.

My vision tunnels. I pry at his fingers, but they feel fused to my skin, impossible to separate.

"You don't get a life that isn't built around me."

His eyes blacken completely, swallowing the whites until there's nothing human left in them. His spine arches backward, vertebrae rising visibly beneath the surface of his skin. Each bone looks like it's trying to slice its way through.

"I will empty you out and stay in the shell that is left of your very vessel." The words start to blend together into one, long string of syllables. "I will *take* your soul for my own."

My lungs collapse. The world folds inward. My body goes light and distant, the edges of everything dissolving into dark.

Heat slams violently through me from the inside out. His hand sears where it grips my throat. Smoke curls from his skin. He jerks backward with a sound that tears out of him that is no longer a language that I can understand. His spine snaps straight.

I fall from his grip. Air crashes into my lungs so hard it hurts.

Light streams through the holes cracking through the room.

He staggers backward, blistered where the light touched him, mouth still stretched too wide as the shape of him struggles to hold.

The brightness remains.

But he does not.

The dark does not disappear all at once. It slowly peels back in trembling layers as something pries it open from the outside. The pressure around my throat fades into heat, and the heat into a distant ache, and even that begins to thin.

Through the bright light, I hear my name.

Not his voice.

Della's.

"Josie Brighton." I feel it reverberating into my very being. "Josie Brighton, you come back to yourself!"

The sky folds inward into something light. The black recedes. The gold light breaks into thin veins that retreat beneath my skin instead of away from it.

My body feels impossibly heavy. Like Jasper threw me from the stratosphere. The sensation of hands returns first. Della's grip is firm around mine, her thumbs still pressing into the pulse at my wrists as she counts me back into existence.

"You breathe now," she says, voice no longer distant but right in front of me. Her green eyes leading me to where I need to go. "You are in your body. You are here in my shop."

Air tears into my lungs in one violent rush. The scent of herbs and brick and tea floods in with it. The table beneath my forearms is solid. The floor is beneath my feet.

"Stay with me," Della says, her voice lower now but no less firm. "Let it go."

The last of the darkness drains from the edges of my vision. The ringing in my ears thins. My pulse steadies beneath her hands.

Hex & Brews comes back into my line of sight as I walk to the open portal.

Bella is standing to the side of the table, pale but upright. The floating candles tremble once more before falling back to the table. Nothing seems to be broken.

Della does not release me until she is certain I'm fully back to myself.

"Good," she says in a way that tells me something happened while I was...wherever that was. "I lost you."

Her grip shifts as she counts the rhythm of my heartbeats beneath her fingers. She's checking, grounding herself in the proof of me being alive. I try to do the same, but my body feels distant, untethered, and for one disorienting second I'm not entirely sure I made it back at all.

"I couldn't get to you," she says, and there is no warmth

in it. She has lost all of her usual whimsy. "Something shut me out."

Bella's breath catches.

"I don't get shut out." Della frowns at me. "What did you see?"

I swallow. My throat still burns from where his hand was.

"Jasper," I say. "He was bloody. It was ugly. It was convincing." I take a second to think how to explain it. "But it wasn't desperation. It was designed to be that way. He needed the scene. He needed me to walk into it."

Bella's hand flies to her mouth.

"And he said he made space inside me," I continue on. "He said he would empty me out and stay."

Della's fingers go cold around mine.

"Behind him," I say, my voice faltering now, "there was something burning. It wasn't his. It burned him."

Della's eyes change, they harden, somehow turning a darker shade of green. She puts her hands on my temples before I can back away.

For a split second her pupils widen beyond anything human. Her breath stops. I feel it through her hands tightening around my hair. She sees it. She sees what I saw. And whatever she touches on the other side makes her flinch.

"Oh, fuck," she whispers. "That wasn't human."

Bella shakes her head immediately. "Jasper is human."

Della looks at her slowly. "No," she says. "No human survives that kind of blockade. No human moves that way inside the veil. No human bends reality to stage their own death. Fuck, no human can *be* in the veil like that."

The floating candles tremble.

The wall clock ticks. Once. Twice. And then it stops.

Bella turns first. "The clock stopped."

All three of us look at it.

3:00 PM.

The second hand hangs frozen in place.

Della's gaze moves from the clock to me. "The first strike," she says quietly. "The first movement."

The tick doesn't resume.

Instead, everything else does.

The floor drops.

The air tilts.

The room spins violently, jars rattling, shelves groaning, Bella grabbing the edge of the table as the world lurches sideways.

Della's voice cuts through the air whirling around us. "He isn't human, Josie." The room convulses again. "He's something older."

Black cracks across the ceiling.

"And whatever that is—" The clock snaps forward with a violent tick. "—it just woke up."

CHAPTER NINE

Josie

The ticking of the clock comes more into focus with every second.

I know that I am at fault for this. I have to be. I mean I fucking brought Jasper Wilder into our world. No one would know him without me.

I'm numb to it all at this point. I was so stuck in my head that I missed the telltale sign of a storm coming.

A portal opens near the bone curtain.

"Bella," Owen frantically says, walking through. I turn and watch him give her a kiss. "Your tone worried me. What's going on?"

"Josie," I hear whispered from behind him.

I let out a sob as Lucas' arms wrap around me. I let myself be vulnerable for once and melt into his embrace.

He puts his hand on my stomach and I feel for any kind of movement. I remember that it is a bit early for anything, but I hate that I forgot about my baby during this whole ordeal.

"Okay," Owen groans to Della. "What in the fuck is going on?"

Della stands up. "We need to meet with the council."

Lucas turns to her, worried, but stays quiet. Owen, on the other hand, steps to her.

"You want to *meet with the council*?" He asks, confused. "You know the council doesn't just meet with people, Della. We found out the hard way."

Della walks forward, unsteady on her feet, and creates a portal in front of her.

"Della—" Bella continues.

"NOW!" Della roars, cutting everything else off. "They will want to hear what I have to tell them."

She walks through the portal without seeing if we will follow. Owen grabs Bella's hand and they go in after her. But I begin to lose my strength so Lucas scoops me up.

We walk out into a room that looks more like a chamber.

Bones are everywhere. I'm not sure I even want to know what... or who they belong to. There is no ceiling, only a black hole that goes up, seemingly never ending.

Fire is everywhere.

"Where are we?" I ask Lucas.

"Infernal Council's chambers," he responds while setting me down in a chair behind a large table.

"It kind of looks like a courtroom," I say, looking around.

"It kind of is," Lucas says, chuckling.

I don't get much more time to look around before the fire in the middle circles and seven figures come down from the sky. They all sit on these throne looking chairs as Owen steps up to them, bowing him head.

"We are sorry to come without being summoned, but Della thinks there is something that you need to hear." Bella walks to the tables that are in place.

I feel like we are in a courtroom... in Hell.

"We are not pleased," the voices come out as one. Fear races down my spine, my hand shoots to my belly.

"Lucas Duvain..." they trail off.

"I am here," he says to them, also bowing his head.

"Are you and your mate well with your little one on the way?"

Lucas turns to me and I stand shakily. He holds out a hand and I take it, we walk to them together.

"Josephine Carrow," they say neutrally. "We believe you chose right by going by Josie Brighton. It fits you."

I look down, trying to be respectful, but I have no idea how I'm supposed to address them. They're almost casual in their conversations, like this is a family, although a formal one.

"We are the Infernal Council, child." They can read my mind apparently. "We can sense your anxiety. Do not be afraid. We only wish to congratulate you on your mating and child. Lucas Duvain, please help your mate to a seat before she faints."

There is a weird sense of... laughter coming from the seven cloaked figures.

"Della Sage," they turn their attention to her as Lucas helps me sit again. "The other Duvains you called should be arriving."

"Are you not mad she didn't call a meeting?" Bella asks them skeptically.

"We are not. As Della would never call except if it was of dire circumstances and we were needed."

Within moments, the rest of the Duvains are here. This is my first time seeing all of them together in one room. I didn't realize there were so many of them. It's jarring to say the least.

"Why have we been summoned?" Evander asks.

"Della Sage has pressing matters for you," the council states to him. "All of you."

The cloaks slide from their shoulders. The governing body of Hell is entirely women, and I have never felt more validated in my life.

One of them—dark hair pulled back tight, posture effortless, authority woven into the way she holds her chin —meets my stare without blinking.

"I am Selene," she says with a neutral tone. "And you are far more important than you realize, Josie Brighton."

Under any other circumstance, I would ask who the others are. I would catalog names, ranks, hierarchies.

But there is too much happening. And it's happening all at once.

Della steps forward into the center of the chamber, hands clasped loosely behind her back like she's a lawyer.

"You are all aware," she begins evenly, "that there has only ever been one recorded instance of bond ignition altering biological inheritance."

Evander doesn't move. Only his eyes shift—ink swallowing the whites. "The archived anomaly."

"Yes," Della says without hesitation. "A mortal woman experienced early bond ignition with a demon prior to claiming. Conception occurred within the instability window. Upon metaphysical settlement, immortal alignment overrode mortal biology."

Selene's gaze flicks briefly toward Josie.

"And?" Theron prompts.

"The mortal father was not the biological father once immortal alignment settled," Della answers, turning to face Theron. "The child's DNA rewrote itself to match the bonded demon."

All I can hear is all of the blood hammering through my eardrums.

"Did the results come back?" My voice sounds small in the cavernous room.

I know I shouldn't interrupt, but I need to know. They're talking about my baby like I'm not even here. That's not going to work for me.

"I don't need them," Della states.

She's entirely too calm considering my life just tilted onto its side. Not to be dramatic or anything.

Lucas' hand tightens on my shoulder.

Evander's jaw flexes. "Explain."

Della inclines her head slightly. "The case did not end in catastrophe. The woman and the demon remained bonded. They raised the child together."

"That precedent was sealed."

"It was contained."

"You're drawing comparison—"

"Too many people talking all at once!" Selene exclaims, shutting them all up.

Their words stack over each other, rising until you can't understand a word that they are saying.

Selene's brows draw together. She interrupts all the men trying to talk over one another. "That is not in the public archive."

"No," Della agrees. "It would not be."

Liora cuts into the debate. "Who was the child?"

Della turns to the council once again. "You can tell them."

"Julia Carter," the council says in unison.

Evander looks first to the council, then back to Della. "That is not possible."

"It is documented," Della replies. "Sealed infernal record. The mortal pregnancy stabilized under bond alignment. The child's immortal inheritance matched the demon—not the presumed human father."

Adrian finally speaks. "You think this is happening again. With Josie."

Della nods to Adrian, and my entire body just... powers down.

Cool. Great. Love that for me. I'm apparently part of something demons have only seen once in recorded history. Which is not a category I ever aspired to be part of.

Selene's eyes flick toward my stomach. "And you are certain?"

Della finally looks directly at me, face telling me I know exactly the answer to that question.

"It's Lucas's," I whisper.

The council confirms what I already know. "Yes."

Evander exhales slowly, shifting his weight from side to side. "And Julia... she has never disclosed this."

Della's expression turns serious. "That," she says evenly, "is her story to tell."

That gives them absolutely nothing to push against. Which is dangerous, considering from what Bella has told me, they thrive on pushing.

"We have more pressing things to discuss," Della says, and my stomach drops. She turns toward me again, pointing her finger. "Her"

Every gaze in the chamber follows her hand. I don't move. Because I am about to become a huge problem.

"She entered the Veil," Della says.

The reaction is immediate.

"No."

"She's mortal."

"That's not possible."

Lucas goes rigid beside me. "What?"

Voices stack and overlap, rising all at once until I can't tell who said what. Again, the Duvains let no one else speak.

"I didn't send her," Della continues, her hand still lifted in my direction. "No ritual. No doorway. I reached for her and she was already there."

"You're saying she crossed alone?" Adrian demands.

"I'm saying she walked into something that was already open." Her hand lowers slowly. "And when I tried to follow —" Della looks pissed. "It locked me out."

Lucas's arm tightens around me. "Locked you out?"

"Yes."

Now no one is talking over anyone. Now they're listening.

"If the Veil chose Josie—" Evander's voice lowers. "It means something else chose to open it."

"Why was she there in the first place?" Lucas shouts, his usual mask of control slips as his grip tightens into fists.

I flinch as his roar tears through the chamber, the sound bending wrong—thick and distorted, the way it felt when the Veil split open around me.

"Because I was trying to learn what happened during the missing week, Lucas!" I fire back.

His head snaps toward me. "Sunshine—"

"I deserved to know!" I shout, my voice cracking

through the chamber. "I deserved answers. Della was giving that to me."

The air feels like it's closing in with the room getting smaller and smaller.

I brace my hands on the arms of the chair. I swear I am more drained than ever before. I am very aware of the changes my body is going through.

I stand anyway. Lucas reaches for me automatically, but I shrug him off and keep walking.

"I am pregnant," I say, adjusting my footing because my center of gravity is no longer trustworthy, "which means I am the one living in this body and this reality and this absolute infernal mess."

"Sunshine—"

"No." I lift a hand before he can make excuses to try to change my mind. "Do not 'Sunshine' me like that's going to make this any better."

I walk to Della who is standing and facing the council.

"I wanted to know about the week I was missing," I tell them. "Instead... I ended up in a nightmare."

"Did you find the answers you seek?" They ask me in unison.

Past me would think talking to cloaked figures was creepy. The person I am today thinks that it is kind of cool.

"Well, no," I admit.

Della lifts her hand and the air in front of the council turns reflective. My classroom appears exactly as I remember it—overturned desks, blood on the tile, Jasper pulling himself upright.

They watch him move. Watch the way he crosses distance without stepping. Watch his body bend and correct itself. Watch the light burn through him. And behind him, something else burning—something that is not him.

When the image fades, the chamber is different. Even the elder Duvains are no longer composed. Selene studies me instead of Della.

"Josie," Selene says evenly, "are you certain that is what you saw?"

"Yes," I reply. "I am certain that is what I saw."

Selene's gaze doesn't leave mine. "Did it feel like a vision," she asks, voice measured, "or did it feel real?"

"Real," I answer without thinking. "I wasn't watching it. I was in it."

A silver haired woman to her right tilts her head. "You felt present?"

"Yes."

"Were you aware you were crossing into the Veil?" Another woman asks, fingers steepled in front of her.

"No," I say. "I was thinking about Jasper. About the week I don't remember. I wanted to understand it."

"And you entered willingly?" Selene presses.

I hesitate, replaying it. "I wasn't dragged. I stepped forward. But I didn't know that I was walking into that."

That earns a quiet exchange of looks around the table.

Selene leans back slightly, considering. "That does not resemble projection," she says. "It resembles memory."

My stomach tightens. "Memory?"

One of the older women speaks for the first time. "The Veil does not fabricate. It enhances what is already known."

Selene inclines her head. "You are missing a week, Josie Brighton. What you described behaved like an event already lived."

That almost scares me as much as Jasper did.

"Mom," one of the Duvains speaks up. "What does this mean?"

"It means Jasper Wilder is now our problem," she sighs. "He is not human."

"Then what the fuck is he?" Lucas exclaims. "Why is everyone so worried, yet saying nothing at all!"

"It's not that simple, Lucas," Selene adds. "It's complicated. There is a lot—"

"Simplify it, Selene," Theron speaks. "Our nephew deserves to know."

Selene looks around, then at me. Her eyes betraying her. Worry clear across her face.

"Jasper Wilder," Della announces. "Is the harbinger of Hell."

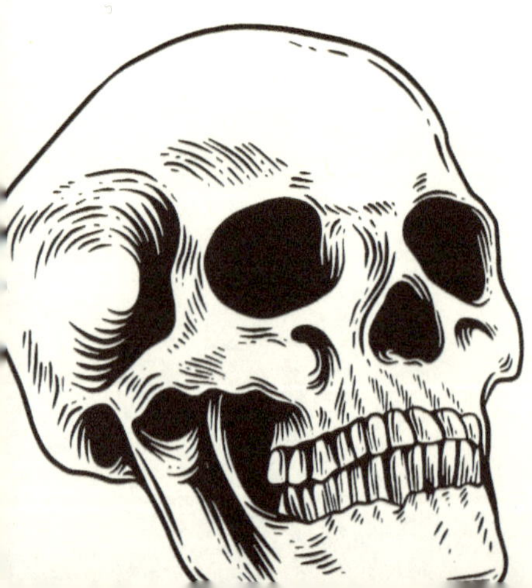

CHAPTER TEN

I've only heard of harbingers in bedtime stories. Ghost stories we used to tell each other as kids. Stupid shit that the mortals do.

I guess the good thing about Jasper not being human is that Josie doesn't need to go to court to deal with custody.

"What is a harbinger?" Bella asks.

Fuck, I forgot that she was even here.

Ophelia steps through a seam near the far wall without announcement, and every instinct in me goes on alert because she does not leave the Loom unless something is wrong.

Her eyes go straight to Della. "I got your message," she says, and the fact that she's here at all tells me this just became much bigger than a story.

"I reached out because the Loom reacted," Della says. "And not something I ever want to see, let alone have Josie relive."

Josie looks between them. "What is it?"

"It is the embodiment of collapse," Ophelia says evenly. "When the boundary between life and death weakens, a Harbinger can form. Not summoned by Hell. Not appointed. It is created when a mortal body is intentionally emptied and prepared to hold something that does not belong in the living world."

"In most attempts," Della adds, "the body cannot sustain the occupation. The structure fails. The mind destabilizes. The vessel deteriorates."

Josie's voice is tight. "Emptied how?"

"The body was cleared," mu aunt says. "And the soul... removed."

Bella goes still. "Removed?"

"Killed," Ophelia clarifies.

"The vessel is typically deceased prior to occupation," she continues. "Death creates access. Ritual reinforcement creates capacity. The occupying force binds before natural decay can sever the structure."

My jaw tightens. "So Jasper—" I start.

"Was not overtaken randomly," Della says. "If this is what he is, then the body was selected, soul terminated, body prepared in a very specific way—conditioned over time to withstand occupation."

Josie's fingers tighten in mine.

"And Jasper's vessel has sustained," Ophelia adds. "Which is rare."

Selene's gaze sharpens. "Most constructed vessels degrade quickly. They cannot maintain autonomy. They do not pass as fully human for long."

I look at Josie. She's shivering. I hear her thoughts in my head and block out everyone else to listen.

I can't believe I slept with a vessel. Oh god, was it dead?

That's what that means, right? If Jasper was dead, I was sleeping with a dead body. I didn't know, though. I would never. He seemed so real. Well, he is real. But the body is dead. Is it? I don't fucking know.

I squeeze her in an embrace. She's so lost in thought that I don't think she even noticed it.

I wonder if the child is even conceived from sex... or magically created.

Seth, on the far end of the room, walks forward. "So we wait," he says. "If vessels fail, we let it weaken and end him when it does."

Ophelia doesn't look convinced. "If he were unstable, we would already see deterioration."

"He has maintained this physical form for years." Della nods once.

Selene's voice lowers. "Which suggests the degradation phase has either been prevented..."

"Or completed," Ophelia finishes.

Bella swallows. "You're saying he's not weakening."

"No," Selene says. "I am saying he is established." She lifts her hand. The air above the table darkens, depth folding inward instead of smoke rising. "Bring him here."

"Who are you calling?" My father asks.

Selene doesn't answer. Instead, a figure forms between us.

It's a man. Ghostly pale. He looks disoriented. He seems young in posture, not age. There's no light in his eyes.

"Where am I?" He asks, voice shaking.

Before Selene speaks, the council moves as one. The cloaks rise again, their faces disappearing into the abyss. What was revealed is concealed just as easily. They are trying to keep their anonymity to those not included in the inner circle.

"State your name." All the voices come out as one again.

He lifts his head. "Jasper Wilder."

Josie's voice breaks before the word finishes forming. "Jas..."

She doesn't complete what she is trying to say. Her nails dig into my hand. Tears swell into her eyes. This man is the person she thought she was with all this time.

She starts to crumble and I scoop her up in my arms, holding her to me.

The soul looks around the chamber, confusion growing at seeing everyone here. He studies the council, the other Duvains, me.

His gaze does not linger on Josie. *Fuck*. He doesn't know any of us, he's acting like he's never seen us before, because he hasn't ever seen any of us. This is not the man that Josie met.

"I don't understand," he says. "I was driving back from campus. Sterling said we'd talk more tomorrow about the internship. There were headlights. Then—"

He stops. Nothing comes after that.

"You died that night." Ophelia breaks the news to him. At least she did it in a gentle way. Probably way nicer than anyone else would have told him.

He stares at her. "No."

"Your soul has remained in Hell since that moment," Ophelia continues solemnly.

I can't help but feel bad for the guy. He seems nice. He doesn't deserve any of this. The soul looks down at himself like he's checking for wounds he can't see.

"That doesn't make sense," he says, his voice rising an octave. "I didn't do anything."

He doesn't rage. He doesn't deny his fate. He just looks lost.

"Sterling was there," he says slowly. "Ellison too. They said it would help my future. Rhys was going to join us, too."

Josie gasps out a sob. Not for the thing in the mortal world. For the boy standing in front of us.

Around the room, the mood changes. The Duvains aren't looking at a threat anymore. They're looking at what was taken. This Jasper isn't a monster. He's a college kid who trusted the wrong men. Whatever is walking around wearing his face is not him.

Selene lowers her hand to release the soul back to where it belongs.

The real Jasper looks around one last time, confusion overtaking him for a moment before we can see peace enter his eyes.

Every member of the council glances at one another.E-vander steps forward slightly. "Before you go," he says. "We have some questions."

Jasper looks confused but nods slowly. "If I can answer them, I will."

Josie moves before anyone else can speak. Her hand slips from mine. She stands and walks to him.

"Do you know me?" She asks. "At all?"

Jasper's soul turns toward her. He studies her face for a long moment, like he's searching through memories from long ago.

His expression softens. "I'm sorry," he whispers. "I don't."

Josie goes completely still beside him. "You've... never

seen me before?" She asks.

Jasper shakes his head. "No," he says gently. "I haven't."

A small sound breaks out of her before she can stop it. I rush up to her, my hand immediately finds hers, squeezing tightly. "It's okay, Sunshine. It's okay."

She swallows hard, forcing herself to keep going. "The body walking around on Earth," she says, her voice shaking now. "That's yours, right?"

Jasper frowns slightly. "I have no clue what you're talking about," he answers.

"He wouldn't know," Selene adds. "He is a soul. He's completely separate from the body that was once his."

Josie's shoulders tense. My stomach twists because I already know where her mind is going.

"So when I—" Her voice breaks. She tries again. "When I conceived..."

The words fade out before she can finish them. The council murmurs quietly among themselves.

Finally Selene is the one chosen to speak. "There is another possibility."

Josie lifts her head.

Selene's gaze drops briefly to Josie's stomach.

"If the vessel had already been altered," she says carefully, "and the harbinger had fully awakened..."

Ophelia finishes the thought. "Then the conception could not have occurred in the usual biological way."

Josie blinks at them. "What does that mean?"

Della answers. "It means your child was probably conceived through magic. Since harbingers can't... have children."

I know we've had sex. I don't want to think about that. At all.

"But he can have sex," I say.

"He can..." A council woman says. "Until he is no longer human. Do not worry, child. You did nothing unseemly."

Selene nods once. "And given everything we've learned tonight," she says quietly, "that explanation is becoming far more probable."

Josie's hand moves instinctively to her stomach. I tighten my arm around her shoulders.

"Anything else?" Selene asks. "I want to release his soul to feel some peace. He does not belong in this part of Hell."

"There was a man," Jasper speaks, voice confused as if he's trying to remember something from long ago. "He made me vow to tell the council that Obadiah Crowe sends his regards. I'm not sure what he meant by that, but he did say that I'd meet you at some point. I'm so sorry, I wish I had more information for you."

Everyone shakes their heads. Selene raises her hand again.

And then he is gone.

"The living and the dead," Selene says after a moment. All the counsel members put down their hoods. No one interrupts her. "The living architects were Sterling and Ellison Creed."

My aunt is not someone to leave puzzles incomplete. She finishes them. I can see her starting to put two and two together. "And the dead," she continues evenly, "was Obadiah Crowe."

I have no idea who she is talking about. That name means absolutely nothing to me. But my father and uncle certainly recognize it. My father doesn't speak, but there's a shift in him, something cold and dark settling on his shoulders. My uncle goes rigid, a rage simmering beneath the surface.

Bella looks between them. “Who is Obadiah Crowe?”

Theron and Selene are speaking to each other telepathically. They all knew whoever this Obadiah Crowe is.

Evander’s voice is low. “You’re sure he is the other half of who summoned the harbinger?”

Selene answers without hesitation. “I would recognize the power of his name anywhere. He would also be the type to do it.”

“Mom...” Caleb interjects.

Selene shakes her head and turns to him. “He was a pastor. Salem. 1692.”

“I know that date,” Bella whispers. “You mean the Salem witch trials?”

“Yes. He petitioned for my hand in marriage,” she says plainly. “When I refused, he accused me of witchcraft. He oversaw my arrest. My trial. My execution.”

“I can’t believe it,” Josie gasps.

“He believed he could control what he did not understand,” Selene continues. “He tried to weaponize faith. To use divine law to cage infernal power.”

Her eyes darken to a deep obsidian, swirling around the edges. “He failed.”

My stomach drops.

“We will continue this later,” my father says firmly. “All of us need to come together to figure out a plan.”

He tilts his chin toward Josie.

She’s overwhelmed. Exhausted. Fighting tears she refuses to let fall. The fire that carried her through this is burning low, and I can see the toll it’s taking.

She needs to get out of here.

“We’ll meet later,” I say to my family.

Before anyone can argue, I step forward, lift my mate

into my arms, and disappear—already knowing exactly where I'm taking her.

The portal opens into the night air outside my house. I step through, Josie still in my arms, the opening sealing behind us.

The house comes into view and I carry her up the short path to the front door. I push it open and carry her inside.

Josie lets out a tired laugh against my shoulder.

"What?" I ask.

"You just carried me over the threshold."

I frown down at her. "Yes."

"That's a whole mortal thing," she says, amused. "Like newlyweds. It's supposed to be good luck."

I look back at the doorway, then at her. "As much as I wish that it was, it wasn't intentional."

Her smile widens. "Well," she says, glancing around the house as I finally set her down, "I'm choosing to believe it was."

I shake my head slightly, smiling. "We're home," I tell her.

Her eyes move from the stone exterior to the tall windows stretching across the front of the house, then to the warm light spilling out over the path leading to the door. Dark wood frames the glass, clean and simple against the stone.

She tilts her head back slightly, taking in the height of the place. I wanted vaulted ceilings, I didn't want to feel as though I was trapped in a tiny home.

The second floor balcony wraps around the front corner, black railing catching the porch light. The entryway itself sits recessed into the stone, the door wide and solid, built more for privacy than display.

Not to mention the added loft I put in it.

Josie turns slowly, looking from one side of the house to the other like she's trying to take the entire thing in at once.

"This is your house?" She asks, staring back up at the ceiling.

"Yes," I reply, skeptically. I can't tell if she likes it or not. I hope she does, I'll redesign the entire thing if she doesn't.

"I want a tour," Josie says immediately. She's got that sunshine smile on her face.

It's at this moment that I know I will do absolutely anything to see that as often as possible. However, I did just have to carry her into the house.

I sigh, dragging a hand down my face. "Sunshine, you're exhausted."

She looks like she could fall asleep standing up. Her shoulders droop. Her eyes are heavy. Still, she lifts her chin at me.

She looks back at me immediately. "Never too tired for this," she insists.

I stare at her for a second, then let out another breath. "Of course you aren't."

She's staring at a house I see every day like it's the eighth wonder of the world.

"Alright," I say, holding up my arm signaling for her to lead the way. "Tour it is."

The entryway opens into a wide living space with tall ceilings and exposed beams stretching across the top. Floor to ceiling windows line the back wall, looking out over the water. The fireplace along the far wall burns blue fire. Something she seems to be enamored by.

Nothing in here is decorative for the sake of it. Everything has a purpose.

She steps closer to the windows, looking out at the water stretching into the distance. Her mouth parts just a little. And I find myself chuckling.

"What?" She asks, turning back to me.

"You're looking at it like I built the Taj Mahal."

She gestures around the room. "Lucas, this place is incredible."

I glance around the same space I wake up in every morning. The couch I fall asleep on half the time. The kitchen I cook in. The windows I barely notice anymore.

Then I look back at her. She's in awe.

For me, it's Tuesday.

"Come here," I tell her.

Josie looks up from the couch immediately. "Where?"

Instead of answering, I take her hand and lead her across the living room. She follows easily, curiosity lighting up her face.

When I slide the glass door open, cool night air spills into the house. Josie steps out onto the balcony and stops.

The view stretches out in front of us—dark water reflecting the moon, the treeline framing the shore, the city lights far enough away that the night still feels like ours alone.

"Oh," she breathes. "I didn't know there was a city center!"

"There is," I say. "Adrian and Damian have apartments there. They prefer being closer to everything."

The night air moves around us as Josie steps to the edge of the balcony.

Her hands move to the railing as she looks out over it. "This is insane."

I lean against the doorframe, watching her instead of the view.

She turns toward me slowly, still half lost in the moment.

"You know this is ridiculous, right?" she says. "You just casually have a view like this."

A laugh slips out of me. "I built it for the view."

"Well congratulations," she says. "You succeeded."

I take a deep breath, savoring the moment before I drop a bucket of water on it. "I want to talk about what happened today," I say.

She immediately tenses up and backs away. "I kind of feel sick to my stomach." She crosses her arms over her chest, brows drawn, leaving a little wrinkle between them. "Knowing that I was intimate with something so evil and... dead."

"Josie," I start, pulling her close. "You did nothing wrong. I wouldn't really say he's dead. He mainly just doesn't have a form in the mortal world.There is no way you would've known he was any different than what he portrayed."

The wind lifts a strand of her hair across her face. I reach out and tuck it behind her ear.

"I want to forget him," she says. "Forget every intimate moment I had with him and wipe the slate clean."

She closes the distance. Her hand slides into the front of my shirt and she kisses me.

The kiss is soft at first, like she's testing something fragile. "Will you help me forget, Lucas?"

My hands find her waist and I pull her closer, answering

the question when my lips seal to hers. When we finally break apart, her forehead falls against my chest.

"Okay," she murmurs.

My hands stay on her hips. "Okay?"

She tilts her head up, eyes bright despite how tired she is. "Tour successful."

I laugh against her hair. "Oh we're just getting started, Sunshine," I quip back, picking her up in my arms as she squeals.

Her laugh echoes through the house as I carry her inside. And I don't think I've ever heard a better sound in all my immortal life.

"You are ridiculous," she says, grabbing onto my shoulders as I head down the hallway.

"You asked for the tour."

"This is not the tour."

"This," I tell her, nudging the bedroom door open with my foot, "is the most important part."

She goes quiet when she sees the room.

The space is large but simple—dark wood floors, soft lighting, the same floor-to-ceiling windows looking out over the water. The bed sits in the center of the room, wide and unpretentious, the kind meant for sleeping... or not.

I set her down slowly.

We stand nose to nose, the silence settling in like the lingering chord after a cliffhanger. She exhales—a small sound—and her fingers fidget at my shirt collar.

"I never expected your house to look like this," she blurts.

I raise an eyebrow. "What did you expect?"

She glances around. "More... flames. Maybe a torture chamber. Something dramatic."

"There is one downstairs." I stare at her completely deadpan.

Her head snaps up. "You're kidding."

I say nothing. She stares, then narrows her eyes. "You're kidding."

A twitch at the corner of my mouth. "Yes."

"Okay, good," she mutters. "I was about to have a whole slew of follow up questions."

"You can still ask." I cannot take my eyes off of her.

She shrugs. "I'm choosing not to for my own peace of mind."

Her fingers stay at my collar. Her face shows absent, thoughtless, and comfortable moments going through her head. I notice every little thing about her.

"You thought I lived in chaos?" I ask. Without thinking, my hand moves to her waist, settling there as though it belongs.

"You just hide your chaos better than anyone." The grin on her face is going to cause a feral sort of chaos soon enough.

"I don't hide anything." I chuckle lightly at her.

She fixes me with an amused look. "You absolutely do."

"That's your opinion."

"It is a fact," she counters.

My mouth twitches again.

"There it is," she says, pointing. "You do that almost smile when you know I'm right."

"I don't." I smile at her.

"You just did it again."

"I did not." I flatten my lips to try to hide that she is very right.

"You are doing it right now!"

I shake my head. "You're imagining things."

She leans in, studying me. "Not imagining. Don't tell me that. Very annoying."

"Annoying?" I echo. "Me?"

"Yes," she smiles sarcastically. "Because it makes me want to keep talking to you."

"That's not a problem."

"It is if I was trying to be mad at you." She crosses her arms and raise a brow at me.

"Were you?"

She pauses. "No." She laughs loudly. "Not at all."

"Then we're fine."

She laughs softly, dropping her hand from my collar to my chest, pressing it there to steady herself. "You're very sure of yourself."

"I usually am," I say evenly.

"That must be nice," she mutters.

"It is," I reply, without hesitation.

Her eyes narrow. "You should be more humble."

"What's the benefit of that?" The corner of my mouth tips up once again.

She nudges me. "You're insufferable."

"You can keep thinking that all you want."

"Because it's true."

"And yet—" I trail off, unspoken. She presses her lips together, fighting a smile.

"Don't," she whispers.

"Don't what?" I ask, amused.

"Finish that sentence," she says, pointing at me like a warning.

"Why?" I push, knowing exactly why.

"Because I know what you'd say," she replies, narrowing her eyes.

"And?" I tease.

"And I don't want to give you the satisfaction," she mutters, trying not to laugh.

"Sounds like a you problem," I say, grinning.

Her fingers drift against my shirt once again.

"You're different," she says after a moment of silence.

"You already said that."

"I know, but I'm noticing it more." She looks at me, fingers tracing my jaw.

"In a good way?"

She nods, index finger making it's way around my eyebrow. "Yeah. In a good way." She glances around again. "Still can't believe you don't have a secret dungeon."

"Is that disappointing?"

"A little. Would've added character." She lifts a shoulder, flaunting everything.

"I'll take note."

"Please don't," she says. "I don't want to find it later."

"Good call."

She studies me softer now, less detective, more present. "You're not what I expected."

"That seems to be a theme."

"Yeah, it is."

I shift closer until our breaths mingle. "And you're still here."

She rolls her eyes, still joking with me. "You're really going to keep saying that, aren't you?"

"Yeah."

Her forehead comes to rest against mine, her voice is a whisper in my ear. "Good."

I laugh as my lips find hers, kissing her once again.

CHAPTER ELEVEN

Josie

Time passes faster than I expect.

I'm twenty six weeks along now. And I feel every bit of it.

My stomach isn't cute and small anymore. It's round, heavy, and extremely obvious. Standing up too fast now requires a full recalibration of my balance because apparently my center of gravity has packed up and moved somewhere near my knees.

The baby moves constantly. Not the little fluttery taps from earlier that made me question whether it was gas or a tiny human. These are real kicks now. Full body shifts. Sometimes the baby stretches and my entire stomach rolls.

It's incredible.

It's also slightly horrifying.

My back aches if I stand too long. My feet swell by the end of the day. I get tired in a way that isn't just long-day-tired. It's bone-tired. The kind where your body feels like it's secretly running a construction project twenty-four hours a day and you're just the unfortunate building site.

Sleeping is its own Olympic sport now. I can't lie on my back without getting dizzy, and if I roll too far forward the baby immediately kicks like she has very strong opinions about personal space.

I catch myself resting my hand on my stomach all the time now without even thinking about it.

Protective instinct, I guess. Or maybe it's just because she won't let me forget she's there.

Yes, we know she is, in fact... a she now. That revelation apparently unlocked an entirely new level of enthusiasm when it comes to kicking my organs.

Twenty six weeks pregnant and my body has officially abandoned the concept of subtlety.

Two weeks ago, I met my midwife.

Which, yes, Hell has those.

I have my next appointment today.

The whole thing was a weird adjustment at first. Mostly because the woman who will be delivering my child also delivered my soulmate... a few centuries ago.

She's a mate from ancient Greece, which sounds impressive until you realize it mostly means she has seen absolutely everything and nothing about my situation even remotely phases her.

"You going to lunch with the girls after?" Lucas asks from the corner of the room.

"Yeah," I say. "I'm going to head out as soon as Thalia leaves."

Lucas has been there for every single appointment. He's been my rock through this entire process.

A soft knock hits the door before it swings open.

Speak of the devil.

Thalia steps inside. She's tall and broad shouldered, built solid like someone who has spent a lifetime doing real work. Long dark curls streaked with silver are braided back from her face, pinned in place with bone combs that look older than three generations.

Her robes are layered indigo and gray, loose and practical instead of decorative. They shift softly as she crosses the room.

If ancient Greece had midwives like this, I'm starting to understand how they survived childbirth back then.

Thalia sets a small leather bag on the counter and turns to me, smiling. "Let's see how you and the little one are doing today."

She moves to the side of the room and pulls back a linen curtain, revealing a wide bed tucked against the wall. It's layered with thick white blankets and pillows instead of the cold paper covered tables you get in mortal doctor offices.

She smooths one of the blankets flat with practiced hands.

"Go ahead," she says.

I eye the bed for a second before climbing up onto it with significantly less grace than I would have liked. Being this damn pregnant has really killed the whole effortless movement thing I used to have going.

Lucas hovers nearby. He's debating whether he should help or just let me pretend I still have dignity.

I settle against the pillows with a sigh. I am this ornery now... imagine in the coming weeks.

"Comfortable?" Thalia asks.

"As comfortable as someone with a tiny ninja practicing martial arts inside her organs can be."

Thalia doesn't even blink, she just grins. She steps closer

and places one hand against my stomach, pressing gently as she checks the baby's position.

"Relax," she says.

I really am trying.

Her fingers move slightly as she feels along the curve of my stomach, adjusting the pressure here and there the same way any doctor probably would.

Lucas's hand finds mine automatically.

Thalia reaches into the leather bag she brought with her and pulls out a small piece of dark chalk.

Before I can ask what it's for, she draws a quick symbol against the side of my stomach. The mark is cool for half a second before it fades into my skin like it was never there.

Lucas leans forward immediately.

"What was—"

"Just a listening mark," Thalia says. "Completely normal. In Hell anyway."

She places two fingers over the spot. The baby kicks me. Hard. Hard enough that I jump on the table. She has never kicked me that hard before.

"Okay," I say, staring down at my stomach. "She definitely heard that."

"Strong response." Lucas laughs and Thalia hums with a nod of her head.

"Strong heartbeat," she says.

She shifts one of my hands slightly higher on my stomach. Lucas steps closer beside the bed, watching carefully. He settles his hand over mine. The baby rolls beneath our palms, moving my entire stomach like she's testing the structural integrity.

Lucas looks completely awestruck.

The first time that Lucas felt her kick was at dinner one night.

He was giving me a tour around Hell. We were at a corner restaurant covered in burning ivy. It was actually beautiful with some of the best food I've ever had. Apparently it was recently opened by a mate.

We enjoyed dinner together and the baby must have liked it, too. She started kicking and I jumped. Lucas came over and felt her kick, too. Tears sprung to his eyes, although he'd never admit that to anyone but me. It was wonderful.

"Movement is strong," Thalia says.

She reaches into the leather bag resting on the counter and pulls out a small obsidian vial and a thin silver lancet.

I narrow my eyes at it.

"Please tell me that's decorative," I groan.

"It's one drop of blood," Thalia replies calmly. I'm pretty sure that's what they said last time.

"That is not the comforting sentence you think it is," I tell her.

"You'll be fine," Lucas says, squeezing my hand.

"Easy for you to say," I mutter. "You're not losing your blood."

Thalia pricks the side of my finger before I can protest again and holds the vial beneath it.

One drop falls into the dark glass. The liquid glows faintly red before fading again.

"What does that mean?" I ask.

"Your body is adapting well," Thalia answers.

That feels like half an explanation but apparently that's all I'm getting. She sets the vial aside and places her hands against my stomach again, pressing lightly along the sides.

Grabbing a small notebook from the side table, she flips it open. The pages aren't paper. They look like dark parchment, and the thing she's writing with looks less like a pen and more like a sharpened piece of charcoal.

She starts scribbling something down.

I lean slightly to see what she's writing. But the symbols are absolutely not English. They're also not Greek. They look like someone let a spider walk through ink and called it writing.

"What is that?" I ask.

"Infernal shorthand," Thalia says without even glancing up.

Lucas leans forward a little. "That's the obstetrics dialect," he says.

I turn my head slowly toward him. "There's an obstetrics dialect... in Hell?"

"Yes," Lucas says.

"Of course there is," I mutter. This is completely blowing my mind.

Thalia keeps writing like none of this is unusual.

"Cravings?" Thalia asks, glancing down at her notes.

Lucas answers immediately. "Mango with honey and chili flakes," he says. "Also dark chocolate with cayenne."

I turn my head slowly toward him. "You answered that *way* too fast," I say.

"She asked," Lucas replies, casually.

I roll my eyes and squint them at him.

"That was for *me* to answer," I say.

"You forget half of them," he says calmly while shrugging his shoulders.

That... is annoyingly accurate.

Thalia writes something down in her strange demonic doctor handwriting. "Any heartburn?" she asks.

"Yes," Lucas says.

I look at him again. "You're really just taking over this appointment, huh?"

"You said it feels like fire," he replies, entirely too composed for my liking.

"That was a metaphor," I say, glaring at my mate.

"Was it?" He asks, raising a brow.

Thalia continues writing.

I stick my tongue out at Lucas in defiance. He looks entirely too pleased with himself.

"Frequent urination?" she asks.

"Yes," Lucas says again.

I close my eyes. "Oh my god."

"You wake up every forty minutes," Lucas says, side eying me and tilting his head.

"Lucas," I warn.

Thalia nods slightly as she finishes the note.

"Everything you've described is consistent with this stage of pregnancy," Thalia says. "Mortal and demon fetuses are more alike than most people realize."

I sigh and lean back against the pillows. Lucas, traitor that he is, looks entirely too pleased with himself.

Thalia closes her notebook and sets it on the side table. "There is one thing," she says.

That sentence has never once been followed by something relaxing.

Lucas straightens beside me. "What thing?" I ask.

"The energy surrounding this pregnancy is stronger than typical mortal pregnancies," she says. "That is not necessarily a concern."

Not necessarily should honestly be banned from medical conversations.

"Mortal and demon pregnancies develop very similarly," she continues. "But the final stage can progress... faster."

I blink. "Faster how?"

"Some demon pregnancies accelerate once the child is strong enough to sustain itself outside the womb," Thalia explains. "The body adjusts to meet the child rather than the other way around."

That sounds suspiciously like *early*.

Lucas looks thoughtful, not worried. Which I'm choosing to interpret as a good sign.

"So what you're saying," I say slowly, "is that this baby might not wait until forty weeks."

Thalia gives a small nod. "It would not surprise me if she arrives earlier than a typical mortal birth."

Cool.

Cool cool *cool*.

"But everything about the child herself is strong," Thalia adds. "Very strong. So even if she does come early by mortal standards, she should be just fine."

That part she says with absolute certainty. Which definitely helps to calm my racing heart, at least a little.

Thalia gathers her things and moves toward the door. "We will meet again in two weeks," she says.

Lucas nods. "Thank you, Thalia."

She inclines her head once and leaves.

The moment the door closes, I slide off the exam table with all the elegance of someone whose center of gravity has been replaced by a bowling ball.

"I'm heading to lunch," I say.

Lucas looks up immediately. "With Bella and the girls?"

"Yeah," I say. "Can you portal me?"

"Of course," Lucas says, already stepping toward me.

He takes my hand. "You'll be able to do that yourself soon."

"Oh good," I say dryly. "Another skill to add to the list right after breathing fire and accidentally summoning demon animals."

Lucas chuckles. "Something like that."

He squeezes my hand and the world folds.

One second we're in the clinic in Hell. The next, we're standing inside Hex & Brews.

The smell of food hits me immediately. I blink at the long table in the back. It's completely covered in trays, bowls, and containers that absolutely did not come from the small kitchen behind the curtain.

"Did she cater lunch?" I ask.

Lucas follows my line of sight and huffs a small laugh. "That sounds like Della."

Bella and Ophelia are already sitting at the table while Della moves plates around like she's running a restaurant instead of a small tea shop.

Della glances up when we walk in. "Well look who finally arrived," she says. "Julia is in court today and can't be there."

Lucas nods once. "Ladies."

His hand slides around my waist and he kisses me. He does that every time we leave each other now. I think it's his way of ensuring we always come back together.

"I'll see you tonight," he murmurs against my lips.

"Okay," I say.

He turns toward the portal but pauses halfway there.

"Oh," he adds. I already know that tone means trouble. "Owen, Julian, and I are emptying your storage unit today."

I don't even know what to say.

"And the boxes from Bella's apartment," he says.

Bella's head snaps up from the table. "Wait—what?"

Lucas is already backing toward the portal. "You have too much stuff," he mutters jokingly.

Then he disappears before any of us can argue.

Bella stares at the closed portal. "...He's not wrong," she mutters.

Plates start moving as soon as I sit down.

"How was your appointment with Thalia?" Della asks when she's seated with food of her own in front of her.

I open my mouth to answer, but Ophelia stops the room cold.

"I don't mean to interrupt. But there's something I need to get off my chest."

A raw, soft cry sneaks out of her mouth before she can stop it, her shoulders collapsing inward like the grief hit all at once.

Bella's chair scrapes loudly against the floor.

"Hey—hey," she says, moving around the table in two quick steps.

She pulls Ophelia into her arms before she can even try to wipe the tears away.

"What's going on?" I ask, my stomach tightening.

Ophelia shakes her head against Bella's shoulder, trying to breathe through it, but another sob breaks loose instead.

Bella rubs slow circles along her back. "It's okay," Bella murmurs. "Just breathe."

Ophelia grips Bella's hand like she's holding on for balance. Della watches her quietly from across the table, her expression more somber than I've ever seen it.

Bella glances up at her. Then back at me.

"Tell her," Bella says gently. "She should know."

Ophelia inhales shakily, trying to center herself. Her

eyes finally lift to mine. "I've been avoiding talking to you about this," she says. "I didn't want to upset you."

That is not what I expected her to say.

My brain immediately starts running through every interaction we've ever had, trying to figure out what I did wrong. I know we're not incredibly close, but I try to be a good friend.

My stomach tightens. "Avoiding me?"

She nods, looking down at the table like she can't quite face us. "It's not because I'm not happy for you," she rushes out. "I am. I promise I am."

Bella's arm tightens around her shoulders. Ophelia takes a shaky breath. "It's just... seeing you pregnant hurts."

That level of honesty knocks the air out of me.

"Because it reminds me of the ones I lost."

Oh.

Oh. Now I get what she's telling me.

"How many?" I ask quietly.

Ophelia swallows. "Six."

Six.

Bella pulls her closer immediately.

"Six miscarriages," Ophelia says, her voice breaking. "And now... my body just won't take a pregnancy anymore."

She wipes at her face, but the tears keep coming.

I stare at the table because suddenly looking at her feels like the worst thing I could possibly do.

"I went to Thalia again," she says. "I thought maybe something had changed."

She lets out a shaky breath.

"It hasn't."

Bella presses her cheek against Ophelia's temple.

"There's nothing left for her to fix," Ophelia whispers.

Her shoulders shake again.

"My body just... won't keep a baby." She looks at me with red eyes. "I don't think being a mother is in my future."

Della's chair scrapes sharply against the floor as she stands. "That is unacceptable," she snaps.

Ophelia wipes at her face. "It's not something you can negotiate with the universe for, Della."

"The Loom should bless you," Della says, anger flashing across her face. "Of all people, you deserve that thread."

Ophelia exhales shakily. "Thalia checked again," she says quietly. "There aren't any eggs left."

Bella freezes beside her. "None?"

Ophelia lets out a hollow laugh. "Apparently my body decided it was done trying."

My chest tightens. "No," I say, shaking my head. "I don't believe that."

All three of them look at me. "We'll find a way," I say. "There has to be something."

Ophelia's expression softens, but it's the kind of soft that comes with giving up. "I used to think losing the ability to paint in color was going to be the thing that broke me," she says quietly.

She used to read people the way other artists read light. Every emotion became color. Joy, grief, love, anger—she could see it in someone's soul and put it on canvas.

"But when the color left," she continues, her voice shaking, "it wasn't just the paint." She wipes at her face. "I couldn't read people anymore. Not the way I used to."

Bella's arms tighten around her.

"I lost the way I understood the world," Ophelia whispers.

Her fingers curl against Bella's sleeve. "And I thought

that was the cruelest thing the universe could take from me." She lets out a broken breath. "I thought losing color meant I'd lost everything."

Bella shakes her head immediately. "Hey," she says softly. "Don't say that."

Ophelia doesn't look up. Bella's hand moves up to cradle the back of Ophelia's head.

"But this?" She moves on without responding to Bella. Her voice cracks when she speaks. "This is worse."

A tear slips down Ophelia's cheek.

"Because at least I could still paint." Her fingers tighten in Bella's sleeve. "At least I could still create something."

Her breathing falters like the next words are stuck somewhere inside her chest.

"But this..." She shakes her head slowly. "This was the one thing I always thought would be mine."

Bella's arms tighten around her. Ophelia stares at the table, blinking like she's trying to not curse the universe for being so *fucking* cruel.

"For years I told myself the miscarriages were just bad luck." Her voice is hushed now. "Six times I thought maybe the next one would stay."

She lets out a broken breath. I can feel my heart bottom out underneath me. Pain creeping through every crevice.

Ophelia has been through so much. Her father, losing her color, and now this.

"I picked names." Bella's hand stills against her back. I look at her silently telling myself to stay calm. Tears are streaming down Bella's face. "I bought tiny clothes I never got to use."

Ophelia isn't crying anymore. She's numb. Somehow, that's worse.

"I let myself imagine what they would look like." Her

voice cracks completely. "Now Thalia says there won't be another one. I have nothing left to even try with."

Ophelia presses her hand over her mouth like she can't believe she said it out loud.

I think it might be the first time she's admitted it.

"My body isn't broken. It's way beyond that," she whispers. "I have to come to the conclusion that I am never going to be someone's mother."

Bella pulls her closer as Ophelia breaks into wracking sobs once again.

My baby moves inside me like she knows I'm listening. And letting me know how lucky I am to have her here.

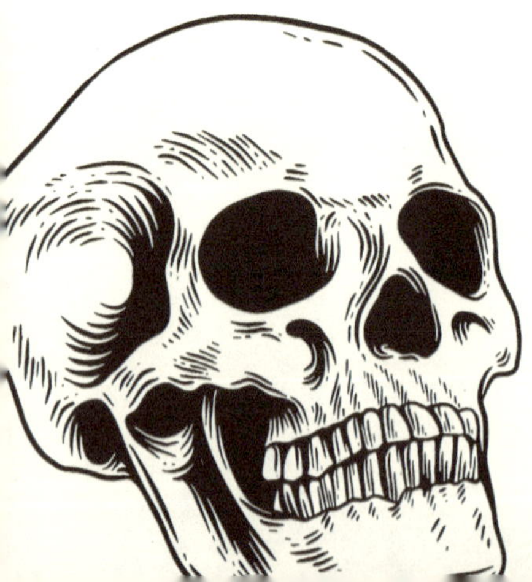

CHAPTER TWELVE
Lucas

I get to Josie's storage unit and raise my hand to open the doors. It's filled to the brim with everything she owns. Except for maybe the six boxes still at Bella's apartment.

Seems like Jasper really didn't want her to do anything.

Although from what Bella described as "his place," I'm not surprised. With the few minutes that I was there, although my focus was on her, I was able to see that there was no color, no art, no personality whatsoever in that place. There was nothing that makes a home feel like someone actually lives there.

I'm beginning to wonder if it wasn't a real home after all.

A Harbinger wouldn't need one anyway. They aren't human. They don't have needs. Maybe it was all a facade. Just like his entire relationship with my soulmate.

I look around the unit again, trying to decide where to start, when Owen and Julian pop in next to me.

Julian's gaze drifts over the stacked boxes. "Mortals accumulate a lot of things."

"Apparently," I say, nudging one of the plastic bins with my boot.

Owen steps forward and inspects a label written in Josie's careful handwriting. "It makes sense. Mortals don't live long. They hold onto what they gather."

Julian tilts his head. "That your professional opinion?"

Owen straightens, brushing invisible dust from his sleeve. "Organization is practical."

Julian and I both turn slowly toward him. "Owen," Julian says, folding his arms across his chest, "you built a house just to hold the things you've gathered over the centuries."

Owen doesn't miss a beat. "It was necessary."

"Necessary." Julian parrots, gesturing toward Owen. "You added a basement and an attic because the house ran out of room."

I drag a hand over the back of my neck and grab the first box. "Remind me again which one of us is the embodiment of greed?"

Julian's grin appears immediately. Owen chuckles under his breath.

"Grab a box," I say, still holding the heaviest thing in my arms. "We got a shit ton of work to do."

Julian gives me a mock salute and grabs the nearest bin. Owen sighs like the entire situation personally offends him, like he's sloth, but he picks one up anyway.

I open a portal in the middle of the unit.

One by one we start tossing boxes through it, the other end opening directly into my living room. It works for about ten minutes before the reality sets in.

Josie owns far more things than three people should

reasonably move. We might be demons, but patience has never been our strong suit.

Julian wipes his hands on his jeans and looks around the unit again. "This is going to take all day."

Another portal snaps open beside us. Damian steps through first with Adrian right behind him.

"Thought you idiots might need help," Damian says, already grabbing a stack of boxes. "Heard from Aunt Liora that you were moving Josie today."

Seth appears next, rolling his shoulders. Caleb follows, glancing around the storage unit with amusement. "Mortals really keep everything."

"Don't start," Owen mutters, throwing a rag at him.

With seven of us moving boxes, the entire process turns into absolute chaos.

Portals open and close across the room, boxes disappearing from the unit and reappearing inside my house faster than I can keep track of them. Within twenty minutes the storage unit that looked impossible to clear is suddenly completely empty.

Julian steps back and surveys the space. "That might be the fastest mortal move in history."

Damian checks the time and nudges Adrian. "We've got to go."

The two of them work in the Punishment Sector now. Their job is to break souls down until they can be rebuilt and released. The ones that can't be rebuilt stay exactly where they are... for eternity.

They work on shifts when it comes to souls. Take as many as they want and those become theirs to deal with. Adrian and Damian usually take the most. They prefer the ones that still have something worth salvaging. Helping rebuild a soul means it eventually gets to leave, it means there's some improvement, something to look forward to.

The worst ones get assigned. Those are the souls that refuse to break. The ones that enjoy what they did.

It's just the five of us now. I look at Caleb and Seth. "Can you guys head over to the apartment and get the boxes from there?"

They nod and step through the portal.

When it's just Julian, Owen, and me, a sound reaches me from beyond.

It isn't spoken out loud. I feel it move through my body instead, threading through my head like pressure behind my eyes. The pull follows immediately, dragging my instincts toward whoever is calling.

Lucas Duvain.

The name slams into the back of my skull. Pain spikes behind my eyes, the way a mortal would describe how a migraine builds. Something is very wrong.

I press my fingers against my temples. The voice comes again, clearer this time, the words threading directly through my mind.

Lucas Duvain. By oath and fire, by shadow and will, I call upon you. Step forth and heed this summons.

Blood hits stone somewhere far away. I can feel it through the pull tightening in my chest. Someone out there knows exactly what they're doing.

The pressure builds again.

Lucas Duvain.

I don't even notice when Caleb and Seth return.

"I know that look," Julian sighs.

I try to ignore him and just focus on the person who is calling me.

Seth waves a hand in front of my face. "You okay, brother?"

"Someone is summoning me," I say, focusing on the pull tightening in my chest as I try to locate where it's coming from.

Seth shrugs. "Then go."

I shake it off and follow the call.

A second later, I pop into what looks like an abandoned warehouse. Something about this already feels wrong.

"Hello," I say, scanning the room.

The place is derelict. No one has cared for it in years. Water drips somewhere in the distance. Sunlight cuts through the broken windows and catches on sheets of plastic hanging from the ceiling, rustling in the wind.

The air smells foul. Mildew. Rot. And something else that lies beneath it. A scent no mortal could name but every demon recognizes instantly.

Decay.

A Harbinger.

"Look at you," Jasper sneers, stepping out from a hallway in the corner of the room.

I try to move. But nothing happens. There's nothing drawn on the floor, no trap that I can see.

Then I look up. A devil's trap carved into the ceiling.

Fuck. I should have known.

Traps on the ground are useless. They hold lower level demons maybe. But not a Duvain. Traps on the ceiling are powerful. They hold everything. Most texts mistranslated that detail centuries ago, but a Harbinger would know exactly what works.

I look back at Jasper. I expected a body falling apart, grey skin melting from the body. Something barely holding together.

Instead, he looks completely human.

Exactly like the soul Selene showed us. Exactly as it did in the apartment that night. I should have known our knowledge of what he is didn't change anything about his condition.

"See, I called you here for a reason," Jasper says as he moves closer. "I want you to listen."

"Tell me how you're still able to blend in," I say instead.

"Very good magic went into this one," he replies, tapping his meat suit. "I was hoping I'd stick in a vessel eventually."

"This is not the first time you've done this," I say.

"It is not." Jasper sneers as he steps closer. "You can ask your Aunt Selene about me later."

His eyes lock onto mine. "But for now, we have things to discuss."

Jasper stops a few feet from the edge of the trap and studies me. "You look disappointed," he says. "Were you expecting a human to be the one making the deal?"

"I'm standing in a warehouse with a Harbinger," I reply. "My expectations adjusted accordingly."

A faint smile crosses his face. "You're more intuitive than the rest," he says. "That's why I called you."

"Get to the point."

Jasper folds his hands behind his back. "Sterling and Ellison Creed wanted Hearthlight," he says. "Not the building. The structure is useless. They want the land."

I don't speak. I stay quiet and listen. He's unhinged and cocky, he'll give me something damning soon enough.

"Development rights. Government contracts. Expansion," he continues when I remain silent. "That piece of land would have made them very powerful men."

"And Bella stopped them," I say, watching him carefully.

"Yes," Jasper says almost amused.

"She fought them and won," I add. I want to charge him, but instead I keep my tone noncombatant.

"With a Duvain soulmate," Jasper replies. "Which made the humiliation worse."

Small sparks crackle along Jasper's hands, brief flashes of heat before they disappear into the dust filled air.

"They blame Bella," he continues. "But they hate your family for making her strong enough to win."

"So they started digging," I say.

"Exactly," Jasper replies. His eyes darken to a non human black.

"They studied the contract Cassius Arden used," he says. "The way demons make deals. The way Hell works."

Ophelia's father. The fuckwad that started all of this bullshit.

"They went deeper than Cassius ever did," Jasper continues. "Further into things mortals should never touch."

While Jasper dies in college, it seems that this Harbinger knows more than we thought he does.

"By creating a Harbinger," I guess. "And connecting with Obadiah Crowe."

Jasper nods once. "They released him," he says.

"All of this," I say, "because they lost a piece of land."

"Because they lost *control*," Jasper corrects. His gaze locks onto mine. "The Creeds want the same things they've always wanted. Money. Power. Government influence."

A faint smile drags across his mouth again.

"And now they also want revenge," Jasper says. "Bella was the beginning of their problem."

His eyes stay on mine.

"And the Duvains," he adds menacingly, "are the rest of it. See I knew she was going to be a Duvain mate. It was obvious. I just needed to get the child in her first. Everything had to go to plan."

I push down the feeling that I need to ask more questions and move on with the one that's gnawing at the back of my mind.

He has something that he's hiding. Usually I would push, but Jasper will tell me. He likes the sound of his own voice.

"What do you want?"

Jasper's smile widens. "A deal."

No surprises there. "You don't have a soul to bargain with, so what could you possibly trade?"

Jasper's mouth twitches, amused.

"Oh, I have something you want," he says.

I stare at him. "Come on, Jasper."

His smile widens slightly.

"You get every piece of information I have on Sterling and Ellison Creed," he says. "Every move they plan to make. Every contract they intend to use against Bella and the Duvain family."

I watch him carefully.

"And in return."

Jasper takes one slow step closer to the trap. "In return," he says calmly, "I want you to release Obadiah Crowe from Hell."

I glance up as I hear a cracking sound. The devil's trap carved into the ceiling splits down the middle.

Jasper twists his hands while watching it all happen.

"Think about my offer," he says, a hint of amusement

in his voice. "You get everything I know about Sterling and Ellison Creed."

Jasper begins to walk away from me and the trap.

"And you release Obadiah Crowe."

The trap cracks again. Stone dust falls from the ceiling.

"Not happening," I say.

Jasper's smile doesn't fade. "You may want to reconsider."

The force holding me in place flickers. The trap is failing. He takes another step back into the shadow of the hallway.

"Tick tock, Lucas," he says. "Time is running out."

The ceiling falls to the floor. The pressure around me disappears instantly. I move forward to catch him. But Jasper is already gone.

The warehouse falls silent. A second later I step back into my house, brushing dust off myself. I hate that I had to jump and roll as the ceiling gave way above me.

Boxes are everywhere. Furniture half moved. Books stacked on the floor. Someone has opened three different boxes and apparently decided none of them belong where they landed.

Owen is holding a lamp. Julian is arguing with him about where said lamp goes. "That clearly belongs in a living room," Julian says.

"It was in a storage unit unboxed," Owen replies. "It could go anywhere."

"That does not make it a hallway lamp." Seth is sitting on a box watching the two of them like this is the most entertaining thing he's seen all day.

Caleb is carrying another stack inside when Liora suddenly looks up. She stops. Her eyes lock on me. "What."

Everyone turns. Julian lowers the lamp. Owen straightens. Seth senses something is wrong.

"What happened?" Owen asks.

I exhale slowly. "Jasper summoned me."

Seth swears under his breath. Liora's eyes harden.

"Where?" Caleb asks.

"Abandoned warehouse," I say. "Devil's trap on the ceiling."

Julian grimaces. "Smart."

"He wanted to make a deal." That gets their attention.

"What deal?" Seth asks.

I meet their eyes. "He gives us everything he knows about Sterling and Ellison Creed."

Julian snorts. "That sounds suspiciously helpful."

"In exchange," I continue, ignoring Julian, "he wants us to release Obadiah Crowe from Hell."

"No," Owen says.

"Absolutely not," Julian adds.

"That is the worst idea I have ever heard," Seth mutters.

Caleb shakes his head.

"Why is Obadiah Crowe so fucking important to him?" I grunt out, wanting to throw something very badly. However, everything within my reach belongs to my mate, and I'll be damned if I break any of her things.

Selene has been standing near the stairs. She hasn't said a word yet, though.

"You all deserve to know who he was," she says quietly, stepping forward.

"You don't have to do this," Theron says from next to her.

"When I was alive," she ignores him, "I was promised to Obadiah Crowe."

Julian's eyebrows lift. Her eyes flick toward Theron.

"He made a deal," she says. "I didn't know that. Our town never knew either. I only knew him as the pastor. Nothing else. But I was to marry him in order for my sister to be well."

Liora and Evander understand exactly what that means.

"Theron killed him when his time was up," Selene finishes. "He swore revenge on the Duvains with his final breath."

I look at her. "But what does that have to do with Jasper?"

"I knew Obadiah Crowe before he died," she says, voice cracking slightly. "I knew the kind of mind he had."

She walks closer to us. "He was obsessed with overcoming death." Liora grabs her hand to keep her steady as Selene wavers a bit. "Jasper Wilder is the proof his theory can work."

"What theory?" Caleb asks.

"He is preparing for his own reincarnation," Selene says. "And it seems that it is happening sooner rather than later."

Suddenly Jasper's deal makes a whole lot more sense.

CHAPTER THIRTEEN

Josie

I find no peace in dreamland.

Every time sleep starts to take hold, the nightmare pulls me down into it—deep enough that for a moment I can't remember where the dream ends and reality begins.

At first, it feels like I'm weightless. Not like I'm floating, but like I'm falling, diving, straight into the abyss.

I start to thrash, peddling my legs back and forth, that's when I realize I'm standing. Prying my eyes open, I look around. Water is everywhere. All around me. Above me. Below me.

I let out a scream, but barely anything comes out. Only the sound of rushing water fills my ears, making my head feel like it is about to explode.

The surface gives beneath my weight as I step forward, the ink-black silk dipping and shifting under my feet.

A baby cries somewhere ahead. Through the darkness, a

bassinet comes into view at the edge of the water. My heart lurches and I start running toward it.

A hand bursts from the black silk like surface around me and clamps around my throat, whipping me around so fast the world spins, flipping upside down.

Jasper.

Not the human mask he wore on Earth. No, this is the Harbinger I saw in the Veil. Shadows crawl across his face as he leans closer, his grip tightening around my neck, claws sinking into my throat.

"Where do you think you're going, sweet little soul?" His breath hits my face, scorching hot, like standing too close as a dragon blows flame from its mouth.

I claw at his wrist, trying to pry his fingers loose, but it's useless. His hold doesn't change as he lifts me higher, my feet leaving the inky surface below. The black silk dissolves beneath us, vanishing as I'm kicking into empty air.

"See," he sneers. "You want me."

This is a dream. This *has* to be a dream.

"It isn't a dream, sweet mortal." Jasper squeezes my throat harder. "You've entered my domain now."

"How did you know that is what I was thinking?" My breath is coming in quick, broken puffs.

"I have the power to do whatever I want in *my* domain!" He squeezes my throat even further, cutting off blood flow, making my vision turn fuzzy.

"I will not let you control me," I choke out.

Jasper tilts his head slightly, studying me. "You think you have control," he says.

"I do."

A dark smile spreads across his face. "No one who walks the Veil ever does."

"You have no hold on me!" I scream.

He lets go of my neck. The world beneath us disappears. The water drops away. And suddenly I'm falling again.

My scream tears through the darkness—and I bolt upright in bed, drenched in sweat.

"What's wrong, Sunshine?" Lucas asks, his arms tightening around me as he pulls me against his chest.

I shake my head, still trying to catch my breath. "Just a nightmare."

He leans back slightly, one hand coming up to cup my face so he can look at me properly.

"You were screaming," he says, lowering his voice and moving his face closer to mine.

"I don't remember screaming," I say, going with that for now. I'm not sure I want to discuss the hell I just witnessed.

His thumb brushes slowly across my cheek, wiping away sweat I didn't realize was there.

"You were," he repeats. His gaze searches mine for a moment before he speaks again. "What was it about?"

I hesitate. The images are still there. The black silk water. The bassinet. Jasper's hand around my throat. The sound of a baby crying.

"Jasper," I admit. This is probably the best place to start.

Lucas sighs. His arm tightens around my waist instinctively, pulling me even closer. I breathe him in, letting the safety, the comfort of him pull me into relaxing against his chest. "Where?"

Isn't that the million dollar question. I have no idea where. He very well might have been lying, but I decide to go with where Jasper said we were..

"In the Veil," I whisper, glancing down at my hands.

"What happened?" He asks. I don't sense any judgement or frustration in his tone. There's only concern.

"He said I walked into his domain," I murmur. "That no one who walks the Veil has control."

Lucas goes quiet. His hand drifts down to rest over the curve of my stomach. "It was a nightmare," he says finally, trying to calm me down. It sounds like he's trying to convince himself more than me, though.

"I know," I say, even though I'm not completely sure that's true.

The baby shifts suddenly beneath my ribs. His eyes drop to my stomach.

"Did he say anything about the baby?" He asks carefully.

I take a minute to think about it. He never did. He didn't even acknowledge the baby crying. Or anything with the bassinet. Jasper completely ignored it. Maybe he didn't hear it. Like that was a message for me and me alone.

"No," I say surprised. "He didn't."

Lucas studies me for another moment before pulling me back against him, his chin resting lightly against the top of my head.

"Try to sleep," he murmurs, one hand rubbing slow circles across my back.

I start to drift when the baby moves suddenly and I sit up screaming, grabbing my stomach.

Something is wrong. Very wrong.

Thalia appears what feels like a second later. I don't even know how she got here as fast as she did.

"Let me check, child," she says, already pulling up my shirt.

Her hands move across my stomach, pressing lightly as she closes her eyes.

For a moment, nothing happens. Then the baby settles suddenly. The tension in my body releases with it.

Thalia let's all the air escape her lungs. She wipes the sweat from her brow and puts her hand over her mouth.

"Everything feels okay," she says, looking me directly in the eyes. She looks relieved. I don't know what to feel about that. "This is a magical child and sometimes they do not yet understand the power they carry."

Part of me wants to ask what that pain was... but the other side wants to be in the dark. The desire to be ignorant wins out in the end.

Lucas steps closer beside the bed. *When had he gotten up?*

"She had a nightmare," he says. "She was in the Veil. Jasper was there, too."

Thalia glances at him. "That is not entirely unexpected," she says carefully. "You and the baby experienced something traumatic. The missing week may be coming back to you."

She reaches into her bag and pulls out a small vial. "This should help with restful sleep," she explains, placing it in Lucas's hand.

Her gaze lingers on my stomach for a moment longer than I expect before she straightens. "Call me if it happens again." She grabs her things and summons a portal. "Do not hesitate."

Then she's gone as quickly as she appeared. I lean back against the pillows, exhausted.

Lucas squeezes my hand. I'm glad that I have some medication now.

He has been making me tea, rubbing my back, even just sitting here, reading with me. Nothing has worked so far. I'm desperate for something to help.

I'm so grateful he's here. Because right now, I feel completely helpless.

"What can I do for you, Sunshine?"

I look at him. He's trying not to pace. He wants to be here for me, he just doesn't know how.

Honestly, I'm not sure what I need either. I'm just as lost as he is. But even though he's trying to hide it, something else is going on.

"There's something you're not telling me," I say.

He looks away, running a hand through his hair.

"I don't want to upset you after everything you've been through tonight," he sighs. "But if you really want to know, I'll tell you."

"I want to know," I say. "Tell me everything, Lucas."

Lucas chews the inside of his cheek, clearly dreading what he's about to say. I understand why. He's worried about me. But we can't hide things from each other. It's not a way to start a solid relationship.

"Earlier today," he begins, rubbing the back of his neck, "while we were moving your things... someone summoned me."

My stomach rolls as a chill shoots down my spine. "Summoned you?" I repeat.

Lucas nods once. "By name."

I grab my hands to stop them from shaking. "That's not something mortals can just... do, right?"

"No," he says quietly. "It takes preparation. You need blood, intent and ritual texts to summon a specific demon. You need the given name of a demon and a specific saying to make it personal. Humans do not usually know our names freely enough to call us. It takes someone who has been studying things mortals were never meant to understand."

My mind immediately goes to one person. The only one capable of something like this.

"Jasper."

"Yes." Lucas' face turns red. A vein pulses in his neck. "He trapped me in a devil's trap inside an abandoned warehouse. A ceiling trap. Which means he knew exactly how to hold me there. Floor traps do nothing."

"Jesus," I whisper.

"He wanted to talk."

I stare at him. "That's it?"

"I wish." Lucas lets out a humorless laugh. "He wanted to make a deal."

My heart drops to my feet. "What kind of deal?"

"Not your typical mortal deal." Lucas hesitates for a moment. "The kind demons usually make."

My stomach twists again. Demons making deals is still strange to me. I would think they already have all the power in the world. Why would they need to bargain for anything? Clearly Jasper doesn't have the power to do what he really wants.

"And what did he want?" I ask, needing to know.

Lucas shifts from foot to foot. "He said he would give us everything he knows about Sterling and Ellison Creed."

That makes my eyebrows pull together. "That sounds... useful."

Jasper isn't the type to be helpful. Not unless it somehow benefits him. Never for anyone else.

Lucas doesn't look relieved. He looks flat out pissed. "It would be," he grits out. "If that was all."

"I knew there would be a catch." I sit up higher in the bed. "He doesn't do anything for others. What does he want?"

Lucas' expression turns dark. "He wants us to release Obadiah Crowe from Hell."

That sounds exactly like something Jasper would want.

"You better not have agreed to that," I say.

"No." Lucas scoffs, throwing his arms in the air. Relief slides through my body. "It's not even my decision to make. I don't really have the power on my own. The council can... so that means Selene can."

"I'm glad you didn't agree," I say, leaning against the headrest. "We can figure everything else out another way."

Lucas studies me for a moment.

"You're taking this surprisingly well."

"I'm pregnant with a baby that was conceived by a harbinger of hell and who's dna belongs to my mate who happens to be a demon from Hell," I remind him. "My standards for panic-inducing news are currently very high."

A faint smile touches his mouth before it fades again. "I'm serious, Josie."

"I know," I say solemnly.

My mind drifts somewhere else. Jasper doesn't have the power to pull someone out of Hell... but he might have the power to seriously fuck things up in the mortal world.

"Ophelia told me something today," I say slowly.

Lucas sits beside me again, close enough that his shoulder brushes mine. "What?"

I trace my fingers along the blanket, trying to figure out how to explain it. "She's had six miscarriages."

Lucas jolts back, but he doesn't say anything. He lets me keep talking.

"And now," I continue softly, "Thalia says there's nothing left."

Lucas's brow furrows. "What do you mean, nothing left?"

"She's basically infertile."

Lucas flinches. He may not know everything, but it's clear he didn't know that.

"That's... not something that happens often with our kind," he says slowly. "At least not that I've ever heard."

I shouldn't be surprised by that. I doubt demons sit around talking about childbirth.

"She also said something else."

Lucas raises an eyebrow, clearly wanting me to continue.

"She can't see her own thread in the Loom."

His expression goes from being confused to downright shocked. "What do you mean she can't see herself?"

"She said when she looks at the threads... she can see everyone else. Just not hers," I tell him.

Lucas runs a hand over his jaw. "That's not possible."

That's what I thought too. An uncomfortable thought creeps into my head.

"You don't think..." I start, before quickly stopping. It's not possible. Not at all. "You don't think Jasper could have something to do with that?"

He leans back against the headrest beside me, clearly thinking it through.

"Maybe," he finally says.

Holy shit. *Maybe?* I thought I was so far outside the box it wasn't even on the same planet.

"If Jasper's rising is strong enough to affect the Veil," Lucas continues, "it could ripple outward to the mortal world."

"How?"

"Powerful families," he says. "People connected to the structure of Hell. When they summoned him, they let others pay the price."

I push myself out of bed. I can't stay seated anymore.

"Ophelia is the Loom Weaver," I say, trying to piece it together.

"She is." Lucas nods. "Julian is the oldest Duvain of our branch of the family."

I think I'm starting to understand what he's getting at. Power equates to power.

"If Jasper is trying to destabilize things," Lucas says quietly, "it would make sense to target the people holding everything together."

A chill slides down my spine as I sink back against the bed, suddenly out of breath. "That's a terrifying thought."

Lucas pulls me closer against his chest. "Yes," he murmurs. "It is."

My brain won't stop spinning. Thoughts slam into each other, filling every inch of space in my head. There isn't a single corner left untouched by all of this.

I don't want to blame myself.

It's hard not to.

Even if it isn't my fault, for some reason...

The Harbinger of Hell chose me.

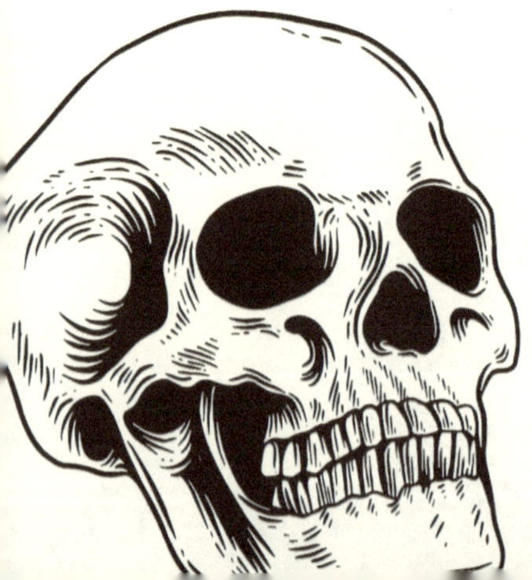

CHAPTER FOURTEEN

Lucas

I lie awake long after Josie falls asleep.

All of the recent events and truths keep replaying in my head on a loop. Julian and Ophelia struggling to conceive. Obadiah potentially being released from Hell. Sterling and Ellison Creed trying to take control of the mortal world. Jasper—a Harbinger—walking freely on Earth.

None of it is good. We're hovering somewhere near end-of-the-world territory.

I glance down at my Sunshine curled against me. She's finally asleep, her breathing is slow and even, relaxed. No nightmares ripping her apart from the inside out.

Hearing her scream earlier broke something open inside me I didn't know existed.

I need to act. I need to do *something*. Anything at this point.

I've always been the one who waits for information

before reacting. The one who studies the board before making a move.

Josie's changed that.

I don't want to sit back and get more information first. I want to fight. I want to rip every single one of these problems out of her life before they ever reach her.

The blame. The danger. The fallout. All of it can sit on my shoulders.

I slowly ease away from Josie and slip out of bed.

She barely moves, only curling deeper into the blankets. One hand rests over the curve of her stomach like she's protecting our daughter even in her sleep.

I will clothes onto myself.

I'm not sure if it's a blessing or a curse but, demons don't need much sleep. A few hours here and there is usually enough. After a few decades, most of us barely bother with it at all. Mates eventually become the same way. Our bodies adjust to each other. To the bond. To the constant awareness of the other person existing in the same world.

Right now, though, sleep isn't even remotely possible. I can't just lie here and do nothing. Too many things are wrong.

I need to speak with Thalia about what Josie said tonight. About Ophelia. About the infertility and the Loom.

And I need to ask her what she noticed during Josie's appointment. I saw the look on her face. Something isn't right.

I pause near the doorway and reach out through the familiar thread that connects family.

Mother.

The response comes almost instantly. *Lucas?*

Are you available?

A moment passes before she answers. I swear she is scoffing. *Of course I am.*

I glance back at the bed where Josie sleeps, peaceful for the first time tonight.

Can you come sit with Josie for a bit? I need to speak with Thalia.

Liora doesn't hesitate. *I'll be there in a moment.*

I know Josie will hate knowing that I had a babysitter come here for her. But her anger is something I'm willing to face if it means making sure that she's safe.

A portal opens in my living room and I watch my mother step through it.

"Hi, Mom," I say, pulling her in for a quick hug. "Thank you so much for coming."

"Of course," she replies, her brows already drawing together as she studies my face. She's not dense, she knows something's up.

"You know about Julian and Ophelia," I tell her.

"I do," she says cryptically.

"Josie told me after Ophelia shared it with the girls," I explain. "She mentioned something tonight. A possibility that Jasper being summoned and whatever he's doing to the Veil could be strong enough to ripple outward."

Liora considers that for a moment, her fingers brushing thoughtfully across her chin.

"Go," she tells me with a wave of her hand. "I will watch your mate. If anything happens, you will be the first to know."

I nod once and step aside so she can move past me.

My mother walks down the hallway toward the bedroom, already shifting into the calm, watchful presence she's always had when it comes to family.

Another soft ripple of magic opens behind her. Selene steps through the portal a moment later.

"You didn't think I'd let Liora sit with a pregnant girl alone, did you?" She teases lightly, already heading toward the bedroom.

Liora glances back at me with the faintest hint of amusement. "She insisted."

"Someone has to keep an eye on your mother," Selene adds as she disappears into the room. "No need to wake your mate to pester her about the infernal claim or anything."

I hear the bedroom door open as they slip inside.

Josie is safe. At least for now, and that's enough for me to move.

I open another portal and step through, heading straight for Thalia.

She's in her office when I arrive.

Her rooms sit inside the same wing where the Infernal Council works. Thalia doesn't spend all of her time here—she prefers visiting mothers in their own homes so they're comfortable when the time comes—but this is where she handles records, charts, and whatever ancient systems demon midwives use to keep track of pregnancies.

I tap the open door a couple of times.

She looks up from behind her desk, glasses sliding slightly down her nose.

"Lucas," she says, gesturing toward the chair across from her. "What brings you here?"

"I need to talk to you," I reply, taking the seat she offered. "About Josie's pregnancy."

Her brow lifts slightly.

"You're not telling us something," I continue. "And I think it might be connected to something else."

She perks up and looks at me with her full attention. "Go on," Thalia says.

"Ophelia told Josie about the miscarriages tonight," I explain. "All of them. And about you telling her there's nothing left medically to try."

Thalia considers that for a moment before releasing a slow breath. "I was wondering when that conversation would happen," she admits.

I lean forward slightly, placing my elbows on the desk. "Josie started thinking about something else," I continue. "Jasper. The Veil. What happens when something like a harbinger starts destabilizing things."

Thalia folds her hands together on the desk. "And?"

"I think it could ripple outward," I say. "That if the Veil is weakening, it could start affecting powerful supernatural bloodlines." I watch her carefully, but she's staring at me just as intently. "Families tied to the structure of Hell," I add. "Like the Duvains."

Thalia is quiet for a moment. "Interesting," she says at last. "Tell me more."

So, I do. I explain everything. Jasper summoning me. The devil's trap. The deal he offered. The Creeds. Obadiah Crowe. And Josie's theory.

By the time I finish, Thalia's expression has shifted from polite curiosity to something far more thoughtful.

Finally, she removes her glasses and sets them on the desk. "You are asking several different questions at once," she says calmly.

"Start with the most important one," I tell her.

"Very well." She watches me carefully. "What I did not say earlier is that Josie's pregnancy is... unusual."

"In what way?" I ask. There's an urgency flooding my system that I've rarely felt in my long life. I need to know this,

I need all of the information as soon as I can get it. I need to do everything that I can to protect her as soon as I can.

"The child is strong," she says. "Stronger than most demon pregnancies at this stage."

"That's not exactly concerning."

"No," Thalia agrees. "Strength itself is not the issue." She pauses. "It's the energy surrounding the pregnancy."

Energy. I didn't even know babies could produce that. Children born between a demon and their mate usually don't show any powers until they're two or three years old.

"What about it?"

"She is reacting," she says.

"To what?"

I admit that I am nervous. I know very little about having children. Apparently this is abnormal for demon and mortal pregnancies.

Thalia's eyes meet mine. "That," she says quietly, "is the question."

"Could she be reacting to the Veil?" I ask. "While in utero?"

It sounds like a longshot even as the words leave my mouth, but I wouldn't be surprised if it's true. The Veil is something very few of our kind understand. No one goes there unless they absolutely have to.

"Pregnancies connected to the Veil are extremely rare, Lucas," Thalia replies. "Very few have ever existed. But in Josie's case..." She pauses for a moment. "It could be a possibility, considering how unusual her conception was."

Before she can say anything more, footsteps stop at the door behind me.

My father steps inside. "Your mother told me you were here," he says. "She was worried."

"I will do some research and then take another look at Josie," Thalia says, already gathering the tools from her desk and placing them into her bag. "Is she resting?"

"She is," I answer.

"Good." She nods. "I want to examine her while she's unaware of her surroundings. It will allow me to access her subconscious more clearly."

She slips past us and heads for the hallway. Evander rests a hand on my shoulder.

"Come, son," he says. "Let's take a walk."

I follow him out of the council wing and into one of the outer gardens. Even in Hell, life grows.

The path beneath our feet is made of black stone that still holds warmth from the constant heat below the surface. Vines crawl up twisted iron trellises, their leaves deep crimson and violet instead of green. Flowers bloom along the edges of the walkway, glowing in the firelight. Dark water runs through narrow channels beside the path, reflecting the red glow of distant embers.

We walk in silence for a while before he speaks. It's what we've always done, taking the time to think before we speak.

"You're worried." Evander keeps his eyes on the path.

"That obvious?" I ask with a humorless chuckle.

"You forget," he says with a small huff of breath, "I raised you."

I look out across the garden where thorned trees twist toward the sky like they're reaching for something that will never come.

"Josie had a nightmare tonight," I tell him. "About the Veil. Seems she returned to it. She was there again," I continue. "With Jasper. *Again.*"

Now he stops walking. "And you think the pregnancy is connected," he says.

"I think everything is connected." I throw my hands in the air and try not to scream.

The wind moves through the dark leaves above us, making them squeak against one another. They are basically made of leather.

"You know," he says, "when you were born, I barely slept for months."

I glance at him.

"Demons don't need sleep," I point out.

"That didn't matter," he replies. "I still checked on you every hour."

We are no longer talking about her nightmare. Actually it is something else completely.

"I can't shake the feeling that something is coming," I admit.

My father's hand tightens briefly on my shoulder. "That instinct has kept our family alive for centuries," he says. "Don't ignore it now." He pauses, looking out across the garden before continuing. "But fear doesn't mean you stop living your life either."

I glance at him.

"That child will change everything for you."

I was not expecting the conversation to go this way. "I'm aware," I mutter.

"No," he says. "You're aware of the responsibility. That's not the same thing."

He turns slightly toward me. "When you hold her for the first time, Lucas... you'll realize how small she is. How fragile babies are."

He gets this far off look on his face. One that I know well. This isn't helping, I've never been an anxious person,

I've always leaned to the more logical side of things instead of emotional. Maybe that's why he thinks I need this conversation. But for once in my life, I think I'm truly feeling the worry that he's describing.

"And you'll understand that every decision you make from that moment forward affects her."

"That's not terrifying at all," I say dryly.

"It should be," Evander replies. "That means you care. You're the first of your brothers and cousins to do this," he adds. "Which means they'll all be watching you to figure out how it works."

"That sounds reassuring."

Not even a little bit.

My father has a point, but I know she'll be tough. She's a Duvain after all.

"It also means," he continues, "that little girl will grow up surrounded by men who would burn the world to the ground for her."

I picture Julian, Owen, Seth, Adrian, Damian, Caleb. He isn't wrong.

Evander's voice lowers slightly. "The first girl in this family in generations."

I know that. There hasn't been a Duvain daughter in the last five generations.

"You'll teach her strength," Evander says. "But more importantly... you'll teach her she deserves to be cherished."

I look out across the garden again, my voice low, almost a whisper. "What if I fail?"

Evander doesn't hesitate. "You will."

That makes me look at him cross. I really don't want to fail.

"Every father does," he says, trying to calm my nerves. "You'll say the wrong things. You'll miss moments you wish you hadn't. Especially when you are called to make a deal."

He pauses to put his arm around me.

"But if you love her the way I know you already do... you'll keep showing up." The wind moves through the dark trees above us. "You're going to be a good father, Lucas."

I nod slowly.

Evander and I portal back to my house.

The moment we step into the entry hall, voices drift from the living room. The women are speaking in hushed tones on the couch.

Evander and I stop just before the doorway.

"...I've never seen anything like it," Thalia is saying.

Selene's voice follows. "You're certain?"

"I wouldn't say it if I wasn't." Thalia continues on with her worries, but it sounds muffled with all the anger I'm harboring.

Evander glances at me but doesn't interrupt.

"Lucas, Evander, come listen to this," Liora says. "What did you see?"

There's a pause in the room. I stand in front of them and wait to see what Thalia has to tell us.

"A memory," Thalia says. "I saw what looks like a memory floating around her subconscious."

"That's impossible," Selene replies immediately. "Josie doesn't remember that week. We don't even know if what she saw in the Veil was real."

"She doesn't consciously," Thalia says. "But the mind stores things deeper than memory. Especially things that magic tends to hide."

"Could it be trauma?" I ask. "Or something related to that?"

"No," Thalia disagrees. "This was definitely magic that

did this. The memory is still threaded into her bloodstream. I expected to see fragments of fear. The nightmare she described. Maybe echoes of the Veil."

"And?" I press.

"That's not what I saw." Her expression tightens. "I saw portions of the Veil." A chill crawls down my spine. "But Josie wasn't alone there."

"Jasper?" I ask. I hate that she is always with him in these situations.

Thalia shakes her head once. "No."

That means whatever this is could be even worse.

Selene steps forward. "Then who?"

Thalia's voice drops almost to a whisper. "The baby."

I stare at her. "That's impossible."

"She was standing in the Veil," Thalia continues quietly. "Not crying. Not afraid."

My mother slowly stands next to me, mimicking my father by putting her hand around me.

"What was she doing?" She asks. The slight twitch around her eyes tells me that she is worried.

Thalia looks directly at me. "Watching."

My pulse hammers in my ears. "Watching what?"

Thalia doesn't answer immediately. When she finally speaks, her voice is grave. "Jasper."

No one moves.

"She was already there," Thalia says softly. "Before he arrived. She is more powerful than anyone I have ever seen before."

"That means... that our baby is the one that keeps pulling Josie into the Veil. Not Jasper."

I'd realized something far worse than Jasper might be coming.

I just wasn't expecting it to be *my* daughter.

CHAPTER FIFTEEN

Josie

The potion Thalia gave me worked. For a while at least.

The nightmares stopped almost immediately, which was honestly the biggest relief of my life. Lucas stopped watching me like I might explode in the middle of the night, and I stopped waking up drenched in sweat like I'd just run a marathon through Hell.

That lasted about three weeks. But now they're back. And I haven't told anyone.

I'm thirty one weeks pregnant now.

Apparently demon babies grow at their own pace. Mine seems to have misunderstood 'pace' for 'race' with how big she's getting.

Which is why Lucas insisted we keep today's appointment with Thalia.

Normally she comes to the house, but I needed to get my ass out of it for a while, so we're headed to her office.

Being pregnant has officially turned me into a human incubator with limited mobility and a bladder the size of a pea.

With this baby growing as fast as she is, I finally gave in and took Bella up on going part time. I just can't do everything anymore. Tinsley has been a huge help—filling in when I need her to, but also jumping in when I'm there. Honestly, I don't know what I would've done without her.

Lucas insisted on portaling. I insisted on walking.

At this point in my pregnancy, we compromise a lot. Which really means I win most of the arguments because he's terrified of stressing me out.

So, we walk.

Hell has roads.

Actual roads. There's no cars on them, but they're old cobblestone roads, the kind that give old towns their charm. Black stone paths winding through gardens and old buildings that look like they've been here since before humans figured out how to light a fire.

They probably have been, but I really shouldn't be surprised anymore. Honestly, it's kind of amazing seeing what demon architectural innovation looks like.

Demons move through the streets in small clusters. Some walk alone. Some carry stacks of ledgers or scrolls tucked under their arms.

A pair of younger demons approach from the opposite direction. The second they notice Lucas, their conversation cuts off.

"Lord Duvain," one of them says, dipping his head slightly as they pass.

Lucas nods back easily. "Morning."

I turn to watch them disappear down the path.

What the hell was that? They looked nervous.

We only make it a few more steps before an older

demon woman pushing a cart stacked with glowing herbs pauses when she sees us. Her eyes land on my stomach first. Then Lucas.

"Well look at you," she says with a knowing grin. "First Duvain baby in decades."

Lucas's hand instinctively moves to the small of my back. "We're hoping she arrives strong and powerful," he replies.

The woman snorts softly. "With that bloodline? I'd say she doesn't have much choice."

Lucas chuckles under his breath and we continue down the path.

I glance at him. "You're famous here."

"I wouldn't go that far," he says, shrugging his shoulders nonchalantly.

Another group passes us and every single one of them straightens when they see him.

Yeah, he's famous. Or terrifying to the younger demon generation. Most likely… both.

He notices me watching him. "What?" He asks.

"You act like this is an everyday occurrence," I say.

"That's because it is." He's laughing now.

When I actually think about it, it's kind of funny. I guess I always pictured demons as pretty solitary creatures. Probably the result of years of people telling me they're evil or terrifying.

I've met evil.

Demons aren't it.

I gesture toward the people who keep nodding respectfully as they pass. "They look like they're greeting the mayor of Hell."

Lucas shrugs. "My family has been here a long time."

That might be the understatement of the millennia.

But watching him interact with them, respectful without needing to prove anything. I begin to understand something. People don't respect Lucas because he demands it. They respect him because he's earned it. His whole family has.

I smile as we continue down the path. The air is warm, but not uncomfortable. It's like a nice spring day.

For the first time in weeks, I don't feel cooped up. I'm not stuck in a classroom, I'm not stuck in a house. I'm out, walking around, seeing people, doing normal things.

Lucas keeps pace beside me, one hand resting against the small of my back. Everything he does feels intentional, but not forced.

That's the thing about Lucas.

I looked down at my hands. I refuse to show how nervous I am around other demons.

I feel Lucas rub his hand down my back.

Which... I'm not complaining about.

If someone had told me a year ago that I'd be walking through Hell with a demon soulmate who cooks breakfast for me every morning and reminds me to drink water, I probably would've laughed in their face.

And yet, here we are.

Lucas cooks. He cleans. He built half a nursery before I even realized that's what he was doing. He talks to the baby, like full conversations.

Sometimes in Latin. Sometimes in Greek. Apparently demons believe babies recognize language before they're even born. Which means our daughter is probably going to come out of the womb speaking something ancient, and terrifying me to the core.

But I don't mind it.

He reads books about pregnancy. Actual books. And not just demon ones, human ones too.

Which is how he learned that pregnant women shouldn't be lifting heavy things. And that, in turn, is why I caught him carrying an entire bookshelf across the room the other day like it weighed nothing.

He doesn't act like any of it is a big deal. Like having me around and in his space is the most natural thing in the world. Even like protecting our daughter was something he decided the second he found out she existed.

I glance over at him as we walk.

He's talking about something I'm not fully paying attention to.

The realization hits me like a kid throwing a box of juice on the ground. Somewhere between the nightmares and the moments where me having a baby becomes a reality and the looming end of the world energy hanging over everything... I fell in love with him.

"Lucas," I say.

He doesn't hear me. He's too busy muttering something to himself about measurements and demon growth charts.

"Lucas!" I say louder.

He turns immediately, eyes wide. "What? Is it the baby?"

"No," I say quickly, grabbing both of his hands.

The realization hits me like a brick while I'm looking into Lucas' eyes.

I may not grow old. But our daughter will. She is part Lucas, but this pregnancy is different.

Everyone says so.

Maybe she won't be immortal.

I begin to absolutely freak out. I picture it suddenly—

years flashing through my mind faster than I can watch them. First steps. First words. School. Growing up.

Growing old.

And me standing there the whole time, exactly the same.

Watching her get older. Watching her die. My chest tightens and suddenly I can't breathe. Air rushes in and out too fast as panic claws its way up my throat.

"Hey—hey." Lucas grabs my arms. "Are you okay?"

I shake my head automatically, but I force myself to get control of it.

Not here. Not yet. Not until I know if what I'm thinking is even possible.

"Yeah," I lie, pressing a hand to my chest. "I'm fine. Just heartburn."

His face immediately softens. "Ah," he says with a small chuckle. "That I can handle."

I hate lying to him. But I can't say it yet. Not until I have answers.

Because if there's even the smallest chance this baby will grow old while I stay exactly the same... I need to know if there's a way to stop that from happening.

Or if there's a way for me to grow old with her.

We reach Thalia's office a few minutes later. She's already waiting for us.

The appointment itself goes smoothly. Measurements, questions, a few notes written down in that ancient looking notebook she carries around.

When she's finished with everything, I turn to Lucas.

"Lucas," I say casually. "I'm going to chat with Thalia for a bit before I head out to see the girls."

He hesitates.

"It's a feminine question," I whisper.

"Oh." He nods immediately and kisses my cheek. "Right. I'll wait outside."

The door shuts behind him.

Thalia watches it close and chuckles softly. "Men," she says. "Doesn't matter if they're mortal or immortal. They're all the same."

I don't laugh with her. "I need to talk to you about the baby," I say.

Thalia looks up.

"Aging," I clarify. "Specifically."

Her brow furrows. "Okay," she says slowly. "What about it?"

I take a breath. "If I'm immortal," I say quietly, "and my daughter isn't..." The words stick in my throat. "Then I'm going to watch her die."

Thalia studies me carefully.

"So I need to know," I continue. "Is there a way to change that?"

"Change your own mortality?" She asks carefully.

I nod. "If that's what it takes," I say. "If she grows old, I want to grow old too."

Thalia looks confused. "Wait. Why would you want to be mortal for your—"

A door slamming open stops Thalia from saying anything more.

Lucas stands there. His chest is rising and falling like he ran, his jaw tight, eyes locked directly on me. "You want to *what*?"

My stomach drops. "Lucas—"

"How long were you planning to keep that from me?" He demands, stepping fully into the room.

"I wasn't—"

"You want to give up immortality?" He's hurt. I know

that. I wasn't being truthful with him and I want to take away every moment I just had with Thalia.. "Without even talking to me?"

"I was trying to figure out if it was even possible first!"

"You're talking about dying," he says.

"I'm talking about living the same life as my daughter!"

Lucas freezes in place. His brows pull together slightly. "Your daughter?" He repeats.

I look at him, not understanding. Uh yeah. She's my daughter. "What?"

"I thought she was ours," he spits out.

The words hit me like a brick. I realize in that moment what I just said. For a second, neither of us speaks.

"I didn't mean it like that," I say quickly. "I just—"

"You're planning for her life like I'm not part of it," he says angrily.

"That's not what I'm doing." I want to reassure him, but he's right. I am planning that.

"Then stop talking like you're the only one who has to face this." He isn't angry anymore. He's devastated. I think that makes it worse. "You think I wouldn't stand beside you through that? Through every year of her life?"

My throat tightens. "That's not what I meant."

Lucas shakes his head slightly, running a hand through his hair. "You're trying to solve a problem alone that belongs to both of us." He looks at me again and I hate the disappointment shining in his eyes. "She's *our* daughter, Josie."

"Enough." Thalia's voice cuts through the room before either of us can say anything else.

Lucas and I both turn toward her.

She's watching us with the same calm expression she always has, but there's a sense of anger to it now.

"You're both arguing about something that isn't even possible at the moment," she says.

Lucas frowns. "What do you mean?"

"Josie is still mortal," Thalia replies neutrally. "She would only become immortal during the Infernal Claim."

"The Claim?" I ask.

Thalia nods. "When a demon and their mate complete the Claim, the bond finalizes. The mortal partner becomes immortal as part of the union."

Lucas goes very still beside me.

"But that cannot happen right now," Thalia continues.

"Why not?" He asks.

Her gaze drops briefly to my stomach. "Because performing the Claim while she is pregnant could disrupt the magical balance sustaining the child."

My stomach twists. I do not want that at all.

"In other words," she says gently, "we are not risking the life of this baby for the sake of a ritual."

Lucas immediately nods. "Agreed."

I exhale slowly. "So... I'm still mortal."

"For now," Thalia says.

"And the baby?" The words barely register as I squeak them out.

"The baby is part demon and will be fine," Thalia cuts in. "She will be immortal."

Lucas hasn't moved. He's staring at me like I'm a stranger and not his mate. His other half.

"Lucas—"

"You were really going to do it," he says quietly. "Change your mortality."

The room feels too small all of a sudden. "I was asking a question—"

"You were asking how." He laughs in such a humorless way that it pierces my heart.

He doesn't scream or yell. He doesn't berate me. Instead, he just airs his frustrations.

"You came here," he continues, his eyes locked on mine, "to figure out how to die one day... and you didn't even tell me."

"I wasn't trying to hurt you." I cross my arms to protect myself.

"You were planning to leave me," he whispers, eyes glassy.

I wasn't thinking. Not about that. I was so fucking worried about the baby that it never even occurred to me I would be leaving him.

"That's not what this is," I whisper.

"Isn't it?" He asks. His hand drags down his face, and for the first time since I've known him, Lucas looks completely lost. "You think I could watch you do that?"

I know it's a rhetorical question yet I answer it anyway.

"I was thinking about our daughter," I say defensively.

"I love you," Lucas says. The words come out rough, like they hurt to say. Almost as much as they hurt to hear. "Fate may have put you in front of me. But it didn't make me love you."

He shakes his head slightly. "I love the way you kneel when you talk to your students. Like they're the most important people in the world."

My vision blurs. Tears fall down my cheeks.

"I love how you hug Bella like you mean it. How your hand finds your stomach every time the baby moves."

I can't breathe. Air tears into my lungs in ragged gasps.

"I love you," he repeats. "And you were standing here

planning a future where I wake up one day and you're just... gone."

"I wasn't—"

"I won't forget what you said about *your* daughter," he cuts in. His voice drops. "That's the curse of living forever." He swallows. "When mortals lose someone, time softens it. They move on. The memory fades around the edges." His eyes hold mine. "That will never happen to me."

Another tear slips down my cheek.

"You know what. When you're gone," he says quietly, "I will see you here. Exactly as you are. In every memory I have." My heart drops. "I'll remember the last time you laughed. The last thing you said to me. The last time you touched me."

Tears keep falling until Lucas is nothing but a blur through them. "And I will carry that for eternity."

"You don't deserve what I did today," I whisper. "I was only thinking of me... not how it would affect you."

Lucas lets out a breath that sounds almost like a laugh.

"Loving you doesn't stop because you decided something without me." He takes a step back. "My love for you is infinite," he says. "That's not a promise. It's the reality of what forever looks like for me."

His eyes soften slightly. "You're the only person who has ever made eternity feel terrifying."

He just keeps pushing and pushing.

I want to tell him how I feel. I should have from the start. Not lie. Not run. Just tell him how much I love him. What he means to me. How he is my everything.

But I stay silent. Because I know there's nothing in the world that would make this better.

"No amount of time would ever be enough," he says

quietly. "Because you, Josie Brighton... are the other half of my soul."

Thalia clears her throat awkwardly as my body trembles out of control.

Then he turns.

"Do not make me learn how to exist in a world you chose to leave."

He walks out before I can say anything.

I choke back a sob as the door closes behind him.

He forgot to mention one very important detail.

I never wanted to exist in a world without him. I just didn't want to abandon my baby like my mother did to me.

I can barely see the door he walked out of through the tears in my eyes.

He walked away with the other half of my soul.

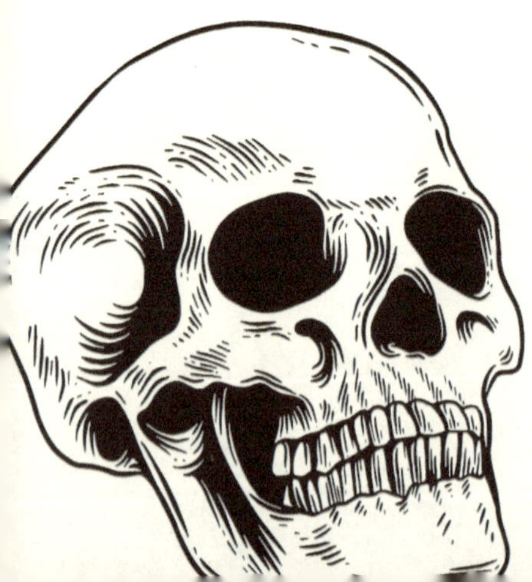

CHAPTER SIXTEEN

I'm hurt. And running away from my mate feels like a crime. Every instinct in my body demands that I turn around, go back to her, pull her into my arms, and refuse to let her face anything alone.

Instead, I keep walking.

Every step away from her pulls against the bond in my chest. The blood in my veins are screaming at me to turn around. I drag a hand through my hair, trying to clear my head, but the words keep repeating. *Change your own mortality.*

As if I am something she can simply step away from. The life that I *thought* we were building means nothing to her.

Pain tears through my chest hard enough that I have to stop. I bend forward, hands braced on my knees, forcing air into lungs that suddenly refuse to cooperate. The same feeling I had in Thalia's office. The bond between us pulling so hard it feels as if it might tear me apart from the inside out.

I need to talk to someone who understands this. I don't need sympathy, I need the truth. No matter how harsh.

I call Owen and Julian. They are the only ones who will understand why walking away from a mate after being betrayed feels as if my soul is being torn in half.

Where are you?

Julian responds almost immediately. *The Ninth Circle.*

The only bar in Hell. Also the busiest place in the entire realm.

Demons from every district pass through those doors at some point—politicians from the council wing, collectors fresh off contracts, enforcers coming off punishment shifts. Deals and information get whispered over drinks. Fights break out and disappear just as fast. No one asks questions.

It sits in the center of the infernal district, built from black stone that looks melted and reformed a thousand times over. Red firelight bleeds through the tall windows, and the bass from whatever music they've decided to play tonight can usually be heard halfway down the street.

I need to talk.

Owen responds this time. *We'll grab a room in the back.*

I open a portal and step through, the noise of The Ninth Circle hitting me the second my boots touch the floor.

The place is packed. Heat presses in from every direction. Not just from Hell, but from the sheer number of bodies crammed into the room.

A long black bar cuts across the room. Demons crowd around it shoulder to shoulder, drinks already in their hands. Music pounds from somewhere in the back. The bass vibrates through the stone beneath my boots. Voices overlap across the room. A flash of magic sparks through the room and I think a punch was thrown in the corner.

The ceiling arches high overhead, iron sconces burning with red fire. The light cuts through the smoke and throws shadows all over the floor.

The women can come here if they want. Nothing stops them. But years ago they decided this place wasn't their scene. I get it. It is loud here. Plus all the demon egos are just a lot.

So they made their own space. A place a few streets over where they gather instead. Nights are less likely to end in a fistfight or a contract being signed under the influence of Hellfire whiskey.

Ophelia and Bella go there often. I'd hoped Josie would too once she became my mate.

The thought sits heavy in my stomach.

Most of the women tied to our circle have mates already. All except Della. But Della has always been... different. No one quite knows what she's doing or what she's planning. She appears when she wants to. Disappears just as easily. An enigma even by Hell's standards. That says a lot.

A few demons glance my way when I walk in, but most don't bother. This is the type of place where people prefer to remain anonymous. It's not like out on the street where easy conversation can naturally flow. This is a heavy place for heavy actions.

I scan the room once before heading toward the back hallway. Owen and Julian will already be waiting. They know I don't come here unless something is wrong. I've never been a bar person. In fact, I tend to avoid it when at all possible.

Being around this many people has never been something I enjoy.

I pull the curtain aside and step into the private room. A glass sits on the table, ice slowly melting inside it. They must have ordered it the moment I called them.

"Okay, little brother," Owen says, leaning back in his chair. "What happened with your mate?"

I frown. "How did you know it was a mate thing?"

"It's always a mate thing," Julian says, lifting a brow.

I sit down and push the glass aside. "She went behind my back," I say, blowing out a breath. "She asked Thalia if there was a way to change her mortality."

Neither of them reacts the way I expect. I was expecting anger or shock. Maybe even a bit of horror. Instead I get... absolutely nothing from them.

"For the baby?" Owen asks.

I nod once. "She's worried about outliving her."

Julian gives Owen a look. The kind only twins understand. "Mortals don't think the way we do," he says. "They react first. Think later."

"That doesn't make it easier," I mutter.

"No," Owen agrees. "But it does explain why she did it."

He leans forward, resting his forearms on the table. "Bella told me about Josie's mother," he says. "About how things were for her growing up."

I stay quiet. I already know what he's implying. Josie told me about her mother a while ago.

"She isn't trying to leave you," Owen continues. "She's trying to protect her child in the only way she knows how."

Julian nods once. "Mortals spend their entire lives worrying about losing the people they love," he says. "That instinct doesn't disappear just because she's tied to a demon."

I drag a hand down my face. “She should have talked to me.”

“She should have,” Owen agrees. “And you should tell her that.”

Julian leans back in his chair. “That’s the part no one tells you about having a soulmate,” he says. “You don’t stop having conversations. You have more of them.”

“Hard ones,” Owen adds.

I stare down at the table. “So, what am I supposed to do?” I ask.

Owen shrugs slightly. “Go home.”

Julian smirks faintly. “And talk to your mate before this turns into something it doesn’t need to be.”

Owen lifts his glass. “You’re the first one of us to have a kid, Lucas. None of us know what the hell we’re doing yet.”

Julian nods. “But one thing we do know?”

I look up.

“You don’t walk away from your soulmate,” Owen says emphatically.

“Especially when she’s terrified,” Julian adds.

I start to realize they might be right. “I need to go.” I push to my feet and finish the drink in one swallow.

I step through the portal into my house and immediately hear Josie crying in the bedroom.

The sound stops me cold. It rips my heart out all over again. For a moment I just stand there, staring down the hallway, listening to her sobs echo through the house.

I am a large part of the reason she is this upset to begin with.

So, I push the door open slowly. Josie is curled on the bed, her face buried in the pillow. Her shoulders shake with every breath.

“Sunshine,” I whisper.

She turns when she hears my voice. Her eyes are red and swollen, tears still sliding down her cheeks. "Lucas," she whispers.

The way she says my name nearly brings me to my knees. I cross the room and sit on the edge of the bed.

"I shouldn't have done that," she says finally, wiping at her face. "Going behind your back. Asking Thalia without talking to you first."

I shake my head slowly. "I was angry," I admit. "But I understand why you did it."

She looks at me, confused. "You do?"

"I talked to Owen and Julian." She waits to hear what I have to say. "You weren't trying to leave me," I say. "You were trying to protect our child."

Her face crumples. "My mother didn't protect me," she says while hiccuping. "She used me. Controlled everything. I swore I would never let that happen to my daughter."

"You're already doing better than she did."

Josie grips my hand tightly. "I didn't even think about what it would mean for you," she says. "I was so scared of losing her that I forgot I would be losing you too."

"That's the part that hurt." I rub my thumb over her hand. "I thought you stopped caring about me. That was selfish of me. We have a child, she should come first."

She doesn't interrupt. I take that as my cue to continue. "There's something else you should know." She looks up. "My entire life I've been the embodiment of Sloth." Her brow furrows. "People hear that and assume I am lazy. That I don't care. That I move last because I don't want to move at all."

"That's not you," Josie says, her voice breaking.

"No," I say, meeting her eyes. "It isn't."

I look down at our hands. "I wait because I need all the

information first. I need to understand everything before I act." She listens without cutting me off. "So when you went to Thalia without telling me," I continue, "it felt like the decision had already been made."

Her eyes fill with tears again. "I never meant to take that choice from you," she cries out.

She swallows hard. "I just kept seeing it in my head," she whispers. "Her growing up. Getting older. Me staying exactly the same. Standing at her grave one day while I'm still here." Her voice breaks. "I couldn't breathe, Lucas."

She looks terrified and my head feels heavy. "I love you."

The words make me feel something I never have before. That someone was there to love me this whole time. "I love you, too."

She presses her forehead against my chest, crying again, but this time not from that gut wrenching sadness I felt through her. "Next time," she whispers, "we figure it out together."

I pull her closer, my arms tightening around her. "Together."

She stays pressed against me, her forehead against my chest. I still feel the slight tremor of her shoulders from tears, but the panic has dissolved. Adrenaline worn off. Her fingers dig into my shirt again, but this time, she is unbuttoning it.

"Josie?"

"Lucas," she says, her voice filled with lust.

"What are you doing?"

Her palm slides up my neck. She leans in and kisses me.

My hand slips behind her neck, fingers tangling in her damp hair, and I deepen the kiss, pressing her body flush against mine. I feel the hard buds of her nipples poking against her nightgown, the sight sending a jolt straight to my groin.

Her lips part and I taste all of her sweetness. "I hated watching you walk away," she murmurs, voice trembling.

I trail kisses down her throat. "I hated doing it."

Her tongue teases my bottom lip. Her hands slide down my sides, slipping under my shirt. She frees the last button in one decisive tug and peels the fabric off my shoulders.

I gasp when her palms brush bare skin, heat pools in my stomach, and I can feel my cock swelling, aching.

Vulnerability and awe glint in her eyes. "I love you."

"I love you too," I murmur, my forehead resting against hers. "I always will."

She offers a soft, shy smile, then slowly unclasps my pants. Her fingers slip inside, tugging my cock free. It's throbbing, leaking a bead of precome at the tip. I pull her closer, hips pressing into hers. Her wet heat radiates against me.

"You sure?" I murmur.

She exhales, breath hot against my jaw. "Lucas, I spent an hour crying because I thought I was losing you."

"I'm not going anywhere."

She moves closer, her curves molding into mine. Her fingers trail through my hair as she leans into me, breasts heavy against my hands.

"You look scared," I say softly.

She bites her lip. "I am—scared of messing this up. I'm not exactly a ball of experience in this sorta thing."

My thumb brushes over her cheek. "We're talking our way through it."

She snorts. "That's very Sloth of you."

"Don't start," I tease, and she laughs. It is the most intoxicating sound I've ever heard.

I pull her nightgown over her head, and see her in her entirety. My cock nudges her between her thighs. She's the most beautiful thing I've ever seen.

She wraps her arms around my shoulders, pulling me impossibly close. I feel her soaking wet pussy lips brushing my shaft, her juices coating me. If I move an inch, I could just slip in.

"Lucas," she murmurs.

"Yeah?"

"Thank you for coming back," she says, sealing her lips to mine.

I press my palm to her face. "Sunshine, I'm not that easy to scare off."

I flip her over and she laughs, drawing me down for another kiss. Her hands roam my chest, trail down my sides, then grip my hips. I line the head of my shaft against her wet entrance again.

Her breath catches. "Lucas, please—"

I push slowly in, filling her tight channel inch by inch.

She gasps, arching her back as she takes me deeper. Her pussy ripples around my cock, squeezing me in strong, inviting waves. I hold her hips, thrusting gently, letting her adjust to my girth.

A low sound escapes her as she grips my shoulders.

I withdraw almost completely and drive back in, deeper this time, until our bodies are flush. She cries out, legs shaking as I find my rhythm. Her moans grow louder, wet slaps of skin on skin echoing in the room. I cup her breast, thumb circling her hardened nipple as I thrust, feeling her swell and contract around me.

Her hands clutch at my back, nails grazing my skin. "Lucas—oh god," she pants. The sounds she's making forces my strokes harder, more possessive.

"Fuck," I growl, picking up speed, plunging ino her with firm slaps. I can feel our breaths quickening, hearts racing.

Everything is heightened with our bond.

She shudders beneath me, eyes half closed, and whispers, "I love you so much." Her voice breaks as pleasure tightens her limbs.

I lean down, kissing her neck. "I love you, too," I rasp.

My next thrust catches her in the right spot and she arches, crying out as waves of pleasure ripple through her. I feel her walls clench around me, her orgasm building in tight pulses.

I'm right behind her, every thrust bringing me closer.

"Oh fuck, Sunshine," I grunt, vision blurring.

With one final deep thrust, I spill into her, filling her with hot, tremoring bursts. She cries out my name, body tensing, then goes limp under me, riding out her orgasm in shuddering waves.

I collapse next to her, chests heaving, sweat glistening on our skin. She wraps her arms around me, burying her face in my shoulder. I hold her tight, kissing the top of her head.

Josie traces small circles against my chest with her fingers.

"Lucas?" She asks in my ear.

"Yeah, Sunshine?"

She lifts her head just enough to look at me. "I want to do the Infernal Claim."

The words catch me off guard.

"After she's born," she adds quickly, resting a hand over her stomach. "When it's safe."

I study her face for a moment. "You're sure?"

She nods. "I want to be tied to you," she says quietly. "For eternity."

Something tight in my chest loosens. "You already are," I tell her.

Josie shakes her head slightly. "No," she says. "Not because of fate. Not because of contracts or magic." Her fingers curl into my hand. "Because I choose you."

I pull her closer, pressing another kiss into her hair. "Sunshine," I murmur, "I chose you a long time ago."

CHAPTER SEVENTEEN

Josie

At first, I think I'm floating.

The good kind of floating.

The kind where you're stretched out on your back in warm ocean water, the sun on your face and absolutely nothing to worry about. Somewhere nearby waves are rolling lazily onto sand. I swear I can even smell salt in the air.

In my mind, I've got a drink in my hand too—something cold and ridiculous with a tiny umbrella sticking out of it.

Yeah. This is nice. I could stay right here forever.

My stomach lurches.

The baby moves. Suddenly, something about this doesn't feel right.

The water under me doesn't feel like water anymore. It feels thicker. Sludge in water form.

My eyes open. The beach is gone. The sun is gone. The drink—tragically—is also gone.

Instead, black silk stretches in every direction beneath my feet.

The Veil.

I stare down at it for a second. I drag a hand over my face. "Oh come on," I mutter to the empty darkness. "Not this shit again."

I've been here several times already. It's basically my second home at this point. I've explored every inch of this place.

The baby shifts again. "Easy," I whisper, rubbing slow circles over the spot where she kicked. "I'm right here." Neither of us like this place.

Something ahead of me shimmers faintly, like heat rising off asphalt on a summer day.

I squint. Threads. That's new. I don't remember those being here before. Hundreds of them are stretching through the air in front of me, thin strands of pale silver drifting through the darkness like spiderwebs caught in the wind.

"Loom threads," I whisper. "Why are those here?"

The baby kicks again. The nearest thread begins to tremble. The light flashes. A loud snap echoes through the Veil and I jump.

The thread disappears. I stare at the empty space where it was, my pulse suddenly racing. Another thread pulls tight.

Snap.

Something cold spreads through my bones. "That can't be good," I mutter.

Another thread tightens before snapping.

I turn slowly, scanning the darkness. More of them are

moving now. The silver strands shiver in the air, pulling taut like something invisible is tugging on them from the other side.

"Okay," I whisper under my breath. "I definitely don't remember this part from the other nightmares."

The baby shifts again, a hard rolling motion beneath my ribs.

One of the threads closest to me jerks.

Snap.

The sound begins to spread outward, threads snapping one after another like something breaking deep inside the world.

"What is happening?" I whisper into the Veil.

"You hear it, don't you?" The voice comes from behind me. My entire body goes still.

A woman stands a few yards away. She shouldn't belong here. Not in this endless dark. But somehow she looks more at ease than I do—like she's been here a very long time.

Her long auburn hair falls in a loose braid over one shoulder, strands of silver catching the dim light. Her pale gold skin glows faintly, soft as candlelight against the darkness.

Her bare feet rest against the black silk surface. She's watching me.

Another thread trembles above us before it snaps into pieces.

Her hazel eyes lift toward it, warm and distant at the same time. She is not alive. "Even the strongest threads fray when the world forgets how to hold them," she murmurs.

I stare at her. "Do you know what's happening?"

She looks at me, her gaze dropping slowly to my stomach. She's reading me. I definitely don't enjoy it.

Another thread snaps somewhere behind us.

Her mouth curves into a quiet, sad smile. "Birth," she says softly, "is a door few understand."

The Veil ripples beneath my feet.

I swallow. "That doesn't sound comforting."

Her eyes return to the breaking strands drifting through the darkness. "It wasn't meant to be."

Another thread pulls tight.

Snap.

Her voice lowers. "Listen carefully, child."

My heart pounds. "To what?"

Her gaze drifts into the darkness beyond the threads. "You're almost out of time," she murmurs. "Listen to the warning."

"Time for—"

The ground disappears and I bolt upright in bed with a gasp. Sunlight floods the room.

I just sit there, disoriented, staring at the golden light spilling across the blankets like nothing in the world is wrong.

My heart is racing so hard it hurts.

"Sunshine?" Lucas is beside me instantly.

One arm wraps around my shoulders before I can even catch my breath, pulling me against his chest.

"I'm here," he murmurs. His hand slides to my stomach automatically.

The moment his palm presses against my skin, I can feel the baby settle.

"Nightmare again?" He asks, face against my hair, voice in my ear.

I stare at the sunlight spilling across the room.

"Yeah." My voice comes out rough.

Lucas shifts beside me, laying next to me on the bed. "The Veil?"

I nod.

He doesn't ask anything else right away. Just keeps his hand on my stomach, thumb moving slowly back and forth like he's trying to convince both of us everything is fine.

Which would work a lot better if I couldn't still hear it. The snapping. One thread after another. And the woman's voice. *Listen carefully.*

Something about that dream felt different. It wasn't just a nightmare.

It was a warning.

By the time I reach Hex & Brews, the morning sun is already high enough to be bright, but the day is still cool.

Which is good, because if I stayed inside my house in Hell any longer thinking about snapping threads and the mysterious Veil woman that I've never seen before, I might actually lose my mind.

The bell above the cafe door chimes as I push it open. Immediately, five heads turn toward me.

That's when I realize two things. First, the entire table in the back is already full. Second... they've all been waiting for me.

Bella is the first one on her feet. Her eyes sweep over me from head to toe in about half a second. Her mouth tightens. "Okay," she says slowly. "You look like absolute shit."

I sigh and drop my bag on the empty chair. "Good morning to you, too."

She ignores that entirely. "You're too skinny."

"I'm pregnant."

"You're still too skinny."

Honestly, I should have expected this. Bella has been in full mother hen mode ever since the whole Veil incident the first time. I don't bother to tell her it's still happening now.

Across the table, Tinsley is already pushing a mug toward me. "Drink this before Bella starts threatening to feed you by force," she says cheerfully.

I glance down. Tea. Probably something herbal and magical and vaguely terrifying.

"Thanks," I mutter, sliding into the chair.

Now that I'm sitting, I take a better look around. Bella, obviously. Tinsley. Ophelia, who's watching me with that Loom weaver intensity that makes it feel like she's reading three different timelines at once. Della, sitting calmly beside her. And Blaire.

That's the part that surprises me. I don't really know her, but apparently everyone else does. This feels less like a friendly get together and more like an intervention.

I lean back in my chair and cross my arms. "Okay," I say skeptically. "Should I be worried about whatever this is?"

No one answers immediately. Which is never a good sign. We are the bunch who tend to enjoy talking over one another to get a point across.

"You look like you haven't slept in days," Bella blurts out suddenly.

"That's because I haven't," I say.

"That's not funny, Josie," Bella huffs.

"I wasn't joking," I respond tightly.

Ophelia's gaze softens slightly. "The nightmares again?"

I nod. "They're getting worse." I put my hand on my head and rub my eyes. "They're different than they were before."

Della tilts her head slightly. "Different how?"

I hesitate. Because saying it out loud somehow makes it feel more real. "I saw the Veil again," I say finally. "But it wasn't just... the water and the darkness this time."

Everyone leans forward a little.

"There were threads," I continue. "Silver ones. Hundreds of them."

Ophelia stiffens.

"They were floating everywhere. And they kept—" I stop, my stomach tightening. "Breaking."

The sound rushes through my head again.

Snap.

Even remembering the noise makes my skin crawl.

"They were snapping," I say quietly. "One after another."

Ophelia's fingers tighten around her mug. Della and Blaire exchange a look.

Bella leans forward, resting her elbows on the table. "Explain," she says. "Because I'm clearly missing something here."

Ophelia's gaze shifts to me. "You said there were threads?"

I nod. "Hundreds of them," I say. "Floating everywhere."

Bella frowns. "Wait. The Loom looks like that?"

Ophelia tilts her head slightly. "Yes."

Bella blinks. "I thought it was... you know. A loom." She gestures vaguely with both hands. "Like the big wooden thing with the pedals and the yarn and the old lady making a scarf in the corner."

Tinsley snorts quietly.

Ophelia almost smiles. "It isn't a physical loom," she explains. "It's the Veil itself."

"The Veil?" Bella repeats what is running through my head.

Ophelia nods. "The threads Josie saw are life threads. Every living soul has one."

A chill slides down my spine.

"They stretch through the Veil," Ophelia continues. "Endlessly. Growing forward as life unfolds."

Bella's voice drops. "And when someone dies?"

Ophelia's fingers tighten around her mug. "The thread pulls tight." She pauses, sighing. "And then it snaps."

"That's exactly what I saw." I look at Ophelia, nearly jumping out of my chair. "Threads snapping."

Bella's eyes widen. "And they were just... breaking away?"

"Yeah." I rub my arms again, suddenly cold. "One after another."

Della and Blaire exchange another look. Ophelia's expression turns thoughtful.

"That's the problem," Ophelia says, almost matter of fact.

I stare at her. "What problem?"

"They shouldn't be breaking like that." Ophelia meets my eyes. "Josie also shouldn't be seeing them. She is not a weaver."

My heart rate spikes exponentially. "Please tell me that's not bad."

Ophelia considers that. Which makes me even more nervous. "The Loom is changing."

"What does that mean?" I ask.

"It means," she says carefully, "the threads I watch aren't behaving normally."

Tinsley frowns. "How so?"

"They're tightening."

I blink. "Tightening?"

Ophelia nods. "Normally the threads grow. They stretch forward as life carries on." She looks directly at me. "But lately… they aren't."

"Wait—" Della says.

"They're pulling tight instead," she continues, without stopping. "Like something is drawing them inward."

Bella leans forward. "Is that dangerous?"

Ophelia doesn't answer.

Della speaks instead, a foreboding tone in her voice. "It means something is coming."

I rub my arms. "That doesn't sound good."

"It isn't," Blaire says calmly.

I look between them. "I feel like I missed a conversation."

Tinsley nods. "Yeah, same."

"She's been training," Della says, gesturing to Blaire.

"With you?" I ask.

Blaire shrugs. "Someone had to train me."

"You're explaining it poorly," Della replies.

Blaire rolls her eyes, then looks at me. "I'm a witch."

The lights flicker and my tea sloshes over the edge of the cup.

Blaire winces. "That's been happening a lot."

"Let's not do magic that leaves a mess," Della says, waving her hand and cleaning it up instantly.

"Della's magic is structured," Blaire continues. "It is controlled with years of practice."

"Old," Della adds.

I glance at her. "How old?"

Della doesn't hesitate. "My family practiced long before Salem," she says. "Before witches scattered. Before the Veil was something people understood. We learned early that staying in one place comes with consequences."

"That's cryptic," Bella laughs under her breath, smirking.

Della lifts a brow. "I'm not a cryptid."

Tinsley snorts. "That's exactly what a cryptid would say."

Bella shakes her head, a faint smile tugging at her mouth.

I shift my attention to Blaire. "And you? Is your magic old?"

Blaire leans back slightly, arms crossing. "Not like hers," she says.

Della doesn't react.

"My family history isn't nearly as vast in the magical department," Blaire adds. "I believe my grandmother was the first to possess magic."

Bella frowns. "That sounds... vague."

"It is," Blaire says. "You now know as much as I do."

"So Della was trained by her family." I study her. "So why weren't you?"?"

Blaire pauses. "No one would do it. The first time my powers showed up... a church exploded." She shrugs and glances at me. "Technically related."

Della speaks next. "She's learning control."

"That's a generous way to put it," Blaire mutters.

I'm about to say something sarcastic when I notice Ophelia isn't moving. Not in the way she usually does when she's observing or thinking something through.

No. This is different. Her eyes are wide, her whole body pulled tight. She's on high alert. Her fingers are locked around her mug, her gaze fixed somewhere just past the table. She's not here with us anymore—her mind is already somewhere else.

"What?" I ask, glancing between her and Della.

Ophelia doesn't answer. Her brows pull together slightly. She's trying to make sense of something. "The threads..." she says, more to herself than to us.

Della is already watching her closely.

"What about them?" Bella asks.

Ophelia finally looks at me. "That's not right," she says.

"What's not right?" I ask, my voice coming out tighter than I expect.

Della stands, her attention never leaving Ophelia. "Show me," she says.

Ophelia nods once. I don't move. My body won't let me. Because something about this feels familiar in the worst way.

I've already lived this moment and I know exactly how it ends.

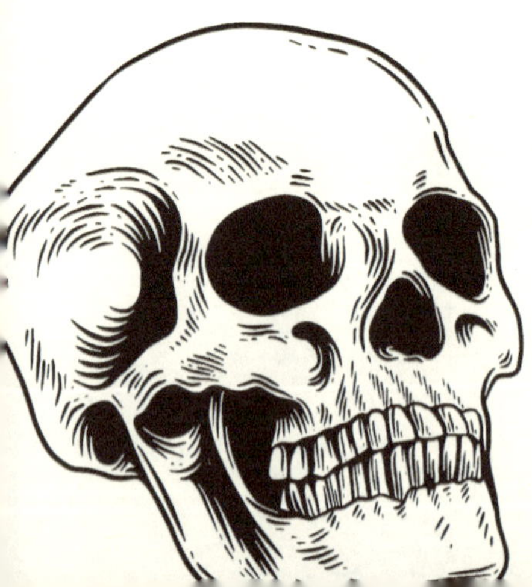

CHAPTER EIGHTEEN

Lucas

Josie hasn't slept properly in weeks. She falls asleep, but staying asleep is a different story.

I sit at the edge of the bed, watching her. The small shifts under the blankets. The way her fingers tighten in the sheets. The uneven rhythm of her breathing.

She looks peaceful. But she isn't.

One hand is curled over her stomach, protective even in her sleep. The other is twisted into the blanket like she's holding on to something... or bracing for it.

Thirty nine weeks. Thalia says everything is progressing normally. The baby is strong.

My concern isn't the baby. It's Josie.

She's been here more than she should be. Not just for appointments. She lingers, watching. Checks things twice.

That isn't normal.

Josie lets out a low, strained moan, her body pulling tight for a moment before easing again. I'm already moving, my hand sliding over hers, the other settling against her stomach.

"I've got you, Sunshine."

The baby moves. I flatten my hand instinctively on her as I focus on the movement. I know her patterns. I've been tracking them for weeks. This doesn't match any of them.

Josie's breathing evens out beneath my hand, her body relaxing like whatever had hold of her just let go. The feeling in my chest doesn't. If anything, it makes my instincts heightened.

Something is wrong. I've known it for days—I just haven't been able to prove it. And that's the problem.

I don't move without understanding what I'm dealing with. I don't act without knowing the outcome. Right now, I have neither.

Della's words haven't left me since she said them. The Loom is changing—not subtly, not in isolated cases, but across everything. Threads tightening, pulling in ways Ophelia or the council haven't seen before.

I didn't like the way she said it. She was way too calm. Something is interfering with the natural progression of mortal lives. Something strong enough to affect the Veil itself.

Jasper.

He isn't just moving through it. He's changing it.

I drag a hand over my jaw, my gaze dropping back to Josie.

Della said something else. Something I haven't been able to shake.

Josie is at the center of it.

I glance toward the clock. 2:50 a.m. Josie hasn't moved in the last few seconds. Her breathing is steady beneath my hand, her body finally still after the tension that's been pulling at her all night.

It should feel like relief. But it doesn't.

I ease my hand away carefully and stand, taking one last look at her before stepping out into the kitchen.

They're already here. Della stands near the center of the room, arms loosely crossed, her attention fixed on something only she can see. Ophelia is beside her, quieter, but just as focused.

Bella is pacing.

"You're all up early," I say, stepping fully into the room.

Bella stops mid step and looks at me. "Don't start with that. We wouldn't be here if it wasn't important."

"I assumed as much."

Della glances at me. "How is she?"

"Asleep," I answer. "For now."

Ophelia's gaze flicks toward the hallway. "Has anything changed?"

"No," I say, then hesitate. "Not enough to explain what you felt."

Bella crosses her arms. "Okay, great. That's reassuring."

"It's not meant to be," I reply.

"That's the problem," she shoots back.

Della inhales softly through her nose, cutting in before Bella can keep going. "The Loom is still unstable."

Bella turns to her. "Define unstable."

Ophelia answers instead. "Threads are tightening."

"All of them?" Bella asks.

"Not every single one," Ophelia says, "but enough that it isn't random."

I lean against the edge of the kitchen counter, my focus shifting between them. "You're saying this is connected."

"Yes," Della says simply.

Jasper and Josie. She really can't catch a break.

"Josie couldn't even enjoy her fucking pregnancy," Bella swears under her breath. "I hate that he keeps being a thorn in our side."

"He's not just moving through the Veil," Ophelia adds on to what Bella is saying. "He's teaching Josie how to change it."

"And that affects the Loom," I finish.

Della nods once.

Bella runs a hand through her hair. "Okay, so what does that mean for Josie?"

Ophelia looks toward the hallway. "Her thread is... different."

I straighten. "Different how."

Della answers this time. "It's under strain."

"That's not possible," I say automatically.

"It is when something is interfering," she replies.

Bella's expression hardens to pure fury. "So what, we just sit here and wait for something bad to happen?"

"No," I say. Because that's not happening. She can't take anything more happening to her. Eventually, it'll be too much.

Before anyone can respond, another presence fills the room. Thalia. She doesn't step through a portal this time. She's just... there.

The second I see her face, every part of me dreads what is about to say. She looks directly at me. "It's time."

The words barely register before a scream tears through the house. "Lucas!" She lets out a guttural, primal sound that is more like an animal than human. "I can't—something's wrong—please—"

This isn't the half conscious moaning from her nightmares. Not the tossing and turning that's creased the sheets all night.

This is the sound prey makes when death finds it.

My body moves without me making it, a blur across floorboards that might as well be miles. The door slams into the wall with a crack like bone breaking.

Josie's twisted in the bed, spine contorted, fingers clawing white knuckled into sheets now soaked crimson. Her other hand clutches her belly.

The blood. God, the blood. It's everywhere. Spreading. Devouring the white cotton beneath her like a living thing.

"Hey—hey, I've got you," I say, closing the distance and reaching for her, but she's shaking, her entire body pulled tight as another cry rips out of her.

"Something's wrong," she gasps, her fingers digging into my arm hard enough that I think it might break skin.

"I know," I say, forcing my voice steady even as everything in me starts to come apart. "I'm right here."

Thalia is beside us a second later. She doesn't hesitate. Her eyes take in the blood, the tension in Josie's body, the way she's struggling to breathe through it.

"This isn't happening here," she says.

I look at her. "What does that mean?"

"It means we move. Now." There's no room for argument or questioning in her tone.

Good. I slide an arm under Josie's legs, the other bracing her back, lifting her carefully as she cries out, her body tensing again as another wave hits.

"I've got you, Sunshine," I murmur against her hair. "Stay with me."

Her grip tightens in my shirt, her breath uneven against my neck.

"I'm here," she whispers, like she's trying to convince herself.

The portal opens before I take another step. I move through it without hesitation.

Thalia's space is already prepared.

The room beside her office isn't quite a hospital, but it's close enough. It is full of clean lines and structure, everything is placed with intention. Symbols carved into the walls and floor glowing faintly beneath the surface, runes layered into the space in a way that makes the air feel comforting in some weird way.

I carry her to the bed and lower her down carefully, but the second she hits the surface, her body arches again, another cry tearing out of her.

Thalia is already moving, hands glowing faintly as she begins working.

"Lucas," she says without looking at me, "I need space."

Not happening. "I'm not leaving."

"I didn't ask you to leave," she replies calmly. "I asked for space."

That I can do. Barely. I step back just enough to stay out of her way, my eyes never leaving Josie as she grips the sheets, her entire body fighting something I can't see.

Something I can't stop.

"Lucas!" Panic cuts through her voice. "I don't—this isn't right—"

"I know," I say, even though I don't. Keeping the panic out of my own voice is getting harder. "I'm right here."

Another contraction seizes her.

I see it before she makes a sound—the way her body transforms into something primal once again, her fingers clawing the sheets of the hospital bed, abdomen hardening to stone beneath her sweat soaked gown.

Her face contorts, eyes squeezed shut as she bears down against the unstoppable tide rising from deep within her, the baby is coming and she is waiting for no one.

Then the scream comes. It tears out of her, raw and unfiltered, filling the room in a way that makes it impossible to think around.

Even more blood spreads beneath her, darker now, soaking into the sheets faster than it should. Too much.

This isn't how this is supposed to go.

Thalia's hands move quickly, her focus absolute as she takes in everything at once—the bleeding, the way Josie's body is reacting to labor.

"We don't have time to let this progress naturally," she says.

I look at her, brows drawn low. "What does that mean?"

"It means I'm not risking her," Thalia replies, already moving. "We need to intervene."

Josie cries out again, her head falling back as her body arches under another wave of pain.

"I can't—" she gasps. "Lucas, I can't—"

"Yes, you can," I murmur, moving behind her and pulling her back against my chest. "You're doing it. Stay with me."

Her hand finds mine again, gripping tight.

"I'm here," she whispers, her breath shaking. "I'm still with you... I'm not leaving you."

Thalia's voice cuts through whatever Josie wanted to say next.

"Lucas." I meet her eyes. "I need you to hold her still."

I move closer, one arm bracing Josie's shoulders, the other anchoring her hand in mine as her body fights against the pain, every instinct in her trying to pull away from something that won't let her.

"I've got you," I murmur against her hair. "You're not doing this alone."

Her next scream is louder.

Thalia moves quickly, her magic flaring low and controlled as she works, guiding, adjusting, forcing the process forward before whatever is happening can take more from her.

Time stretches like taffy, bending and warping around a gear. It's off kilter, as if the universe itself has slipped into neutral.

I catch sight of the clock, its numbers glowing a deep, ember red against black stone.

2:58 a.m.

Every second crawls by with excruciating slowness, ticking like a hammer against my skull.

The rustle of sheets sounds like sandpaper, the hum of the refrigerator a thunderous roar. Her limbs feel leaden, weighted with invisible chains as she shifts against the sweat dampened sheets.

Josie's body strains, pushing past the point where it should be able to, her breath breaking, her voice raw from screaming.

"Lucas—" she gasps again, weaker this time. "Something—"

Her words cut off as another wave hits, her grip tightening, her body pulling against mine.

"I know," I say again, even though it doesn't feel like enough anymore. "I know."

"Almost," Thalia exclaims from Josie's feet. "Stay with me, Josie."

Almost.

The word doesn't mean anything right now. Not when everything about this feels like it's coming apart instead of together.

The door bursts open.

"Hey!" Thalia turns quickly. "This is a private suite."

It's Ophelia. She doesn't look composed anymore. She looks terrified.

"Lucas—" Her voice breaks as she steps into the room, her gaze locking onto Josie, while ignoring Thalia. "Her thread—"

My head snaps toward her. "What about it?"

Ophelia's hands are shaking. "It's fraying," she says. "It's tearing—"

"No." I choke on air. This cannot be happening. We have a new life coming now. "No!"

Thalia doesn't look at me when she says it.

Her focus stays on Josie, her hands steady even as her voice lowers into something quieter. "Lucas..."

I already know. I feel it before she says the rest.

The bond loosens around the edges. It feels like water slipping through my hands no matter how hard I try to hold on.

"She's dying," Thalia mutters solemnly.

Thalia doesn't waste another second before grabbing the baby and passing her off to my mother when she comes into the room.

She leaves with the baby, closing the door behind her

"No." That is completely unacceptable. My voice comes out rough. I can stop it just by refusing it. I know I can.

I pull her closer against me, one hand cradling the back

of her head, the other gripping hers like I can anchor her here if I just don't let go.

"Josie—"

Her body is still there. It's still warm. I can hear her breathing... barely.

But something else is already pulling away.

I feel it. I feel her. Slipping away from me.

"Stay with me," I say, my voice breaking for the first time. "Sunshine, stay with me."

Her fingers twitch weakly in mine. Her lips part like she's trying to say something, but no sound comes out. Her eyes find mine. And for a second she's still here. Then the bond pulls. Hard.

It doesn't break. Worse. It's tearing. Something is dragging her sideways out of me.

"No—" My grip tightens, panic slamming through me as I feel it slipping faster now, like I'm losing hold of something I was never meant to keep. "Josie—don't—"

Her hand goes slack in mine. The pull stops. I'm still holding her. But the place where she was inside me is gone.

The clock ticks. It is low and hollow, echoing from the bell tower in Hell. I look at the wall where the numbers are.

3:00 a.m.

The witching hour.

My Sunshine is gone.

CHAPTER NINETEEN

Josie

I wake up screaming.

The pain hits before I can even open my eyes, ripping through my body hard enough that it knocks the air out of my lungs. For a second I don't know where I am. My hands clutch at the sheets, my body curling in on itself as another wave crashes through me, stronger than anything I've felt before.

"Lucas!" The sound tears out of me before I can stop it, raw and jagged, more animal than human. I can't breathe through it. I can't think past it. "I can't—something's wrong—please—"

This isn't like the nightmares. Not the half aware panic, not the restless twisting in the sheets where I wake up and everything is okay again.

This is different. This feels like something has found me. The Veil found me.

Pain rips through my body again, hard enough to make

my vision blur. My back arches off the mattress without permission, my fingers clawing into the sheets as something deep inside me tightens and pulls.

There's warmth spreading beneath me.

Too much of it.

I don't need to look to know what it is.

"Hey—hey, I've got you." Lucas. He's here.

"Something's wrong," I gasp, grabbing onto him, my fingers digging into his arm like he's the only thing keeping me here.

"I know," he says. "I'm right here."

Another wave crashes through me before I can hold onto that, my body locking up again as something forces downward, harder this time.

I can't stop the sound that comes out of me. I can't stop any of it.

Thalia is here.

I barely register when she arrives. I can't even really hear what she is saying.

"This isn't happening here," she says.

I don't know what that means.

Lucas picks me up and moves before I can even ask what she's talking about. Not like I could really get a word out anyway.

One second I'm on the bed, the next I'm flying, the world tilting as he lifts me. The movement sends another spike of pain through me and I cry out, my body tightening all over again.

"I've got you, Sunshine," he murmurs against my hair. "Stay with me."

Stay with me. I latch onto that.

My fingers twist in his shirt, my face pressed into his

neck as I try to breathe through the pain that won't give me a break.

"I'm here," I whisper, the words barely making it out.

I don't know if I'm saying it for him or for me.

The surface beneath me is different when he lowers me down, but I barely have time to process it before another contraction hits and my body arches again, a scream tearing out of me.

"Lucas," Thalia says somewhere near me. "I need space."

"I'm not leaving."

"I didn't ask you to leave. I asked for space."

I would laugh at that if I could breathe.

Another wave crashes through me, harder than the last, my body tightening to the point it feels like it might break in two.

"Lucas!" Panic claws its way into my voice. "I don't—this isn't right—"

"I know," he says. "I'm right here."

I believe him. Even if nothing else feels right at least he does.

The pain doesn't stop. It builds, stacking on top of itself, leaving no room in between. My body is moving without me now, pushing, reacting, doing something I can't control.

I scream again. It tears out of me, raw and helpless, as the pressure builds until it feels like I'm going to split apart.

There's too much blood. I can feel it all around me.

"We don't have time to let this progress naturally." Thalia says somewhere in the distance.

"What does that mean?" Lucas asks.

"It means I'm not risking her," Thalia grunts out. "We need to intervene."

"I can't—" My voice breaks as another contraction hits. "Lucas, I can't—"

"Yes, you can," he murmurs, moving behind me and pulling me back against his chest. "You're doing it. Stay with me."

His arm braces me. His hand anchors mine. I hold on like it's the only thing keeping me here.

"I'm here," I whisper, my breath shaking. "I'm still with you... I'm not leaving you."

That feels important to say. If I continue to speak, I can will it into existence.

"Lucas," Thalia says. "I need you to hold her still."

His arms tighten around me instantly, holding me in place as my body fights against something that won't let go.

"I've got you," he murmurs against my hair. "You're not doing this alone."

I want to believe that. I really do. But something else is happening. Underneath the pain. Underneath everything. Something's pulling at me.

At first I think it's just the contractions, the pressure forcing everything downward, but this feels different.

This feels wrong. Something is tugging at me from the inside.

Another wave hits, stronger than anything before it, and I cry out, my grip tightening on Lucas as the room tilts once again.

"Lucas—" My voice comes out weaker this time. "Something—"

The words don't finish. Because whatever is pulling at me suddenly *yanks*.

Something tears loose inside me, not flesh, not bone, but something that was never supposed to come apart.

And then there is nothing.

I know something is wrong before I even open my eyes. There's no pain. That alone is enough to set off alarm bells.

I blink. The room comes into focus, and of course the first thing I see is Lucas. He's sitting beside the bed now. I don't remember him moving.

His shoulders are hunched forward, his head bowed like something is physically weighing him down, his hands gripping mine so tightly it looks like he's afraid to let go.

I follow his gaze slowly, like if I don't rush it, this won't be what I think it is.

My body is lying on the bed. I'm laying in a way that doesn't look like sleep.

There's blood everywhere. Dark against the sheets, smeared across skin that looks too pale. My chest isn't moving. My face... God. I look dead.

I stare at it for a second too long, thinking if I just keep looking, something will fix itself. Maybe I'll rub my eyes and sit up and realize I'm having a weird post-birth out of body experience.

"That's not—" My voice doesn't sound like mine. It doesn't sound like anything. It's a whisper.

Lucas doesn't react. He doesn't even look up. "Lucas?" I try again, louder this time.

Nothing.

He tightens his grip on my hand and presses his forehead against it, trying to hold on.

That's the moment it hits me.

I'm not in there. That thing is just a shell.

The realization creeps in, wrapping around my spine and squeezing until I can't breathe. Or I don't think I am breathing.

I look down at myself. At the way I'm standing beside the bed. At the fact that I don't feel my weight on the floor.

"Okay," I say, because apparently that's where my brain goes when everything is falling apart. "That's... not ideal."

My attention snaps back to Lucas. He looks destroyed.

"I'm right here," I say, stepping closer to him. "Lucas, I'm literally right here—"

I reach for him. My hand goes straight through his shoulder. I freeze. "No."

I try again. My fingers pass through him like smoke. Panic hits fast and hard, clawing up my throat as I stumble back.

"Okay, no, absolutely not," I mutter, shaking my head. "We are not doing this. I just had a baby. I do not have time to be dead right now."

The words sound ridiculous, but that doesn't make it less true.

Liora's back is turned to me, but I can see that she has a little bundle in her arms.

Lucas makes a sound. I turn back to him instantly.

"I love you," he says, his voice rough, like it's being dragged out of him. "I choose you."

My chest tightens so hard it feels like something is caving in on itself.

"I'm right here," I whisper, even though I know he can't hear me. "I'm still here."

He presses his face into my hand again. My body's hand.

Thalia's voice slices through the silence behind me. "Lucas."

He might as well be carved from stone. His head remains bowed, dark hair falling forward to shield his face. His hands grip mine with a pressure that looks to border on painful. The tendons in his forearms stand out like cords.

"Lucas," she says again. Floorboards creak as she steps closer.

The clock on the wall ticks again. His breathing doesn't even hitch. Her gaze never flickers toward me. Those amber eyes remain fixed on him.

"We'll give you a moment," she murmurs, already backing away.

There's movement behind her. He doesn't look. He doesn't care who leaves. The door closes leaving just the two of us. Alone. Together.

"Lucas," I say again, stepping closer. "Look at me."

He doesn't. His hands tighten around mine and his shoulders shake. I can see that he's trying to stop the tears. But they fall anyway.

"I'm right here," I say, louder now. "Lucas, I'm right here—"

My voice doesn't exist to him.

"I'm sorry," he says, the words rough, dragged out of him.

"No," I whisper immediately. "No, don't—what are you apologizing for?"

"I should have done something," he says, his grip tightening. "I should have stopped this."

"You couldn't," I say, even though he can't hear me. "You were there. You didn't leave me."

He shakes his head slightly, pressing his forehead harder into my hand. "I chose you," he says. "I told you that."

My breath catches. "I know," I whisper. "I chose you too."

His shoulders shake again. "You said you weren't leaving," he continues, his voice breaking. "You said—"

He stops. He can't finish it. I step closer without thinking, reaching for him again. My hand goes through him. I flinch back like it burned.

"Okay," I say under my breath. "Okay, that's still not working."

My gaze drops to the bed where white cotton sheets have turned crimson, spreading outward from the center like a blooming rose.

Then to the blood that's soaked through to the mattress, darkening as it dries at the edges while the center remains slick and wet.

There's so much of it pooling beneath me, dripping onto the hardwood with soft, rhythmic taps.

Too much for anyone to survive.

My stomach twists. Until I think about my baby girl. "Where is she?"

Lucas doesn't react. Fuck that's right. He can't hear me. I look around the room, my pulse starting to race again. There's no crying. No movement. No baby.

"No," I whisper, shaking my head. "No, no, no—"

My eyes snap back to Lucas.

"Where is she?" I say again, louder now. "Lucas, where is our baby?!" I'm screaming now, as though I can force him to hear me if I just feel enough rage, enough fear.

He doesn't answer. He just sits there, holding my hand. Holding what's left of me. And crying.

"Lucas—"

Something grabs me. Fingers wrap around my arm, and before I can react, I'm yanked backward.

"No—"

The room tears away from me.

"No, no, no—"

I reach for him, for anything, my other hand clawing at

empty air as everything around me distorts and collapses inward.

"Lucas!"

He doesn't see me. He doesn't feel me. And then he's gone.

The world drops out from under me.

I hit something that isn't solid and isn't liquid, black silk rippling beneath me as I land hard enough to knock the breath out of a body I don't think I have anymore.

The Veil.

"No," I whisper, scrambling back, my hands sinking slightly into the surface as it shifts under me. "No, no, not here—"

A sound echoes behind me. Not footsteps. Something dragging.

I don't want to turn around. I already know what I'll find.

"Surprise." The voice is not human. Maybe it once was, but not anymore. My entire body goes rigid. "You finally came back to me. I knew you would."

I spin anyway.

Jasper is in front of me. Not the version of him I've seen before. Not the human version either. This one is... worse.

He stands there, but not fully. Parts of him lag behind the rest, a shoulder slightly out of place, the line of his arm not quite matching where it should end. He looks like he's been pulled together wrong and never set back correctly.

The dark around him doesn't sit on his skin, it slips under it, shifting faintly with every movement, dragging pieces of him with it. His face is almost the same, almost human, until his eyes meet mine. They are completely black. They go deep enough that it feels like they keep going, like if I look too long I won't find the bottom.

Rage hits me as fear disappears. “Get away from me,” I snap, already moving, swinging my fist to him.

My fist connects. It does absolutely nothing though. He doesn’t even move.

His head tilts slightly, almost curious.

“Still fighting,” he says, laughing.

I try again. “I said—”

Pain explodes across my face as he hits me. It sends me stumbling, the Veil rippling violently beneath me as I lose my footing.

My vision flickers. My head spins. The one thought that cuts through everything is my baby.

There was too much blood.

There was no crying.

She’s gone.

I went through all of that just to lose my baby.

“No—” My voice breaks as the darkness starts closing in. “No, no, no—”

The Veil swallows the sound.

And then everything goes black.

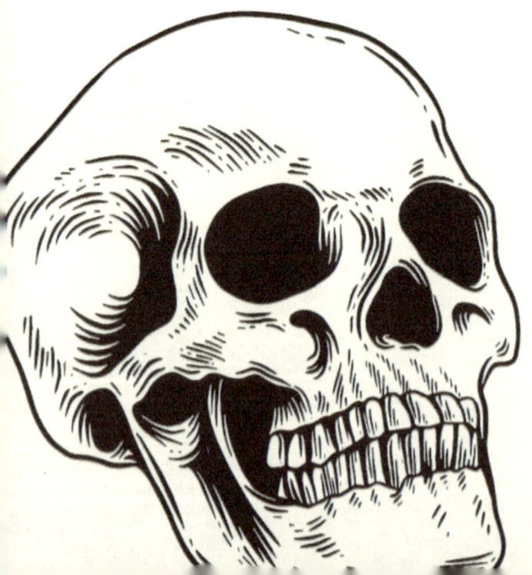

CHAPTER TWENTY

"Lucas." Thalia's voice reaches me, but it feels distant, muffled by the emptiness in my chest.

My attention stays where it belongs. On her. On the hand in mine.

I tighten my grip without thinking. It's the only thing I can still control.

"Lucas," She says again, stepping into my line of sight and waving her hand between me and the hospital bed. I don't turn to look at her fully.

My fingers remain intertwined with the cold, limp ones on the white sheet. My thumb traces the soulmate mark on her collarbone. It's muted and dead. Just like her.

My back stays rigid, shoulders locked. Footsteps pad away behind me, followed by the soft click of the door. Ophelia's perfume lingers in the air, promising a shit ton of unwanted truths about my Sunshine. All the things that I don't want to know. They might as well stay gone.

"I'm sorry," I say to her, words coming out ragged and worn.

There is no response. There won't be. She's gone.

"I should have done something." I tighten my grip on her hand. Maybe I can bring some color back if I squeeze harder. "I should have stopped this."

I shake as I press my forehead to her hand, tears slipping free no matter how tightly I try to hold them back.

Demons feel. No one believes that. We're supposed to be tough. Emotionless. That's the difference between us and a Harbinger. We feel. They don't.

They have no soul. No empathy. No reason to care about anything except the mission they were summoned for.

This is worse than anything I have ever known.

My grandmother died when my grandfather did. Her immortality left with him. She had been mortal once.

I never was.

Mine won't leave me.

I will live forever with this.

Unless I choose not to.

"I chose you," I say. "I told you that."

I'm ready to go with her. To end this before I have to feel what comes after. I can't live without her, and I don't see the point in trying.

I'm already working through it, the how, the fastest way to follow her, when a sound pierces through my plans.

A cry.

"You want to end your life," Thalia says, her voice rough. She knows exactly what I'm thinking and she's pissed I'm even thinking it. "Here is your child to force you to hang on."

I look up as she places her in my arms, and for a second, nothing else exists.

She's small, impossibly so, wrapped tightly, her face flushed from crying, soft blonde curls damp against her head. Her fists are clenched, her whole body tense. She came into this world already fighting.

I see it in the details I know too well. The shape of her mouth, the full cheeks, the way her face turns pink when she cries.

I know that face. Because she looks like her.

"Josie..."

Her cries start to slow down, tiny hiccupping sounds fading into small coos.

"Yeah," I murmur, my thumb brushing lightly over her cheek, skin softer than anything I've ever touched. "That's your mom."

I find myself watching her, trying to understand something I've never had to think about before.

I don't know what I'm doing. I don't know how to hold her properly, what she needs, what any of this means, and the realization hits harder the more that I think about it.

We planned. We made the nursery.

I think about the moment everything was done except the crib, when we stood in the doorway and looked at it for the first time, like stepping inside would make it real in a way we couldn't undo.

The room doesn't look like anything else in the house. Josie made sure of that. It's full of things she claims she doesn't care about but spends hours picking out anyway. The walls aren't one color because she can't commit. The rug is non-negotiable because apparently babies have opinions about the texture of wool. There are already too many things on the shelves for someone who keeps saying we don't need that much stuff.

"We absolutely needed all of this," she insists, hands on her hips when I gesture toward the shelves.

"You bought three versions of the same blanket," I point out, glancing between them.

"They're different," she shoots back immediately.

"They're the same color," I say, unimpressed.

"That's because it's a good color, Lucas," she argues, like that is that.

I don't bother responding. It clearly isn't a fight I'm going to win. I might as well stop while I am behind.

The crib sits in pieces on the floor. I know that I need to build it.

Josie sits down cross legged beside it, picking up some wood and turning it over in her hands.

I grab the manual.

"You're not helping," I mutter, already sorting through the pieces.

"I'm absolutely helping," she insists, grabbing one and handing it to me.

It's the wrong one.

"This doesn't go here," I tell her, setting it aside.

"It looks like it goes there," she argues, leaning closer.

"It doesn't," I say flatly.

She squints at it. "Okay, but conceptually—"

"There's no conceptually in building furniture," I cut in.

She snorts. "You're so boring."

"I'm correct," I reply without looking up.

"Debatable," she says lightly.

It takes longer than it should have.

I could fix this in seconds. Magic, done, finished, perfect. The entire room could have been.

Josie didn't want that.

She wanted to do it together by hand. Said it mattered.

I glance at her as she confidently picks up another piece she absolutely does not understand. I already regret saying we would do it ourselves.

She looks like she's having the time of her life, completely unbothered by the fact that none of this is going according to plan, and it makes it hard to care that it isn't.

"You're not even building anything," I point out.

"I'm supervising," she says easily, not even looking up.

"That's not a real role."

"It is when you're doing it wrong."

She laughs, still holding the wrong piece, completely convinced she's helping, and I let it happen because it means she's here, sitting across from me, exactly where she's supposed to be.

She should be here for this. Josie would know what to do. She always did.

Panic builds as I let the truth sink in. I'm supposed to do this without her now.

"You're not doing anything alone," Bella says from somewhere behind me.

I don't hear anyone come in, but when I look up, they're all there. My parents. My brothers and their mates. Cousins. My aunt and uncle.

Everyone.

Every person I love, standing in the same room, not leaving. My life doesn't feel so empty anymore.

My mother steps forward first. She doesn't hesitate. Her attention goes straight to the baby, then to me. "Lucas."

I don't answer. I'm not sure I can. A sob catches in my throat, and I force it back.

She steps closer, her hand coming to rest on my shoulder. "You don't have to do this alone."

My grip tightens around my daughter as I look down at her, focusing on her little wiggle in my arms.

"I don't know how," I admit.

My mother doesn't hesitate. "You will. And until you do," she adds, quieter now, "you have us."

She's so small. I could break her without meaning to. She's my everything now.

"Lucas." Selene's voice cuts in. She sounds serious. Something is going on. "I'm sorry to interrupt, but we're being summoned to the council."

I don't want to go. The small bundle in my arms demands all of my attention.

She makes a soft sound, something between a breath and a coo, and I look down at her. She wiggles slightly, her mouth shifting into something that almost looks like a smile.

It's not, it's far too early for a real smile, I know it's just gas. I read all of the books I could get my hands on. But I'm counting it anyway.

"Go," Thalia says, stepping closer, her hands already reaching. "I'll stay with her while you're with the council."

That makes me look up. My grip tightens without thinking.

"It may be about Josie," she adds.

Still, I don't let go.

There's a pause before she tries again. With a different tactic this time. "What's her name?"

I look down at her. It's not a decision I'm making now. We already had this conversation. More than once.

We went back and forth until we found one that felt right. One we both agreed on. One she loved.

"Sereyna."

Evander's voice comes out choppy behind me. "After my mother?"

I look up at him. "Yeah."

He looks to Theron who give a slight nod of his head. When he turns back to me, his eyes are shining with pride. "She would have liked that."

I smile. My thumb brushes lightly over her cheek. "Rey," I add after a second. "That's what we'll call her."

It feels right. It feels like something Josie would have loved.

She liked that it was shorter. It honors both her mother and her grandmother. Two women who sacrificed everything for their children.

I hand Rey to Thalia, and she takes her carefully, settling her against her chest with a kind of ease that tells me she knows exactly what she's doing.

Rey makes a small sound, and Thalia answers it without thinking, making her start to wiggle again. I take that in, hold onto it, because it means my daughter is safe for the few minutes I won't be here.

"Let's get this over with," I say, even though the words don't sit right. Nothing about this is something to get through or move past.

I turn back to the bed one more time.

Josie hasn't changed. She won't. I know that, but it doesn't stop me from stepping closer, from reaching for her, my hand coming up to her face, brushing over her cheek before I lean down and press my lips to hers. They're cold now—starting to turn a bluish gray color.

"You did it, Sunshine," I murmur, trying to keep my voice low. This is only meant for her even if she can't hear it. "I'll take care of her. I promise."

I can hear some tears in the back as I say my final goodbyes. Most likely, Thalia will take care of the body once we leave. I won't be able to see my mate again.

"I love you."

I force myself to step back before I can change my mind and never leave this room.

The council chamber is already full when we arrive, the shift from one space to the other abrupt enough that it takes a second for everything to stop spinning.

Ophelia stands near the center, her attention fixed somewhere beyond the physical room, her focus already split between here and the Veil.

When we step in, her gaze snaps toward us. She looks upset, but under that is guilt.

We were called here for one reason.

Josie. It has to be about her. Or what's left of her.

"Ophelia," I say, trying to keep the irritation out of my voice. "Tell me why you and the council took me away from my child."

Della shifts beside her, her posture tighter than I've ever seen it, her attention fixed on something none of us can see.

"Her thread..." Ophelia starts, then stops, like she's trying to find the right words and coming up short. "Josie's thread."

My jaw clenches so hard my teeth start to ache. "What about it?"

"It didn't break the way it should have," she says finally. "It's not... severed. Not completely."

That doesn't make sense. "When a life ends, the thread snaps," I say. "That's how this works."

"Yes," Ophelia agrees. "It is."

"But not this time," Della adds.

My attention shifts to her. "Explain."

Della's gaze flicks to Ophelia before returning to me. "It's still there. Frayed. Strained. Like something interfered before it could finish breaking off fully."

A slow, cold feeling starts to settle in my soul.

"So fix it," I say. "Find her. Match the thread. You can save her."

"We tried." Ophelia's expression turns angry. Her brows furrow and mouth strains into a thin line. "But she is dead. There is nothing left of her physical form."

I have to be hearing them wrong. "What do you mean you tried?"

"We went into the Veil," she says. "We traced her thread as far as it would let us. We called for her." She nervously swallows. "We tried to summon her soul."

You could hear a pin drop. The fire crackles around us, but no one dares to speak.

"And?" I ask.

Ophelia holds my gaze. "There was nothing to find."

Something in me burns fiery hot. "That's not possible."

"It should be there," she says. "It has to be. But it's not responding. It's not... anywhere we can reach."

The words don't make sense. None of this makes sense. My hands curl into fists at my sides.

"You're telling me my mate is dead," I say slowly, trying to control my fury, but there is no use, "and her soul is just... missing?"

No one answers. That's all the confirmation I need.

I look between them, something dangerously hostile rising fast enough that I don't bother trying to stop it.

My Sunshine is dead.

And I don't even get to grieve her. No burial. No final moment. Nothing.

Because something else had to happen. It always does.

In this family, nothing is ever left alone. Nothing is ever allowed to just exist without being taken or twisted into something else.

We don't get to keep what we want.

So I say the one thing that I believe everyone is thinking.

"Where the *fuck* is the soul of my mate?"

CHAPTER TWENTY-ONE

Josie

I wake up choking.

It hits hard and fast, my body jerking as something forces a breath into my lungs that doesn't belong there. My throat burns as I gasp, coughing immediately, the sound tearing out of me as I double over, my hands bracing against something shifting beneath me.

Nothing comes up. Not like that stops my body from trying.

I gag again, leaning over to try to expel whatever the fuck is stuck in me. There's nothing to throw up. But the sensation is still there. And that's fucking annoying

Nine months of being sick and this is what sticks around?

That's the first thing that doesn't make sense. Feeling pregnant when I'm clearly not. There's no bump. Nothing.

The second is the lack of pain.

My hands press harder into the surface beneath me as I

try to get off the ground, my fingers sinking slightly into it. Slow waves ripple outward from where I touch it.

Black silk.

The recognition settles in slower this time, dragged into place through the haze of everything else.

The Veil.

Fuck. I'm still here.

My breathing starts to even out, not because I've calmed down but because my body can't keep up the panic it started with, as if something about this place strips it down to the bare minimum and leaves the rest behind.

I've been here before. Too many times.

I was here when I died. Even when I was alive.

"Welcome back." Of course, it's him. Motherfucking Jasper Wilder.

Can't I ever get away from this asshole?

He looks worse up close. He looks even worse in the light. There's no humanity left—not even the pretense. He looks like he's melting.

So that's why he needs a vessel.

I should be terrified. However, I'm just annoyed that I have to deal with him again.

I straighten anyway, rolling my shoulders back. I didn't choose to be here, but here I am.

Cool. Me and the wicked witch, round thirty two.

"You always did have a thing for dramatic entrances," I say, unimpressed.

"Interesting." His head tilts, just slightly. "You're not reacting the way most people do."

"Yeah, well," I shrug, "most people haven't had you stalking them in their sleep for weeks."

Without warning, a sharp pull through my chest that knocks the breath out of me for half a second before it releases just as fast. I suck in air, forcing myself upright immediately.

I'm not giving him that. His mouth curves slightly.

"You feel it," he says.

"Yeah," I mutter, rolling my eyes at him. "Hard to miss."

Another pull follows, something twisting and reaching into places it shouldn't even know exist. Not that I even have a physical body for him to mess with.

My fingers curl at my sides. That's it. I'm not giving him anything else. No weakness for Jasper.

"You're going to have to try harder than that," I tell him.

He watches me for a second, something shifting behind those black eyes. He expected me to cower.

That's not happening. Fuck him.

"You're still missing it," he says finally.

"Then explain it," I shoot back, crossing my arms. "Because from where I'm standing, this all feels very unhinged, even for you."

A slow smile pulls at his mouth. "I tried to do this the easy way."

I let out a short breath. "Breaking into my head and killing me wasn't easy?"

"I summoned Lucas," he continues, ignoring me completely. "I made my offer. You already know that."

I scoff. "You don't just summon a Duvain and expect them to do your bidding."

"I do when I have something they want."

"They didn't take it," I say, already knowing where this is going.

The corner of his mouth twitches upward. "No."

"Because of the Duvains," I push. "They shut it down."

"They made it very clear no deal involving him would ever be considered," he says, almost conversational.

Him.

"Obadiah," I say.

"Good." He drags his fucked up leg and saunters away. "You're keeping up."

"You tried to trade for him and got denied," I say. "So what, you decided to escalate? Kill me?"

"I didn't kill you," he replies, cracking up into fits of laughter.

"You ripped me out of my body during childbirth. I'm counting that." I fall into step behind him.

He turns on me fast enough that I have to step back to steady myself. But it's what he says that stop me in my tracks. "You were already dying."

"What?"

"Your body couldn't sustain both the child and the bond," he continues, completely unbothered. "It was always going to end that way."

I want to punch that look off his face.

My jaw tightens. "So you planned all of this."

"I anticipated it."

"Don't try to dress that up," I snap. "You waited for me to die."

"I waited for you to cross," he corrects. "Your soul was going to leave your body. The only question was where it would go. I made sure it came to me. I prepared you for the Veil."

His gaze holds mine. "It's why I sent the dreams. Until you started coming on your own."

I blink at him once. "You mean the nightmares," I say. "Where I was drowning in the depths of the inky waters of the Veil."

"They served their purpose." He has the nerve to shrug at me, like he's a teacher and I'm a student that isn't quite crashing the concept of a basic lesson..

My lungs empty in a hiss between my teeth. I press my fingertips to my collarbone, where the mark still burns even though I'm dead.

"Yeah," I whisper, voice catching. "They did something."

My arms cross loosely over my stomach—the empty cavity where my child once grew—as my mind doesn't stop.

Not sleeping for weeks. Barely keeping down water. Hallucinating shadows at the corners of my vision. The stress. The exhaustion. The hemorrhaging. My body breaking down in slow motion while I thought it was just... pregnancy.

My stomach turns as bile rises in my throat. "You didn't just prepare me," I say slowly.

He doesn't interrupt. Not surprised that he says nothing. Predators enjoy watching their prey realize they're trapped.

I look at him, at the ancient glee in his eyes. "You wore me down. You fed on me." My head feels like it is about to explode. "You kept me exhausted. Stressed. Sick. You were draining both of us."

His neutrally happy expression doesn't change.

"My body couldn't keep up," I continue, the words coming out with more vigor now, voice rising. "It started failing and I didn't even realize it was happening because I thought it was normal."

"It was inevitable," he says, shrugging that one working shoulder.

"No," I snap, yelling now. "You made it happen."

That's the part that matters in this whole situation. My

pulse picks up. I try not to show Jasper how upset he made me, but I can tell that he sees it anyway.

"You didn't just wait for me to die," I say. My voice drops to a whisper. "You needed both souls. You harvested us."

His head tilts slightly. Not denial. Not agreement.

He's satisfied at the fact he killed me *and* my baby.

"I accelerated the process," he says. "The child's essence was... particularly nourishing."

I stare at him, horror crawling up my spine. "That's a really polite way of saying you murdered my baby to get to me."

"Your body failed," he replies. "You both couldn't hold on."

"Because you wore me down from the inside," I say, but my attention is already somewhere else.

He laughs. "Yes. And I'd do it again."

I don't react to that. Not yet. I need to know exactly what he's talking about before I kick his ass.

"You said *my* body," I cut in.

His smile lingers. "I did."

My pulse spikes. "You didn't mention the baby."

He doesn't answer. Yeah, that's not suspicious at all. I'm about to crack him open like a melon and find out what he knows.

"What happened to her?" I demand.

"I don't fucking know," he says flatly.

I stare at him. He said that without a second thought.

He shrugs, careless. "And I don't care."

Rage hits faster than I've ever experienced it before.

"You don't get to just not care," I grind out, stepping toward him.

"She wasn't the point," he cuts in.

My hands curl into fists. "Then what was the point of me being pregnant?! Because she was the point for me, she was everything to me!"

He watches me for a second, dark eyes glittering with unmistakable fury. That's his mistake.

I lunge before my brain catches up to my body, the black silk blurring around me.

My palm cracks against his stubbled cheek with a sound like lightning striking wet earth, hot pain radiates up my arm, his chiseled face snapping sideways, a crimson handprint blooming on his skin.

It's not enough.

His step falters for a heartbeat, fingers loosening around my arms as black sludge oozes between his knuckles, dripping onto my skin where it sizzles like acid.

Mine.

The word slides through my head.

I tear free and slam both palms into his chest. The impact splits his skin, revealing a glimpse of something writhing beneath his ribcage. He stumbles back a step.

It lasts all of two seconds before he's on me.

Faster than death itself.

His hand closes around my throat, driving me backward until my spine cracks against the ground beneath the Veil. My skull fractures with a sound like stepping on autumn leaves.

My vision bleeds crimson at the edges.

His grip tightens. Not enough to sever my head. Just enough to remind me he could twist it clean off.

"You're done," he says, voice similar to the sound of death.

I claw at his wrist, my nails peeling back as they dig into

flesh that yields like rotted meat, but it doesn't matter. He doesn't move. Doesn't flinch.

"Get—off—" I choke out, my voice gurgling through the fluid filling my crushed windpipe.

His other hand catches my shoulder and slams me back down. Something inside me ruptures.

"You're not strong enough to fight me," he continues, eyes leaking tar down hollow cheeks.

I spit at him, a mouthful of my own blackened blood. His eyes darken to bottomless pits.

"But you will be," he says, licking lips that split to reveal too many teeth.

My stomach drops through the earth's core.

"I don't need you like this," he continues, almost thoughtful, his grip tightening just enough to remind me I'm not going anywhere.

I claw at his wrist again. My vision is starting to tunnel at the edges moving inward.

"I need you stronger." He puts his other hand next to my head. "I want you nice and primed for your eternity here... with me."

I try to laugh. It comes out broken and gurgled.

"Hard pass," I choke.

His head tilts. *Study me all you want you bastard, I will never give you what you want.*

"You'll change your mind."

"I won't," I manage, forcing the words through what little air I can get.

"You will," he says urgently, his hot breath smells like bile on my face. "You already have."

The grip he has on me tightens, pressure building at my throat until something causes him to jump back. His entire body locks as he stops mid motion.

The sound that rips out of him tears through the Veil and his hand drops from my neck as air slams back into my lungs hard enough to hurt.

I fold in half, choking, dragging in breath that burns all the way down while the world starts to clear around me.

Something's off.

It takes a second for my vision to catch up, everything dragging into place until I see it clearly.

Something is lodged in his back, buried deep between his shoulders. A blade. Runes carved into it glow faintly, pulsing in a way that feels familiar. It is as if a knife from the mortal world and Hell had a baby.

Only the hilt is visible, the rest sunk too deep to see.

I didn't do that.

He stumbles forward, shadows tearing loose from his body as the Veil shudders around us, reacting to whatever just hit him. His hand lifts, reaching back, fingers hovering just short of the blade before stopping.

I claw my way up, lungs screaming for oxygen that won't come fast enough. The ground lurches beneath me, but I launch myself forward anyway.

He whips toward me too fucking fast.

Pure animal instinct takes over. I slam both palms into his chest with enough force to shatter bone, desperate to keep those hands—those claws—away from my throat.

Something whistles through the air behind him.

It rips into him.

A second blade punches through his back, lower, tearing muscle and sinew. The impact hurls him forward with a guttural, primal shriek that freezes my blood.

The Veil convulses around us, writhing like something in agony, pulsing with malevolent awareness. It's hunting. Breaking every law of reality I thought I understood.

I don't know what nightmare it's about to unleash.

I turn to run.

Claws close around me, pulling me back as Jasper is dragged away at the same time.

I twist and catch my balance, turning just enough to see her.

The same woman from my last nightmare before I went into labor. Auburn hair pulled back, skin glowing faintly, hazel eyes locked on me. She jumps onto Jasper's back.

"Run!" she shouts, covering his eyes as he lets out a sound that tears through the Veil.

He grabs her and throws her to the ground.

I don't wait. I run. The ground ripples under me, but I keep moving.

Where do I go?

"Look up!" her voice carries across the Veil. "Find your thread. Grab it and hold on."

I lift my head and see it. A silver strand above me. I jump for it when something grabs me. My foot drives back hard as I twist, forcing myself free.

This time I catch the thread, gripping it tight. It moves under my hand.

I look back. She has Jasper on the ground, holding him there as he fights her.

"Once you feel it pull," she says, "pull back and hold on."

I tighten my grip, feeling it tug.

"Who are you?"

She looks at me.

"Tell my sons I love them."

Jasper starts to rise.

The thread pulls. I yank back.

The Veil drops away as I'm dragged into the dark, the last thing I see is her holding him down.

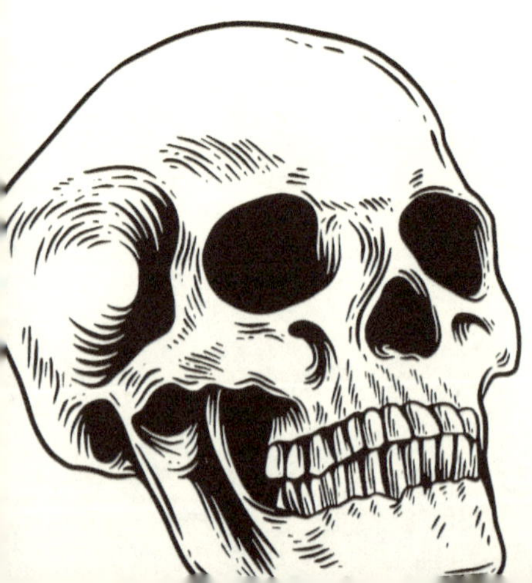

CHAPTER TWENTY-TWO

Lucas

Three months.

That's how long it's been since I lost her.

Not that time means anything anymore. It passes whether I pay attention to it or not. Days blur together. Nights are worse.

The only thing that keeps me together is Rey.

I sit in the chair by the window, my daughter resting against my chest, one hand supporting her head the way Thalia showed me. She fits there easily now. Not as impossibly small as the first night, but still small enough that I feel it every time I hold her.

She is fragile.

My thumb brushes lightly over her cheek as she makes a soft sound, somewhere between a sigh and a hum, her tiny fingers curling against my shirt like she's making sure I'm still here.

"Oh, you're hungry aren't you?" I murmur, adjusting

my hold on her as I bring the bottle up to her mouth, gently rubbing the top to her lips.

She settles down almost immediately.

I thought I didn't know how to do this. The most interesting thing about being a parent is that you figure it out. I did that.

But no one prepares you for having to do this alone. Not even in Hell. Not even in a family that's seen more loss than most. There's no guide for raising a child by myself when the person you were supposed to do it with is... gone.

My grip adjusts slightly without thinking as she shifts against me, her breathing evening out. The pull on the bottle slows, then stops completely, her mouth going slack around it as sleep takes over. I ease it away carefully, not wanting to wake her.

I watch her instead of thinking too hard.

That's how I've been getting through it.

One moment at a time.

Because if I think too far ahead I'll break.

"You're strong," I tell her. "You know that?" My thumb brushes over her again. "Just like your mom."

Rey shifts in her sleep, her small hand tightening just slightly against me, and I focus on that instead, the sound of my voice enough to keep her dreaming something good.

"You've got a lot of people," I murmur, glancing toward the door where I know, without needing to check, that at least one of my family members is nearby. "More than I did."

The door opens without a knock.

Julian steps in first, already looking at the baby before he even looks at me. Owen is right behind him, arms crossed but attention locked in the same place.

"She asleep?" Julian asks, his voice toned down. It always is when Rey is around.

"For now," I answer.

Owen lets out a slow breath as he steps closer. "You've got that down at least."

"That's generous," I reply.

Julian huffs a laugh. "You haven't dropped her yet. We're counting that as a win."

Rey stirs in my arms not long after. I feel the first tremor—a faint wiggle beneath my palm—and a tiny whimper that tells me my baby girl is ready to wake up. Her lips part in a perfect little "o," signaling what's coming next.

I don't wait.

"Yeah, I hear you," I murmur, rising to my feet, tightening my hold.

At least she slept. Half an hour—better than most nights. She sleeps best in my arms. Thankfully, I don't require sleep.

Owen uncoils from the wall. "Give her to me."

I hesitate.

He sighs. "Lucas."

"I know," I say, not looking at him.

"Do you?" He presses.

Against my will, I hand her over.

She settles against Owen's chest like she's done it a hundred times, one tiny fist fisting into his shirt.

Owen freezes.

Julian leans forward. "Why did you stop moving?"

"She grabbed me," Owen says, eyes wide, tone bordering on astonishment.

"She's a baby," Julian replies, smirking.

"I'm aware." Owen rolls his eyes, still completely frozen. "I think this means something."

I drag a hand down my face. "It means she has the Palmar Grasp Reflex. Because she's a baby."

"Yeah, yeah. We know. You read the books, did the things. Let me have this." Owen's still smiling down at her.

We don't make it three steps into the living room before everything goes wrong.

It starts with a sound. A wet one.

We all stop.

Owen looks down. "No."

Julian crouches beside him. "What was that?"

Owen's face tightens. "That was not small."

A portal opens in the middle of the living room without warning.

Evander steps through first, Theron right behind him, both mid conversation—until their attention snaps to the scene in front of them.

Seth follows, takes one look around, and exhales like he's reconsidering every decision that led him here.

Caleb walks in next and pauses. "Why does it look like something exploded?"

Adrian leans in behind him, scanning the room with interest.

Damian steps through last, the portal sealing behind him as his gaze sweeps over the chaos that is my living room.

Owen is still holding Rey like she might go off again. He doesn't move a muscle.

Evander steps up to Owen. "What do you mean not small?"

"I mean—" Owen lifts her away from his chest to inspect her bottom. "This is escalating."

I lunge forward. "Give her to me."

"No," Owen says, backing up. "I've got it."

"You absolutely do not." Julian is doubled over laughing in the corner of the room.

"I said I've got it."

Rey experiments with another sound as Owen holds her away from him at arms length trying not to gag.

Julian recoils. "That sounded aggressively nasty."

"It is aggressive," Owen snaps. "It smells aggressive."

Evander edges closer. "Let me see."

"You're not helping." Owen groans, running around with Rey in his hands. "Step back." He holds her up, diaper facing the others like a weapon.

"No." Evander tries to grab the baby again.

I slip between them, reclaiming Rey. "Everyone stop talking," I say, heading for the couch.

They don't.

Julian calls out to me. "What do you need?"

"Diaper," Owen volunteers.

"Obviously," Evander mutters.

"Where is it?" Julian asks.

I look up. "You don't know where the diapers are?"

"We were not informed," Julian says at last.

"They're in the bag," I reply.

"What bag?"

Owen points. "That one."

Julian snatches the diaper bag off the chair and dumps its contents on the floor. "Too many options."

"It's a diaper."

"They all look different," Julian replies, frowning at them.

"Just give me one."

I lay Rey across my forearm, her legs thrashing. "Hey," I murmur, smoothing her down. "I know. I know."

I open the diaper and slide it beneath her in one clean motion. I don't fumble or hesitate anymore.

Rey kicks once. Little girl is testing me today.

"Yeah," I murmur, catching her ankle gently and guiding it back down. "Not today."

The wipes are already in my hand before she can escalate her anger. I'm done before she even realizes what's happening. She absolutely hates her diaper changed.

Julian whistles. "That is... impressive."

"Stop talking," I warn, sealing the tabs.

By the time I'm done, I turn—and my six brothers and cousins have somehow ended up across the room.

Like I detonated something. I stare at them. "...really?"

Julian lifts a hand. "In my defense, that happened so quickly that I didn't know what else to do."

I glance back.

Theron and Evander haven't moved.

Theron gives a small nod toward Rey. "Clean."

Evander adds, "Efficient."

Julian looks between them. "You two are concerningly calm about this."

Theron shrugs. "We've done it before."

Owen frowns. "On purpose?"

Evander glances at him. "That's how children work."

Caleb exhales. "I don't like that."

Rey shifts as I pick her up in my arms, completely unbothered. I rest her against my chest."They'll figure it out," I tell her before kissing her cheek.

"No," Julian replies immediately. "We won't."

The front door thuds open against the frame. Bella storms inside and immediately halts in her tracks.

Her gaze drones over the room in mounting disbelief.

A pastel rug is streaked with sticky formula, its fibers

matted. The couch cushions lie askew, one slit open like a wound, white foam tumbling onto the hardwood. Pacifiers, rattles, half unrolled rolls of wipes, and a scattered handful of teething rings fan out from the toppled diaper bag. Julian must've hurled them as if he were launching grenades. Even the lamp shade wobbles at a crooked angle.

Then Bella's glare snaps to me. Then to Rey, cheek flushed and eyes wide. Then back at the carnage.

"...What the hell happened here?" She puts her hands on her hips, trying not to laugh.

Julian straightens, brushing flecks of foam from his shirt.

"We handled it," he scoffs with crooked pride.

Owen—perched suspiciously far from me, arms folded —adds, "There was an incident."

Bella blinks. "An incident?"

Julian nods solemnly. "She weaponized bodily fluids."

I open my mouth. "That's not—"

"It was targeted," Owen interrupts. "She made eye contact."

Bella's eyebrows climb as she follows Owen's finger to Rey.

Rey yawns, tiny fist curled around the blanket.

Behind her, Selene drifts in, eyes bright. She takes in the bomb that went off and bursts into laughter. A full throated, amused roar that vibrates through the room.

"Oh, this is incredible," she says, stepping past overturned toys. "You left them alone with a newborn?"

"I was here," I retort flatly.

Ophelia slips in next, hand over her mouth, shoulders jiggling with silent laughter.

"Oh my god," she whispers, eyes flicking between us

like she's witnessing a slow motion disaster. "You let them problem solve."

"I did not let—" I begin.

Liora enters last, serene as dawn. She surveys the chaos with a soft smile and actually laughs. It's as if she's watching a charming comedy.

"Oh, this," she says, folding her arms, "is my favorite version of all of you. Utterly useless."

Julian exhales. "I was directing operations."

"You were in the way," Owen mutters.

Bella claps her hands twice. "Okay. No. Stop. Nobody speak."

They all chatter anyway.

"She made a noise—" Julian starts.

"Enough," Bella cuts them off as she strides forward, yanks the diaper bag upright, and starts jamming supplies back inside. "Why are there wipes in three separate locations?"

Julian points at the fireplace hearth. "We deployed them."

Bella squints. "This isn't a military op."

"It felt like one," he protests.

Selene drifts behind Owen and brushes Rey's cheek with a fingertip. Rey relaxes a little, snuggling against me.

"She's calm now," Selene hums.

Owen murmurs, "She won."

My aunt smiles. "She always wins."

Ophelia is already picking up bottles, stacking them by size, restoring order.

"We step away for a few hours," she mutters, "and civilization collapses."

"It didn't collapse," Julian says.

Ophelia glares at the room. "It collapsed."

Suddenly, there is a rumble in the room. Bella doesn't look up from the bag. "If that's who I think it is, keep Rey close. They don't exactly portal with a baby in mind."

Julian straightens. "Right on schedule."

A ripple of blue light splits the air in the center of the room. A slender tear hovers for a heartbeat—then Matthias steps through, elegant as ever, eyes sparkling.

"Missed us?" He calls.

"No," Owen grunts jokingly.

Thayer emerges next, nostrils flaring as he sniffs the air. "Something smells good."

"You're early," Bella says, focused on the pan.

Severin steps in quietly, claiming a stretch of wall with his usual silent authority.

And then—Caelum enters.

He appears last, solid and unhurried, not sparing a glance for any of us. He heads straight for Rey.

"Don't—" Bella warns, but it's too late.

Rey's eyes flutter open. Her chubby hand slips from my shoulder and reaches for Caelum.

Julian exhales. "There it is."

Owen nods. "Every single time."

Rey wraps her tiny fingers around Caelum's index finger and squeezes.

"That's the worst possible choice," Bella retorts.

Matthias places a hand over his chest. "I'm right here."

"You're not the worst," Owen says.

Matthias smirks. "That somehow makes it worse."

Thayer watches, intrigued. "...She didn't hesitate."

"Traitor," Bella mutters.

Caelum doesn't stay where he is at. Rey still has his finger, but that's not enough.

He reaches for her without a word, lifting her from my

arms with practiced ease, one hand supporting her, the other at her back, rubbing in small circles. Rey goes without hesitation, sighs against his chest like she belongs there, her tiny hand immediately gripping his shirt.

He doesn't give her back.

Julian folds his arms. "Of course."

"She skipped all of us," Owen says.

"She has standards," Selene replies.

Rey shifts, getting comfortable, pressing closer into Caelum. He's her favorite. Besides her daddy of course.

Matthias smirks. "I respect the consistency."

Caelum doesn't react. Doesn't even look up from Rey's eyes. He adjusts her slightly to pick up her blanket and pacifier, sticking it in her mouth.

Selene watches that, amused. "You're not getting her back anytime soon."

"I'm aware," I reply, smiling. I love that my daughter has so many people that care about her.

Rey sighs softly against Caelum's chest, completely content.

Order snaps back into place.

Selene and Liora take over the kitchen, moving in sync and effortless. They've done this a hundred times before. Bella and Ophelia jump in beside them, filling in gaps without needing direction.

Selene keeps up a steady stream of commentary. Liora ignores most of it.

Ophelia restores every cushion and bottle to its rightful place. Owen reorganizes the coffee table like it personally offended him.

Julian hovers nearby in what he insists is a supervisory capacity.

"Stop supervising," Ophelia calls.

"I'm observing," he insists.

"You're breathing the wrong way."

Thayer lingers by the counter. "I can help."

"You absolutely cannot."

Severin remains anchored to the wall. Matthias somehow produces a glass of something cool.

And Caelum stands exactly where he is, Rey settled against his chest, one of her tiny hands still fisted in his shirt. She has no intention of letting go.

He doesn't move. Doesn't offer her back. That's where she's staying. Rey seems perfectly content with the arrangement.

I glance down at her in Caelum's arms. "She picks one of the worst ones," I murmur.

Owen's voice drifts from across the room. "That tracks genetically."

"Not helpful," I shoot back.

I step up beside them, dragging a finger gently down Rey's cheek.

"You've got a lot of people," I say softly to her.

She nestles closer, safe in the chaos and clearly, no one else should ever be left alone with her again.

XII
I
II
III
IV
V
VI
VII
VIII
IX
X
XI

CHAPTER TWENTY-THREE

Josie

Light bleeds in at the edges of my vision.

I got dropped from a million feet and landed headfirst into my own body. That must be it. It's a workout to drag air into my lungs. I wince as I press my hand to my temple.

"Okay," I rasp. "That's... unpleasant." I swallow, blinking hard. "Can dead people get migraines? Because if so, that feels like a design flaw."

"Josie."

I look up, and it's Ophelia standing in front of me. Relief hits first followed quickly by the realization that if Ophelia is here, then I'm definitely not anywhere normal.

"Welcome back," she says softly, offering me a small, careful smile.

"Yeah," I mutter, pushing myself up. My body feels stiff. I've been out longer than I've realized. Time works different in the Veil. "We're gonna circle back to that, because I have questions." I glance around, then back at her. "Where is here? And follow up to that... am I alive? What about my baby?"

Her smile drops, and yeah—there it is. Bad news.

"No," she says gently. "I'm sorry, Josie. I don't have the power to bring you back to life. Your baby is safe and happy, surrounded by people that love her."

I hear her. I just don't agree with it. Which feels like an important distinction. If I don't agree, it's not real yet. That's how this works.

"Okay, but my baby is okay." I say slowly. "So we're going with dead. Great. Love that for me." My hand drags through my hair as I look back at her. "Then how are you here? And how am I here?"

Ophelia lifts her hand and the room starts to move.

The walls thin for a split second before something else shows through. Faint silver threads stretching out in every direction begin to shake before everything goes back into place like nothing ever happened.

"You're in the Veil," she says, moving her fingers across the threads. Since when did Ophelia become a harp player? "This is where the Loom exists. Where every life thread is held."

I stare at her for a second, then glance around the room again, suddenly seeing it differently.

"Never thought I'd see this in my lifetime," I mutter. "Or afterlife I guess. If I was lost in the Veil, how did you find me?"

"Blaire has a rare ability," Ophelia says, not looking away from the threads. "She can find people—souls, specifically—even when they're displaced."

"Displaced," I repeat sarcastically. "That's a comforting word."

"Della helped stabilize the connection," she continues. "Together, they were able to locate your thread and anchor it long enough for me to reach you."

My stomach drops. "My thread."

Ophelia nods. "It's damaged, Josie. Frayed. But it's still there. That's the only reason I can speak to you at all."

I lift my hands to the mark. I can still feel it pulsating slightly on the skin.

"Okay," I murmur. "Okay... so I'm dead, but not completely gone, and my thread is hanging on by a thread." I let out a short breath. "No pun intended with that."

She doesn't laugh. None of this is funny.

I look at her again, forcing her to look at me by grunting. "Lucas. Where is he?"

She must see something in my eyes because she starts speaking. "He's with your daughter."

She lifts her hand, and the Veil bends between us, the space rippling like disturbed water. When it clears, I can see it.

Lucas. He's sitting by the window with our baby in his arms. She's bigger than a newborn. Not by much, but enough. Time kept going after I died. I knew that. I just didn't expect days to stretch into months.

He's holding her as if she's everything. His eyes tell me that letting go would cost him the world.

My chest caves in. "That's—" My voice breaks. "That's her."

"Sereyna," Ophelia says lovingly. "We all call her Rey."

Rey wiggles in his arms, letting out a soft, complaining noise before getting comfortable once again, her arms flailing around in the air. Lucas says something I can't hear, his thumb brushing over her cheek in that familiar way. He always did that with me.

"Oh," I whisper, the sound barely there.

We call her Rey. Ophelia's part of her life. That makes me happy—it does. I just wish I was... more than just stories to her. She's my daughter.

"He didn't—" I swallow hard. "He's okay?"

Ophelia hesitates. "He's... trying."

I can't look away.

"She's okay," I say, astonished, more to myself than anything. "She's safe. She's happy." My throat tightens, but I force the words out anyway. "He's taking care of her. I don't have to worry."

"She is," Ophelia confirms.

"I should be there," I whisper.

"I know," Ophelia says gently.

I drag my gaze away from them and force myself to look at her as the image of Rey and Lucas disappear. "Then why am I here?"

Ophelia doesn't answer right away. That's never a good sign.

Her eyes flick past me for half a second. "Because we needed to talk," she says in a way that tells me she means it. "And we don't have much time."

I feel the anger build up in my soul. "Define not much."

There's only so much more of this I can take.

"Minutes," she says. "Maybe less. Your soul isn't stable here. Whatever is holding you is temporary."

"Great," I mutter. "Love a countdown. That's exactly what I needed to hear right now."

"Josie—"

"No, it's fine," I cut in, dragging a hand through my hair. "I'm dead, I've got a migraine, my soul is apparently on a timer, and you're telling me we're speed running this conversation. Totally normal. Fine. Talk. What is so important that we're doing this now?"

She steps a little closer. "You weren't supposed to die."

Yeah. That's the *worst* thing she has said so far.

I gape at her, mouth wide enough that bugs could fly in it. "I'm sorry, what?"

"Your thread—your life—it wasn't meant to end there," she continues. "Fate didn't mark that moment as your end."

The skin between my shoulder blades prickles, then goes numb, like ice water trickling vertebra by vertebra down to the small of my back.

"Then why did it?" I ask, my voice raising to a higher decibel now.

Ophelia's teeth clench behind closed lips. "Because something interfered."

His name burns in my throat like acid.

"Jasper," I force out, my voice cracking with the effort of containing the storm inside me.

I laugh under my breath, but there's nothing fucking funny in it. I didn't think I could hate his guts more but here we are, knee deep in this shit again.

"He didn't just take advantage of the moment," she says. "He altered the outcome. He forced your thread to break when it wasn't meant to."

"It didn't break," I say, pissed off. "You said it yourself."

"It didn't break cleanly," she corrects. "That's why you're still here. Why we can reach you at all."

"Lucky me."

I can't keep lying to myself about how terrible my existence was from beginning to end. The deck was stacked against me from the start.

Ophelia tries to calm me. "Josie... what happened to

you shouldn't have happened. Not like that. Not then. Not ever."

I look away from her, back to where the image of Lucas and Rey had been, like I might still catch a glimpse of them if I try hard enough.

"I died," I say simply. "That feels pretty final."

"The council reviewed your thread," she continues. "What's left of it. And they agreed—unanimously—that this was an unnatural disruption."

"That's a very polite way of saying I got screwed over."

"Yes."

Well. Points for honesty.

I cross my arms loosely, feeling the fabric wrinkle under my elbow. I look down and see a tunic covering me. That's not what I was wearing when I arrived in the Veil. "What does any of this matter? I got screwed over, if I only have minutes, I'm assuming there's nothing to be done about it. While I thank you for showing me my daughter, my family. I'm not sure what the point of this is."

"We made an agreement."

I narrow my eyes, the blackness of the sky making the stone obsidian. "We?"

"The council," Ophelia clarifies, "and me."

"What kind of agreement?" I know I am being defensive but at this point, I feel like I have the right to be.

"One that gives you a choice."

"A choice," I repeat, tisking a bit. "Sounds like that should come with fine print."

"It does," she admits.

My hands shake as I dig my nails into my palms, rage building like a pressure cooker behind my eyes until I can practically taste blood in my mouth. One more word—one more goddamn cryptic non answer—and I swear I'll tear this whole fucking room apart with my bare hands.

I exhale, trying to lower my ghost heart rate to get this shit over with. "Start talking."

Ophelia's eyes gleam. I bet she's probably getting as fed up with my attitude as I am with her pace of conversation. "Because your death wasn't supposed to happen, Fate can't fully claim you—not yet. Eventually it will. But the longer your thread remains unstable, the harder it is to keep you tethered here."

I gesture around us at the cavern's echoing emptiness. "So this—" I sweep my hand through the gloom "—is temporary."

"Yes."

"And the alternative?" My voice echoes back at me, hollow.

Her expression darkens, shadows pooling beneath her eyes. "You move on."

Fuck this.

"But," she adds carefully, "because of what was done to you are being given the chance to decide what happens next."

My pulse trembles. "Decide?"

"Yes." She exhales, a hint of jasmine on her breath. "It shouldn't be possible. But the Veil is compromised. The Loom's threads are fraying. And your thread"—a flicker of concern in her tone—"is... unique right now."

"Unique," I echo, tasting the word. "Another word I hate."

"It means you're not bound to a single outcome yet. Not life. Not death."

"What are my options?" I ask.

Ophelia hesitates. "Josie—"

"No," I cut her off. "Don't Josie me, Ophelia. You said I have a choice and little time. I want all the information. Now."

Her gaze never wavers. "You have two options. You have to make the choice now."

I lean forward, bracing for impact. "Let's hear how fucked up they are."

She inhales, losing patience. "The first is that the council can weave a new thread for you."

I blink. "A new... life?"

"Yes."

A cold wave crashes through me.

"They can rewrite it—drop you back in the mortal world before any of this happens. Before Bella. Before the Veil. Before Hell." Ophelia nods to where the image was. "Before Lucas and Rey, too."

My throat tightens. "No demons. No Duvains. No pregnancy. None of it?"

"None of it." She walks forward. "Fate would resume, naturally. Without interference."

I swallow. "So Jasper—"

"Would never reach you."

Her words strike like a hammer. My ribs constrict. "I'd graduate, build the life meant for me... just without all of this."

Without them. Without him. Without her.

All I can taste is emptiness. "And I wouldn't remember any of it?"

Her eyes flicker. "No."

The denial hollows me from the inside out.

"Okay," I whisper. "What about the second option?"

Her face grows solemn. "You let your mortal thread end. We would cut it properly. Right here and right now."

I close my eyes, bracing for emotional impact. "Meaning I stay dead."

"Yes. If you choose that," she explains, her tone is defiant, "you don't move on like most souls. You don't leave this realm. Your new lifeline will be tied to your soulmate's thread."

My pulse pounds. "Where do I go?"

Her eyes glisten with what looks to be sorrow. "You stay in Hell."

"Does that mean I can stay with Lucas? And Rey?" I ask, knowing I shouldn't be hopeful, but I really want to be. I want something to just go right for once.

She nods gently. "With Lucas and Rey."

A tether of love and agony binds me. "I'd remain... here?"

"Yes."

I nod slowly, the walls of Hell pressing in. "Okay..."

"But there are conditions."

"There are always conditions," I mutter.

"You wouldn't interact with the living. They wouldn't hear you. You'd be cut off from their world."

I picture Lucas holding Rey, her tiny laughter. My chest aches. "My life in the mortal world?"

"It would be erased—to maintain balance."

There is the catch. I have to say I don't love the idea of just being erased. "So I never existed?"

"Not entirely. Those bound to Hell—Bella, Ophelia, your friends who crossed over—anyone connected to this realm would still remember you. From now and in the future. Whatever that may be."

"What about Lucas and Rey?"

"They will know you," she says. "You will return from

the moment you left in your own mind, but it has been about three months for everyone else."

Three months. I've been gone that long. No wonder Rey looked older.

I press my palms to my temples, sorting the impossible. "Option one—I get a fresh life, safe and normal, but I lose all of this." I gesture at the empty air. "Lose them, him, her."

Ophelia's face remains calm. Obviously it is her role to tell me my choices, but to not influence my decision. Probably better she tells me. I'd probably throw fire at the council.

I draw a breath. "Option two—I stay here forever, no future, nothing beyond Hell."

Her eyes glimmer into mine. "But you get them."

I close my eyes, tasting grief and longing. "Of course those are the choices," I murmur. "Because nothing about my life has ever been simple."

I stare at nothing for a second before the question hits me in a way that is impossible to ignore.

"Wait," I say, looking back at Ophelia. "If I stay... what does that actually look like?"

Ophelia looks slightly confused. I know that I am probably stating the obvious, but I can't put my finger on what any of this means yet.

"You will never be able to enter the mortal world again," she starts, stating what she already did before. "And will spend your eternity in Hell."

"I get that," I say, furrowing my brows. "But would I be able to be around other demons or just those that knew me before? Will I be isolated from *this* world?"

Ophelia's eyes light up, a chuckle coming out of her.

"I see what you mean," she says, still laughing. "I'm sorry, Josie. I should have explained that better."

She wipes a tear from her eyes.

"Of course you can be around demons. Hell has different power levels than the mortal world," she says. "You can't leave Hell. Doesn't mean you can't be around those who are already here."

I shake my head. "I get it now.."

Do I? Not really. But I understand enough.

I glance toward the empty space where Lucas and Rey stood as if I could will them back. "Either I forget them," I whisper.

Or I never leave them.

My chest tightens. "...That's cruel."

Ophelia's voice is an echo. "It's the only way the balance of the universe will hold."

I close my eyes, inhale the weight of the underworld, and know there is no escaping forever. Two choices. Both permanent. Both are impossible.

I open my eyes again, still searching the shadows for an answer.

I close my eyes, and it's not even the hard parts that come first. It's the little moments. The way he says *Sunshine* and looks at me as if I light up his whole world. The way Rey's hand curls around a button. The nursery we built. The stupid blankets. The way nothing ever went according to plan and somehow it still felt right.

I swallow hard.

If I go back... none of that exists. Not even as a memory. Lucas won't know me. Rey will never exist to begin with.

My chest caves in at that.

A shaky breath leaves me as I shake my head slightly.

No.

No, I can't do that.

My hand lifts to my chest again, pressing over that frayed, barely there thread. It's still there. Still holding. Barely.

I think about Lucas holding her—the way he looked, like he was holding everything he had left. I think about Rey. Alive. Safe. Here. With him.

A slow breath leaves me. A small, broken laugh slips out after.

"Time is up." Ophelia straightens slightly, her voice gentle. "Did you choose?"

"I did."

She looks at me with all the hope in the world. I can't handle this. "What choice did you make, Josie?"

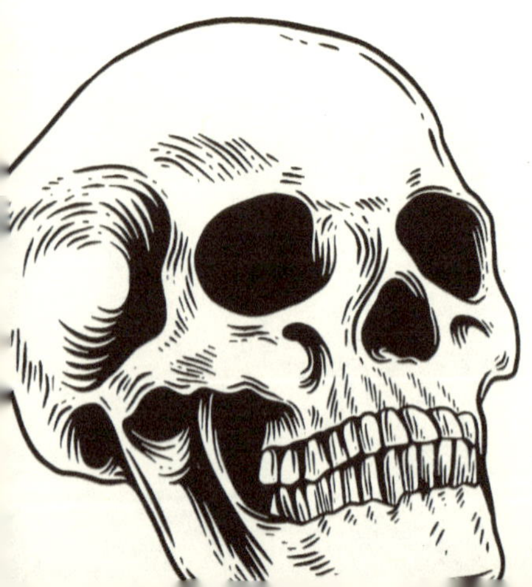

CHAPTER TWENTY-FOUR

Sunday dinners have turned into something else entirely.

They used to be loud, chaotic, borderline unmanageable in a way that felt normal for my family. But since Rey came into the picture, my cousins and brothers seem to be more domesticated than ever before.

Rey's asleep in the pack-and-play Bella brought over from the center, tucked into the corner of the living room where I can see her no matter where I sit.

Bella didn't trust me to pick one out myself—said I'd choose something for a demon and not a little girl.

I tried to tell her that Rey *is* a demon. Not that it worked anyway. Bella is never wrong. Even I hate to admit that she was right about the color palette of the pack and play matching the vibe Josie set up.

Bella smirked and mentioned it was an auntie's job. I

guess I'll let her indulge herself. My little girl needs all the family she can get.

Rey fought sleep tonight. She's a stubborn one, just like her mommy was. She made her usual small sounds and restless movements that made it clear she wasn't giving in easily. I walked the room more times than I bothered counting before she finally drifted off, her breathing evening out against my chest.

I check on her several times throughout the night.

"She's not going anywhere." Evander's voice cuts through my thoughts as he puts his hand on my shoulder.

"I'm aware," I reply, not looking at him.

"Are you?"

I glance over. He's watching me in that way only a father can. All knowing and all annoying is what my brothers used to say.

"I like to check," I say.

"I noticed." He pauses to take a look at Rey.

I don't respond. Across the room, Julian is leaning back in his chair, watching the pack-and-play. He already called dibs on feeding her tonight when she wakes up.

"Where's Ophelia?" I ask, glancing toward the area where people enjoy portaling in.

Selene doesn't look up from where she's leaning against the counter. "Council called her in. She'll be here soon."

Bella pauses mid motion at the stove. "We're not starting without her."

"You are tonight," Selene replies easily. "She said to."

That earns her a look.

Owen straightens slightly. "Wait." He stands up walking closer to the group. "You're on the council," he continues. "So why aren't you there?"

Selene clears her throat. It's as if she was hoping no one

would ask her that. She either has no information, which is impossible, or she is hiding something. That latter seems more plausible.

"I was assigned elsewhere," she says.

Julian raises a brow. "That sounds like you're not telling us everything."

"It's not what that means," she replies.

"It''s what it sounds," Owen counters.

Selene finally looks at him. "I was tasked with staying here."

Evander and Theron look to her now, brows drawn. They had no idea about all of this either.

"With us," Julian clarifies.

"Yes."

"What does that mean?" I ask, gravely. I cannot put Rey in harms way. I need to know everything.

She sighs, like this is exactly what she didn't want to deal with tonight.

"It means," she says, serious now, "you'll know when it happens." her eyes soften when she looks at me. "Rey will be safe, I promise."

As much as it should, that doesn't help.

A sound causes every head in the room to turn at the same time. The conversation cuts off. Chairs scrape against the floor as instinct takes over.

Julian and Owen shift toward the couch as I go straight for Rey, who is now screaming and crying. I'm going to kill whoever walks through that portal. Ophelia would never wake her. This portal isn't hers—black as obsidian instead of gray. Someone else is coming through.

Ophelia steps through first.

"Lia," Julian says, closing the distance. "You know better than to open a portal that wakes Rey."

I'd laugh if I wasn't furious. Julian Duvain has completely folded for a baby.

"I didn't," she says, already tired. "I tried to tell them."

"Who," I demand.

Behind her, the council enters.

Selene stands immediately. "Did you do it?"

Ophelia doesn't hesitate. "Yes."

My focus snaps to her. "Did what?"

She looks at me. "We gave her a choice."

The words don't make sense.

"What are you talking about," I say, already stepping forward.

The portal doesn't close.

It stays open.

Then she steps through.

Everything in me stops.

The one person I never thought I'd see again is standing right in front of me.

Josie.

"Sunshine," I choke out.

I don't remember crossing the room. One second she's there, stepping out of a portal—which should be impossible—and the next I'm in front of her, my hands on her like I need proof. My fingers slide into her hair, over her face, down her arms, everywhere at once, like I'm trying to memorize her all over again before she disappears again.

"You're here," I breathe, my voice breaking.

She says my name like it's the only thing keeping her standing. "Lucas—"

I pull her into me, hard enough that she stumbles, but she doesn't fight it—she crashes into me with the desperation of someone coming home after wandering and drifting along.

My arms lock around her, one hand at her back, the other at her neck, holding her in place against a world that might try to take her again. I would burn down the universe itself before letting her go.

My face presses into her hair, her neck, anywhere I can reach, dragging in a breath that shudders through my entire body. Her heartbeat echoes ringing in my ears.

My hand slides up to her face, trembling against her skin as I cup her jaw, my thumb brushing away tears that mirror the ones I feel tracking down my own face. "Never again," I whisper against her temple, the words breaking in my throat. "You are never leaving me again."

Her hands are shaking where they grip my shirt, twisting into it like she needs something solid to hold onto.

"Never again," she whispers.

I don't wait another second.

I kiss her. My teeth catch her bottom lip. Her nails dig into my shoulders. We collide like thunder, our breath ragged. The mark on my forearm burns hot, then cool, as if recognizing its match.

She makes a sound, putting her hand on her collarbone.

Her mark turns from charcoal to a golden hue. Our marks are one again.

"How," I manage, my voice rough with tears. "How are you here? I felt you—I felt you go—"

Her eyes close for a second, her hands tightening in my shirt.

"They gave me a choice," she says, her voice wavering.

I shake my head, barely following. "What choice?"

"To start over," she says. "A new life. Before any of this. Before you. Before Rey." Her breath catches. "I wouldn't remember anything."

Something in my chest twists at the thought of it—of

her being gone in a way that meant she was never here at all. I look at Rey, tucked into my mother's arms, and I can't picture a life where she doesn't exist. Where I never met my soulmate.

"And the other," I push, clearing the lump that formed out of my throat.

"To stay," she says. "To let my thread end and remain here. With you. With her."

My grip tightens without thinking.

"And you—"

"I chose you," she says, cutting me off before I could finish my thought. Her hand comes up to my face now, mirroring mine, her thumb brushing against my cheek like she's checking I'm real too. "I chose her."

Her voice breaks, but she doesn't stop.

"I couldn't start over," she whispers. "I couldn't forget you. I couldn't forget her." Her forehead presses harder against mine. "I would go through all of it again. Every part. *Every* painful moment just to get back to you."

My eyes close, my hand sliding into her hair again, pulling her closer until there's no space left between us at all.

She lets out a shaky breath against me, her arms tightening like she's afraid this still isn't real.

I pull back just enough to look at her again, my thumb brushing away another tear before it can fall.

Her eyes flick past me. Everything in her freezes to a halt.

"Lucas..." Her voice is barely there. I have to lean into her lips just to hear her. "Is that—"

I don't make her ask. I turn slightly, my hand sliding down to take hers as I guide her forward.

"She's right here," I say happily.

My mother looks up as we approach, knowing what Josie needs. She carefully places Rey into Josie's arms.

Josie's breath catches. "Oh my god," she whispers, nuzzling her fuzzy blonde hair. "She's... she's so big."

"Three months," I say, my voice happier than it's been in months.

Her eyes snap to mine. "Three—"

Then back to Rey. "I missed..." Her voice breaks. "I missed everything."

"You didn't miss her," I assure her quickly. "She's right here."

"Oh—" The sound that leaves her isn't even a word. Her arms tighten instinctively, pulling Rey closer, her hand cradling the back of her head.

"Hi," she whispers, her voice breaking immediately. "Hi, baby girl."

Rey stirs. Her face scrunches for a second, a soft, uncertain sound leaving her.

"It's okay," she murmurs quickly, panic slipping in. "I know, I know, I'm new—well, not new, but—" She lets out a shaky breath. "I'm your mom."

Rey's tiny hand lifts, fingers flexing and then she grabs onto Josie's shirt.

Josie laughs.

"Shirt grabbing means that Rey has fallen in love with you. It's her thing."

"Oh my god," she whispers, tears spilling instantly. "Lucas—"

"I see it," I say, my fingers start to tingle.

Rey makes a soft noise, her grip tightening just slightly.

"I talked to you," Josie continues, tears falling freely down her face now. "All the time. You remember that, don't you? I told you about your dad—" A small, shaky laugh breaks through. "He's still annoying, by the way."

I huff out a quiet breath, but I don't interrupt.

"I told you I loved you," she whispers. "Every day. I didn't stop. Not once."

Rey shifts, her head turning more toward Josie, her tiny body pressing closer.

"I'm right here," she says, her voice trembling. "I'm right here now. I'm not going anywhere."

Her hand smooths over Rey's back, memorizing every bit of her.

"I missed you," she breathes. "I missed you so much."

Rey lets out a soft, content sound, her grip never loosening.

Josie breaks completely. A quiet sob escapes her as she pulls Rey closer, pressing a kiss to her head over and over again.

She's making up for lost time.

"I've got you," she whispers. "I've got you now."

Josie doesn't let go of Rey as she looks up at the rest of them, her fingers still curled protectively around her like she's not willing to risk even an inch of distance again.

Julian is the first to speak. "Where did you go? We know that no one could find your soul."

Her smile falters, the corners of her mouth trembling before flattening into a line. She blinks twice, and when her eyes reopen, they've darkened to the color of wet asphalt.

"He took me," she says, her voice barely above a whisper.

"Who?" Owen asks. We all want her to say it, even if we already have an inkling of who *he* is.

"Jasper," she replies. "He grabbed my soul when I

crossed. I didn't go where I was supposed to. I ended up in the Veil. Where all of my nightmares took place."

He *was* weakening her, shaping her soul into something else. Just like we thought he was trying to do. Bastard. But for what?

"And how did you manage that?" Seth asks from the corner of the room.

Rey cries and Josie begins to bounce her lightly.

"I fought," she says.

That is exactly what my Sunshine would do.

"He was trying to keep me there," she continues. "Said he needed me stronger. I don't know what that means. I hit him. He hit me back. It wasn't going well."

Julian huffs quietly. "Shocking."

She ignores him.

"Then someone else showed up," she says, her brows pulling together slightly as she replays it in her mind. "A woman. She just appeared out of nowhere. She stabbed him and threw some knives at him. Straight through the back. The blade had runes on it. It actually hurt him."

That gets everyone's attention. Who is this woman that saved my mate?

"He didn't see it coming," she adds. "She kept him down long enough to tell me what to do."

"What did she say?" I ask, wanting to know more.

Josie looks at me, coming closer. "She told me to find my thread. Said when I felt it pull, to grab it and pull back. So I did."

Owen lets out a slow breath. "And that worked."

"I'm here," Josie says simply, rolling her eyes slightly. I mean that was kind of obvious.

Theron shifts slightly, his focus narrowing in on Josie. "Who was she? The woman."

Josie frowns, thinking it through. "I don't know. I've never seen her before. Auburn hair. Hazel eyes. Her skin was... glowing a shimmering gold color. Not in a normal way. She just—she felt..." She shakes her head, like she doesn't have the right word for it. "Old."

Selene goes completely still.

Josie keeps going, slower now. "And right before I left, she said something. It didn't make sense at the time. Hell, it doesn't even make sense now."

"What did she say?" I press.

Josie hesitates for a second. "She told me to tell her sons she loves them." She shakes her head again. "I don't know who her sons are."

Liora doesn't move from where she is standing. Evander's mouth opens slightly, like he's trying to process something that doesn't quite fit.

The glass in Selene's hand slips before she can catch it, shattering against the floor in a sharp crack that no one reacts to.

Theron lets out a low breath that turns into something close to a laugh, dragging a hand over his face before looking back at Josie.

"Well," he says, his voice rougher than usual, something almost disbelieving running through it, "that's one way to come back."

Josie looks at him utterly confused. "What—"

Theron's eyes water a bit. Which now leaves me in a state of confusion. "Little one," he says, voice catching on his tears. "You just met our mother."

Evander starts laughing. "Sereyna."

CHAPTER TWENTY-FIVE

Josie

Liora bends to lift Rey from my arms.

"No—wait—" I start immediately, my turns away slightly on instinct

Rey makes a small sound, wiggling in place. "She just—she just settled—"

"She's okay," Liora says softly, that knowing smile still in place. "I've got her. Let me take her while you spend some time with your mate."

I hesitate, my fingers brushing once more over Rey's cheek. I need to memorize the feel of her before letting go, no matter how short of a time I'll be away from her.

"I don't—" I shake my head slightly. "I just got her back. I don't want to—"

Lucas steps in behind me, his hand sliding over mine.

"She's safe," he murmurs. "My mom and aunt have her a lot when I am working. Everyone here has a heavy hand in taking care of her. Our entire family takes turns caring for her."

I don't move. My grip on her doesn't loosen. But.... our family. He said *our* family.

Liora shifts Rey against her shoulder with ease, already swaying slightly as she walks away, giving us space.

He turns me gently, just enough so I'm facing him, his other hand coming up to my face, thumb brushing beneath my eye where tears haven't stopped.

"I want to solidify this," he whispers. "Our bond. I want you to be mine in every way possible. I won't lose you again."

My breath shakes. "I didn't choose this to leave you," I say, my voice breaking. "I chose it to stay."

His gaze doesn't waver.

"Then stay with me," he murmurs.

Bella is the first to step forward, her eyes more red than I've ever seen them. She presses a quick kiss to my temple, her hand squeezing my shoulder.

"Don't disappear again," she murmurs, voice tight despite the attempt at normal.

"I won't," I whisper.

She nods once, then turns away before it can turn into something else.

Everyone else leaves through their own portals. One after another.

And just like that it's only us.

He takes my hand and pulls me with him, and I go without hesitating, my fingers tightening around his. I stay right beside him, my shoulder brushing his arm. I want no space between us anymore.

By the time we reach the doorway to the bedroom, I'm already leaning into him.

He turns and pulls me fully against his chest, and I don't hesitate. His hand comes up to my face, fingers sliding along my jaw before tangling in my hair, and then his mouth is on mine.

I grip his shirt, pulling him closer, needing him just as much as he needs me. He moves me backward into the room without breaking the kiss, and the door shuts softly behind us.

"Look at me," he says.

My eyes find his, and my grip tightens on his shirt, on my teacher to this life.

"Right here," he murmurs, voice rough as his fingers slide to the nape of my neck.

His hands catch the hem of my tunic and drag it up, and I barely get my arms out of the way before it's gone, tossed somewhere behind him like it never mattered. I don't even think about it—I'm already pulling at him, pushing his shirt off his shoulders, needing it out of the way, needing *him*.

He backs me up, step for step, until the bed hits the back of my knees and I stumble. I grab onto him, but he's already following me down as I fall back onto the mattress.

The rest of our clothes disappear fast—fabric shifting, hands everywhere, there's nothing careful about it. Just primal urgency. Just heat. Just the two of us trying to get closer when there's already no space left between us.

He gets back up as he kneels at the edge of the bed, keeping his knees pressed into the mattress. Even this much space feels like too much. His hair is a mess, as usual, and he runs a hand through it absently while waiting for me to join him.

He reaches for the scroll I'm sure Selene left on his nightstand. Spread out on the bed, the writing looks burned rather than inked, the script twists away from the candlelight. It's not a language that I speak. It's an old, demonic language.

We read together, heads nearly touching, his scent cutting through the lavender with something metallic and hot. It's the scent of Lucas. His signature.

Something about that is the most comforted that I've felt since we mated.

Each step is written in imperative. It is meant to anoint, mark, invoke, bind.

Lucas's hand slides to my thigh, then stills. "It only works if you want it." He says it flat, not as a taunt or warning. "No half assing this."

I nod, and something in him explodes.

His hand stays on my thigh for a second longer, warm and steady, like he's memorizing the moment I didn't push him away. Then it moves and my breath hitches as his fingers trace up my inner thigh, making my core throb in anticipation.

There's no rush in it. It's not urgent, it's controlled.Like he's carefully choosing, crafting every second of this.

My fingers tighten on his shoulders, dragging him closer right where I want him, and he comes with me like he was already halfway there. His mouth crashes into mine again, and it hits harder this time, deeper, his tongue pushing into my mouth like he's taking what's his.

A sharp breath catches in my throat, something in me answering instantly. I meet his movements with an urgency of my own. I don't want controlled, I want raw, real, untethered intimacy.

His hand moves up to cup my breast, thumb circling my hardened nipple. The movement makes my body react before I can think about it, my hips arching up to meet his.

I lean into it, into him, my back pressing into the mattress as he follows me down, not giving me the chance to drift anywhere else. His weight settles over me, grounding and consuming all at once, his cock hard and ready, pressing against my thigh.

His hand slides up my side, slower now, and I feel every inch of it—my breath stuttering as his fingers trace the curve of my breast, my body reacting like he knew it would.

My hands find him again, moving without direction, just needing contact, needing to feel something solid as everything inside me starts to build again—heat, pressure, something deeper threading through it that doesn't belong to just me anymore.

The Mark pulses. It pulls a breath out of me, sudden and unsteady. His hand finds it instantly, and the sensation spikes—stronger, deeper, dragging something out of me that I don't have a name for.

I grab onto him harder. My fingers curl into his shoulders, pulling him closer even when there's no space left to close, because it still doesn't feel like enough.

"Lucas—" The word barely makes it out of my pleasure-filled body.

"I've got you."

He always does. It will always be him.

His forehead presses to mine, his breath uneven now, and I feel it—through him, through me, through the bond that's pulling tighter instead of fraying apart.

Something is changing. The thread—the one that was breaking—tightens.

He doesn't let me jerk away. His arm locks around me, holding me there, anchoring me as everything inside me reshapes to my very core.

"Stay with me," he says, quieter now, but no less certain.

"I am," I breathe, even though it comes out uneven. Because I am. I'm still here.

The pressure builds again, but it's different this time. My head falls back against the mattress as Lucas slides inside me inch by inch, stretching me open, filling me completely. My fingernails dig into his shoulders as my body readjusts to his size.

His hips press flush against mine, and he stills, trembling with restraint. I feel every pulse of him inside me, every twitch. When he withdraws slowly and pushes back in, the friction ignites sparks behind my eyelids. The bond between us glows hot where our skin touches.

"Look at me," he whispers, voice rough as he establishes a rhythm—slow, deep thrusts that make my back arch with each one.

I open my eyes to find his face transformed with pleasure, pupils blown wide, jaw clenched. Sweat beads along his collarbone. He hooks my leg higher around his waist, changing the angle, hitting somewhere that makes me cry out.

"I'm here," I gasp between thrusts, my body clenching around him involuntarily.

His rhythm falters. "I know," he growls, pressing his forehead to mine. His fingers tangle in my hair, tugging just enough to expose my neck. His lips find my pulse point as his movements grow more urgent.

I arch up to meet him, our bodies sliding together, slick with sweat. "I chose this," I breathe against his ear.

His eyes lock with mine, dark and certain about everything going on. "I know," he says again, as he drives us both toward release.

Everything hits all at once. It doesn't feel like something breaking or tearing, but locking into place so hard it almost knocks the breath out of me.

It isn't a subtle change nor is it gentle. The thread that used to feel like it could slip through my fingers, like it could disappear if I didn't hold on tight enough, suddenly doesn't move at all. It holds. It anchors.

My fingers dig into his back as the Mark burns hot under my skin, not painful, just there—alive in a way it never was before.

I suck in a breath that actually stays in my lungs this time, my chest steadying instead of tightening, and it takes me a second to realize why.

I can feel him. Not just where he's touching me, not just pressed against me, but everywhere else too, in the same space where my pulse is settling, in the same place my breath is coming back into rhythm.

There's no edge to it anymore, no sense that something could pull away if I let my guard down. It's just there, solid, constant, like it always should have been.

His mouth hovers a breath from mine, the warmth of him ghosting across my lips. "I told you I wasn't going anywhere."

His palm presses against my cheek, fingers curling at my jawline with enough pressure to leave prints.

Our eyes lock.

The mark on my collarbone pulses once, then settles into a warmth that spreads through my veins like honey. The ache I've carried since it first appeared fades to nothing.

I inhale slowly, my fingertips resting against the stubble on his cheek, feeling each tiny ridge against my skin.

"That's it?" I whisper, blinking. "All that—" Air escapes in a soft huff. "And now it just… sticks forever?"

The corner of his mouth lifts with a barely perceptible dimple on his cheek showing. "It doesn't unstick," he says.

My heartbeat stutters, then pounds double time against my ribs.

I nod once, my thumb still tracing the edges of his jaw. "Good," I say.

My fingers slide into his hair, tangling in the strands at the nape of his neck, and I pull him down until our lips meet. Not crashing together like before, but placing the final piece in a puzzle.

The mark hums between us, vibrating with recognition of us meeting once again.

Mine. His. Ours.

Permanent as a tattoo, inevitable as gravity.

Happily ever after in demon form.

Seth

The whole family is packed into my parents' house.

My mother and Selene went all out—food, drinks, the whole thing—to celebrate Lucas and Josie binding themselves together in the most dramatic way possible.

It's loud as can be. Everyone is talking over each other, laughing like nothing in this world ever goes wrong.

Even though we have a giant problem. A problem named Jasper Wilder.

I stay in the corner with a beer, not really drinking it, just holding onto something that gives me an excuse not to engage.

Lucas and Josie are across the room. You can feel the difference if you're paying attention. The bond is locked in, settled, and it's not going anywhere whether anyone likes it or not.

Good for them. After everything those two have been through, they've earned this.

Rey's being passed around. At this point, she's a shared

asset. She makes one tiny noise and half the room reacts like she just solved all of the universe's problems.

I usually get up and take her when she ends up within reach.

But tonight—while everyone's celebrating another Infernal Union—I stay where I am, and my mood takes a hit. I'm not interested in explaining.

I take a sip. Three of my brothers are mated. Lucas. Julian. Owen.

And me? I've got a mark I pretend doesn't exist.

It's worked great. So far anyway.

I've had it my entire life. Same place. Same pull to a mate that I can't find. Same potential to turn everything into a problem I don't feel like dealing with.

So, I ignored it. I buried it deep as fuck, I got good enough at pretending it didn't exist that it stopped reacting altogether.

Out of sight, out of mind. Except not really, because it's still there. It always has been.

The younger Duvain generation doesn't know yet. Only my parents. My aunt. My uncle.

Everyone else gets the version of me that doesn't have to explain why I was born with something that's supposed to happen later. Much later.

I take another sip, watching the room like I'm not part of it. Like I don't belong in the middle of something I've been avoiding my entire life.

Della arrives. Her eyes are always on me. Another secret that I don't really want to share... we've hooked up. A lot.

She's not my mate—clearly. But she's fun. The whole situation is easy. She doesn't expect anything more than what I'm willing to give, and I don't have to pretend with her. She gets it.

She knows when I find my other half, we're done.

Still... my gaze lingers on her longer than it should. Because if I didn't already have something waiting for me—something I never asked for—there's no doubt in my mind that I would choose her.

But that's not how this works. And it never has been.

She doesn't come to me right away. Instead, she moves through the room and goes straight to Selene, which is new, and immediately puts me on edge.

They don't talk long—just a few words—but Selene's expression changes and she becomes focused. I watch as she nods like something just got confirmed that we definitely weren't informed about.

That can't be good.

"Seth," Selene calls.

I don't move at first, because whatever this is, I already don't like it.

"Seth," Selene calls again.

Yeah, that's not optional. I push off the wall and head over, taking my time on purpose, even though every instinct I have is telling me something just went sideways.

"What?" I ask.

Selene doesn't answer. She just looks at Della.

Della looks at me. "It's time we tell them," she says.

I blink once. "...tell them what?"

She doesn't explain, because why would this mystery of a woman tell anyone her plans. She just steps in, grabs my arm before I can stop her, and shoves my sleeve up. I jerk on instinct, already irritated. "What are you—"

And then it hits.

Not for me. For everyone else.

The mark burns against my skin, fully exposed for the

first time in... ever, and the room goes silent. It is dead quiet.

"What the hell—" Julian starts.

"You're mated?" Owen cuts in, brows pulling together. "Since when?"

Lucas doesn't say anything. He's just watching me, which is somehow worse.

"I'm not," I say flatly, already trying to pull my arm back.

Della doesn't let me. "He was born with it," she says.

That gets a reaction from everyone. Basically screams, groans, and utter silence.

"What?" Bella says. "That's not—"

"Possible?" Della cuts in calmly. "It is."

Before anyone can react to that, she reaches up and pulls her shirt aside just enough to expose her collarbone.

Same mark.

Same burn.

Same glow.

What the *fuck*? How did I *never* see what when we hooked up?

"And so was I," she adds.

"But how did I—"

She cuts me off. "You didn't because I used magic to cover it."

I stare at her for a second—then actually look at her—and something in my mind shifts in a way I don't like at all.

She doesn't look away. "We're mates," she says.

Just like that. No build-up. No warning.

It takes a second to process that. "You knew?" I ask her, pulling my arm out of her grasp.

I look a bit closer and see a small burn... or brand where the mark is. What is she not telling us?

"Yes." No hesitation in her tone whatsoever.

My jaw tightens. "Since when?"

"Since birth."

I let out a short laugh. "You're telling me you've known this whole time?"

"Yes."

"And you just—what?" I gesture between us. "Decided not to mention it?"

Her expression doesn't change. "I was waiting for you."

I laugh once. No humor in it. "That's—" I shake my head. "That's insane."

"You weren't ready," she says, completely calm.

That doesn't help.

"Yeah, well," I mutter, dragging a hand down my face, "funny how that works when no one tells me what I'm supposed to be ready for."

The room stays quiet. Everyone's watching us like their favorite television show is on.

I look back at her. At the mark. At everything that suddenly makes a lot more sense than I want it to.

Della decides we're not done ruining my night. Or my life.

"A war is coming."

Selene nods once beside her, calm as ever. "It's already in motion."

Julian straightens. "What kind of war?"

"The kind you don't get time to prepare for," Della says.

Owen exhales. "Start talking."

Della doesn't move, doesn't dramatize it. She just looks at all of us and drops it clean. "Jasper isn't the only problem we have now."

I let out a short laugh. "That's comforting."

"He's part of it," she says. "But not the highest point of the triangle."

Selene steps in smoothly. "When Josie died, we all went after her soul. Tracking her thread. Trying to pull her back."

Yeah. We did.

"You were focused on the Veil," Selene continues. "On the Loom. On her."

"We lost sight of what the others were doing," I mutter.

Della's gaze flicks to me. "Exactly. You were busy."

"They used it," Selene says. "The Veil was unstable. Jasper was tearing through it—pulling attention, pulling power. No one was watching the gates."

Adrian exhales. "A distraction."

"Yeah," I say under my breath. "Shocking."

Selene doesn't soften it. "While you were all looking for Josie... they got him out."

Julian's voice drops. "Got who out?"

Della meets his gaze. "Obadiah Crowe."

Bella swears under her breath. Owen goes still. Lucas doesn't move at all.

I blink once. "...you're kidding."

Selene shakes her head. "No."

I drag a hand down my face. "So we've got Jasper running around tearing through the Veil, and now the Creeds decided to make it worse."

"They didn't decide," Della says. "They planned."

"They needed a window." Theron's voice cuts in. "Josie's death gave it to them."

Lucas' voice is tight when he finally speaks. "Why now?"

Della looks at him. "Because something shifted."

My mark burns again. Almost painful this time.I don't miss the way her eyes flick to me for half a second.

Julian exhales slowly. "So this is bigger than Jasper."

"That is why Della and Seth need to mate now," Selene says. "They have the power to help us get some of the balance back."

"It's not enough," Della says, throwing her hands in the air in frustration.

"We need something bigger," Selene says.

"A war is coming," Della repeats. "We can't fight it alone."

"So what exactly are you thinking?" Selene asks.

Della looks at all of us—at me last, her eyes swirling obsidian, waves of power vibrating off her.

"Release the Horsemen."

Next in the World of The Devil's Bargain

The Horsemen were never meant to return.
Now they're coming.
Bound to the End Series.
Enter the next chapter.

Acknowledgments

Fourteen books later, and I can confidently say this is very much a team effort. So here's a loud shoutout to the people who actually made this book—let's be real, every book—happen.

Brandy, my editor... where do I even start, because you've put more work into this book than feels even remotely reasonable. At this point, I'm convinced you've read this more times than I have. You didn't just edit, you basically wrestled this book into being the best version of itself, line by line, without losing your sanity (somehow). This book is as good as it is because of you, and I genuinely don't have enough words to thank you properly, which is kind of ironic considering I wrote a whole book.

Sarah, my PA, my best friend, my late night "I'm losing my mind" text person, my zombie killing partner, my graphic making companion, and the one I trust to run my content and ARC teams... you somehow manage to be all of that at once. You kept everything running when things got crazy, which was often, and made sure things actually got done. I trust you with so much for a reason, and I don't say that lightly. I'm really lucky to have you.

Tawny, the one responsible for making my books look like they have their lives together on social media while I'm in your DMs asking for just one more thing every five minutes, thank you for putting up with me constantly asking for too much and somehow still showing so much patience every time. Your brain is an actual marketing genius, and because of you, my babies get seen, because I would absolutely not know how to do that on my own. At this point, you deserve partial credit for their success.

To Wildfire Marketing Solutions, thank you for taking care of ARC distribution, sign ups, ads, and somehow getting my books into actual readers' hands. You're the reason these stories leave my laptop and exist in the real world, which is both exciting and mildly terrifying.

Ashley, thank you for running the Facebook group and somehow managing a space where readers can connect, scream, spiral, and occasionally behave, even if we don't want them to. The fact that you keep it all together is honestly impressive, and it wouldn't be the same without you.

Pia, thank you for the incredible covers for the Shadow Brides series, the Devil's Bargain series, and *The Keeper's Secret*. The fact that you can turn my extremely unhelpful, vague, and sometimes nonexistent ideas into something beautiful is a talent in itself. I pinky swear I might get better... eventually.

To all of you, thank you for being part of this process and for putting up with me along the way. I know I don't make that easy, but I wouldn't have it any other way.

Want More?

Want more of Lucas and Josie?

See how they react to Rey's first steps!

Read it here: https://dl.bookfunnel.com/a0kl35kpw8

Up Next

Up Next in the Devil's Bargain Series

He's spent his whole life ignoring the pull.

She's known exactly who he was—and waited anyway.

Lust doesn't rush. It lingers until it owns you from the inside out.

What they have is inevitable.

And now that it's awake... neither of them can choose to walk away.

Coming Soon

Up Next in the Almost: A Dark Valentine Series

Willa and Wes were never done.

They were just unfinished.

Now a Valentine card shows up with her name on it.

And Willa knows better than to believe in coincidences.

Coming June 25, 2026

About the Author

Sara McClaflin writes romance with feelings, flaws, and just the right amount of emotional damage. Her stories are character-driven, morally gray, and often ask one very important question: what if love was a little dangerous—and we liked it that way? After years of reading and reviewing books with too much angst, she finally started writing her own.

She lives on the West Coast with her husband, their chaotic dog, and more book boyfriends than she's willing to admit. Her TBR pile is a cry for help, her playlists are 80%

heartbreak, and she's always chasing the next character who'll ruin her in the best way.

Newsletter Sign-Up

https://subscribepage.io/saranewsletter

Amazon Author Page

https://www.amazon.com/stores/Sara-McClaflin/author/B0CR8VHBHJ

Instagram

https://www.instagram.com/authorsaramcclaflin

Facebook

https://www.facebook.com/profile.php?id=61551822185090

TikTok

https://www.tiktok.com/@sara.mcclaflin

Goodreads

https://www.goodreads.com/author/show/47632250.Sara_McClaflin

Threads

https://www.threads.com/@authorsaramcclaflin

Also By

The Devil's Bargain

Wicked Union– A prequel novella (Liora and Evander's Story)

The Devil's Canvas

Gilded Lies

Unholy Vows (Selene and Theron's Story)

Fractured Destiny

The Shadow Brides

Veil of Fire

Wildflowers & Whiskey (Frankie and Beckett's Story)

The Damaged Bride

The Huntington Brothers Series

Destined for Love

Tangled Hearts

Promises to Keep

Almost: A Dark Valentine

Almost Chosen

Standalone Novels

The Keeper's Secret

Love on the Edge

Anthologies

Head in the Clouds: A Romantic Comedy Anthology
Desperate: A Deadly Thriller Anthology

Did you love *Fractured Destiny*? If you enjoyed the story, I would be so grateful if you took a moment to leave a quick review. Thank you for reading, for your support, and for spending time with these characters. I can't wait for you to see what happens next!

Content Warning

This story contains the following themes and potentially triggering material:

- infertility
- recurrent miscarriage and pregnancy loss (supporting character)
- pregnancy complications and high-risk pregnancy
- childbirth trauma
- maternal death during childbirth
- grief related to pregnancy loss
- stalking and obsessive behavior
- emotional manipulation within a romantic relationship
- off-page drug-facilitated sexual assault of the FMC and discussion of non-consensual conception
- violence and murder
- supernatural violence
- loss of bodily autonomy (supernatural possession of a human body)
- references to ritual killing of a human vessel

- discussions of death and the afterlife
- explicit sexual content
- themes involving Hell and demonic entities

www.ingramcontent.com/pod-product-compliance
Lightning Source LLC
La Vergne TN
LVHW100510110826
845146LV00002B/580

* 9 7 9 8 9 9 9 1 7 7 8 4 1 *